Children of Time

Books in the *After Cilmeri* Series:
Daughter of Time (prequel)
Footsteps in Time (Book One)
Winds of Time
Prince of Time (Book Two)
Crossroads in Time (Book Three)
Children of Time (Book Four)
Exiles in Time
Castaways in Time
Ashes of Time
Warden of Time
Guardians of Time
Masters of Time

The Gareth and Gwen Medieval Mysteries:
The Bard's Daughter
The Good Knight
The Uninvited Guest
The Fourth Horseman
The Fallen Princess
The Unlikely Spy
The Lost Brother
The Renegade Merchant
The Unexpected Ally

The Lion of Wales Series:
Cold My Heart
The Oaken Door
Of Men and Dragons
A Long Cloud
Frost Against the Hilt

The Last Pendragon Saga:
The Last Pendragon
The Pendragon's Blade
Song of the Pendragon
The Pendragon's Quest
The Pendragon's Champions
Rise of the Pendragon

Book Four in the *After Cilmeri* Series

CHILDREN OF TIME

by

SARAH WOODBURY

Children of Time
Copyright © 2012 by Sarah Woodbury

This is a work of fiction.

Cover image by Christine DeMaio-Rice at Flip City Books

To my sister
(who is nothing like Meg's sister,
even if they live in the same house)

A Brief Guide to Welsh Pronunciation

c a hard 'c' sound (Cadfael)

ch a non-English sound as in Scottish 'ch' in 'loch' (Fychan)

dd a buzzy 'th' sound, as in 'there' (Ddu; Gwynedd)

f as in 'of' (Cadfael)

ff as in 'off' (Gruffydd)

g a hard 'g' sound, as in 'gas' (Goronwy)

l as in 'lamp' (Llywelyn)

ll a breathy /sh/ sound that does not occur in English (Llywelyn)

rh a breathy mix between 'r' and 'rh' that does not occur in English (Rhys)

th a softer sound than for 'dd,' as in 'thick' (Arthur)

u a short 'ih' sound (Gruffydd), or a long 'ee' sound (Cymru—pronounced 'kumree')

w as a consonant, it's an English 'w' (Llywelyn); as a vowel, an 'oo' sound (Bwlch)

y the only letter in which Welsh is not phonetic. It can be an 'ih' sound, as in 'Gwyn,' is often an 'uh' sound (Cymru), and at the end of the word is an 'ee' sound (thus, both Cymru—the modern word for Wales—and Cymry—the word for Wales in the Dark Ages—are pronounced 'kumree')

Cast of Characters

The Welsh

David (Dafydd)—Prince of Wales
Lili—Ieuan's sister, David's wife
Llywelyn—King of Wales, David's father
Meg (Marged)—Queen of Wales, mother to David and Anna
Anna—David's half-sister
Math—Anna's husband; nephew to Llywelyn
Cadell—son of Anna and Math
Gwenllian—daughter of Llywelyn
Ieuan—Welsh knight, one of David's men
Bronwen—American, married to Ieuan
Bevyn—Welsh knight
Nicholas de Carew—Norman/Welsh lord

The English

Edward I (deceased)—King of England
Eleanor of England—Edward's daughter
Joan of England—Edward's daughter
Humphrey de Bohun—Regent of England
John Peckham—Archbishop of Canterbury
William de Bohun—Humphrey's son
Maud de Bohun—Humphrey's wife
Edmund Mortimer—Lord of the March
Gilbert de Clare—Lord of the March

1

15 November 1288

Meg

"You know what you need to do, don't you?" Llywelyn said.

In the growing darkness, Llywelyn and David faced off on the balcony that overlooked the Wye River, while Goronwy and I watched from a few feet away. The sun had fallen behind the castle, not that we'd seen much in the way of sunlight on this gloomy November day.

I glanced at Goronwy, looking for help, but he refused to meet my eye, knowing better than to get involved in this argument. Llywelyn and David had come to a blessed agreement since Llywelyn had agreed to David's marriage to Lili. Especially now that Lili was pregnant, Llywelyn approached life with a certain smug satisfaction. But sometimes their conversations still gave me a tickling sensation in my stomach that wasn't my baby kicking or fluttering its hands. It told me that neither man quite trusted the other yet. It was as if the memory of those bitter months of estrangement, even if the original disagreement was resolved, continued to hover over their future.

"I need to see William and Joan off to a good marriage," David said. "That is why we're going to London. That's the *only* reason."

"We could do more," Llywelyn said. "Even with marriage to one of the royal daughters off the table, all is not lost. You could be more, and by doing so, protect Wales from a time when England again has a strong king. You could be that strong king."

Dreading the repeat of this argument, I glanced towards the water roiling below us, heading towards the Severn Sea. Chepstow Castle had been built on solid rock above the Wye River. The storms of the last week, coupled with the tidal surge that had churned upriver in the last hour, had caused the water to run high. At that moment, it lapped only forty feet below the bottom of the castle wall, instead of the usual seventy. England lay on the opposite bank. It was something that nobody at Chepstow Castle could ever forget, even if, at present, England and Wales were at peace.

What hurt my heart most was that Llywelyn was right. I knew what the future might hold for Wales once England found itself a strong king. We had been lucky that England had lost King Edward at the very moment of our ascendancy. In my old world, the few times that Wales had managed to overcome or withstand English invasions had been when it had a strong leader, like Llywelyn, and when it had the support of England's enemies. The last Prince of Wales, not Llywelyn but Owain Glyndŵr, had fallen in the end because once his allies had deserted him, the English king proved stronger and more agile, with better access to men and munitions. Wales hadn't stood a chance.

David folded his hands in front of him and rested them on the wall. I wanted to reach out, to touch him, but stopped myself. He was a grown man, and this was his decision.

In order to reach the balcony on which we stood, we'd come through the kitchen, down a set of stairs, and into a wine cellar. The reason Roger Bigod, the original owner of the castle, had installed the balcony in this location was not for the beautiful view, or the quiet, but to allow fortification and provisioning of Chepstow from the river in times of war.

We used it now to speak in absolute privacy, and had gone so far as to clear the cellar and stairs of companions and guards. David had even excluded Evan, who shadowed him everywhere he went since David had promoted him to captain of his *teulu*. Only Goronwy stayed with us, silent in the shadows.

"I know what you want, Dad," David said.

"Do you?" Llywelyn said. "Why can't you see how a claim from you to the English throne could change the course of Wales' future forever?"

"I can see it," David said. "But on what basis would I make such a claim, and who would I have to betray in order to make it? Humphrey and William? The Norman barons who have allied themselves with us?"

"It wouldn't have to be that way," Llywelyn said. "Everyone knows that the English crown is in doubt and the kingdom in disarray. None of the barons has the support of enough of his

3

peers to make an outright claim, and even those who ally with Valence can't envision him—or one of his lackeys—on the throne."

Valence was the Norman lord who had incited the war against us in August. He hadn't gone away in the intervening months, despite a loss of face at his stunning defeat in the Severn Estuary. Both David and Llywelyn were in agreement that they couldn't count on that same luck a second time, were Valence to contrive another plot against Wales. Thus, Llywelyn's entreaty that David throw his name into the hat for the English crown.

"I have no royal blood, Dad. On what grounds could I possibly rule?"

"As High King—"

David gave a mocking laugh, not letting Llywelyn finish. "But I wouldn't be High King. We're not talking about uniting England and Wales under my rule—at least not today. We're talking about a claim from me to the throne of England."

Llywelyn tried again. "I admit that's true for now—"

"Even if a claim to the English throne held any water at all with the people of England, how would my rule of them be any different from what we've suffered for centuries under the Norman boot?"

"You can't seriously be comparing your potential rule to King Edward's," Llywelyn said.

"In the mind of the English, how would I be any different?" David said. "Welsh rulers who have reached too far, who have stretched their hand over the lowlands of England, more often than not have died fighting in wars to the east, over land none of our people have cared about since the Romans left."

"Those lands were ours, once." Llywelyn said.

"They were," David said, "but this isn't the dark ages and I am no Arthur, no matter what the people say."

"And I say you are. It isn't about the blood in your veins," Llywelyn said. "You *are* the rightful High King of Britain—"

"Please don't say that—" David stepped closer to his father, his hand out.

"—and it is Arthur's spirit that runs in you, even if half your blood comes from another world."

David made a disgusted noise in his throat. "Dad—stop—you know talk of Arthur makes me feel like a fraud." David scrubbed at his hair with both hands and then dropped them.

"I know," Llywelyn said. "I'm sorry if it makes you uncomfortable. It shouldn't." Llywelyn glanced at me.

I interpreted his look as a request for support and closed the distance between us. "It's an explanation for your difference that the people can understand and accept," I said. "That's why we haven't discouraged it. It's been to protect you."

"It doesn't feel that way to me," David said. "I've long since given up on letting my people know about where I came from, but I've striven to be myself, regardless of how odd it makes me."

"It's not that you're odd, Son," Llywelyn said. "You're different from everyone else because it is that difference that Wales needs. That's why you came to me six years ago. That's why your family is so special. England needs you now, too, to prevent a civil war from tearing the country apart for the second time in a generation."

Llywelyn was talking about a repeat of the Barons' War, which for a time had deposed King Henry in favor of Simon de Montfort, his brother-in-law. Llywelyn had allied himself with Simon, and ultimately married his daughter, who had died while birthing their daughter, Gwenllian.

It had become clear to us in the last three years, since England had relinquished its claim to Wales, that the Norman barons were awash in disunity. A given baron might have his supporters, but none had enough to overcome an alliance of his enemies. The regency had been a temporary measure, a compromise until one baron gathered enough power to himself to take the throne outright. The alliance of Bigod, Valence, and Vere had been such an attempt.

Although that attempt had failed, how many barons had thought to implement something similar until Valence's defeat had forced them to reconsider? Clare had been waiting for Llywelyn's death to launch his own assault on Wales. He had viewed David as weaker than his father. Victory would have given him the upper hand over the other barons. But now, even he supported David.

David looked away. As I'd feared, the old argument threatened to consume them again. Between two equals, there was no tie-breaking vote, not even if it was mine. Wanting to diffuse the tension, I put a hand between David's shoulder blades and rubbed gently. It was a mom's attempt to cut through the discord that I couldn't stand to feel between him and his father a second longer. While I fought for what to say to him—anything that would ease the premature lines of care that had formed around his eyes—David bent his head to mine and sighed.

I didn't know that I'd ever get used to having a son eight inches taller than I was, but my heart still melted when I looked at him, as it had when he was a chubby boy of three. He would be twenty tomorrow. I had to shake my head in disbelief when I thought about how much David had grown since the day he came to Wales with Anna. It was a man who looked down on me now.

I put a hand to either side of his face. "What I wish for you, more than anything, is for the burdens you carry to wear on you less, and that you could learn to live more lightly. That's not fair to ask of you, because you carry all of Wales on your shoulders, but we used to have *fun*, remember?"

"God—I know, Mom." David touched his forehead to mine. "I'm no good for Lili half the time. More like a bear than a husband. And now with the baby—"

Llywelyn reached across me and gripped David's shoulder. "Son—" he said, but then didn't finish his thought. Instead, the skin on his knuckles whitened and he held on more tightly.

"Llywelyn! What is it?" I touched his arm.

The muscles in Llywelyn's face tightened and the tendons in his neck stood out. "*Cariad*—" Llywelyn clutched at his chest with his right hand. Then his knees gave way and David and I staggered with him, striving to hold him up as our hips hit the wall behind us.

"My lord!" Goronwy, who'd been watching without interruption while we talked, sprang forward.

"Help me—" Llywelyn clasped my hand and fought for breath.

I tucked my shoulder under Llywelyn's arm while David took his other side, and between us we settled him on the ground at the base of the battlement.

"What's happening, Mom?" David said.

"I-I don't know for sure," I said.

"I'll get Aaron." David sprinted for the doorway that led to the wine cellar.

I huddled beside Llywelyn, who continued to clutch at me.

Goronwy crouched in front of us. "It has to be now, Meg. We have to do this *now*."

"I know, Goronwy, I know." Tears pricked at my eyes, but I blinked them back. This wasn't a time for weeping. In my head, a mantra repeated itself over and over again until I feared I would scream it instead of bottling it up inside me so I could be strong for Llywelyn: *Oh God, don't let him die. Don't let him die. I can't live without him!* "Help me get him up."

"What—what—what are you doing?" Llywelyn spoke in a breathy whisper. His eyes didn't seem to see me, even as he swallowed hard and repeated his question, his voice strengthened this time with indignation.

"It's time to go, my love." I pressed my cheek to his, feeling the rough scruff of his beard on my skin.

"No!" Llywelyn tried to push me away. "I won't let you."

8

"We've talked about this," I said. "It's this or you die."

"It's not worth the risk," Llywelyn said. "Not to you. Not to the baby."

"Isn't it?" I looked to Goronwy. "Help me hold him up. We're lucky this happened right here, near the low wall, instead of in the hall or our rooms, or I'd never manage it."

"You're not strong enough to do this by yourself, you know," Goronwy said. "No more than Llywelyn would, I won't let you go alone."

"Of course I'm not going alone. I'm taking Llywelyn—"

I broke off as Goronwy lifted Llywelyn in his arms as if he weighed no more than a child. Llywelyn had been ill off and on since the battle in the Estuary in August. He'd tried to hide it, but I was his wife, and I knew. He'd lost weight, no matter how much he tried to deny it to David. I wouldn't have said his weight loss was so much, however, that Goronwy could carry him.

I gritted my teeth. Llywelyn was wrong. It was long past time we went, whether he liked it or not.

With a grunt, Goronwy used a fallen rock as a step up and climbed to the top of the waist-high wall that overlooked the Wye River. He glanced down at me. "Are you coming? It's not as if this will work if I do it by myself."

"Yes, yes, of course I'm coming!" I lifted my skirts so they wouldn't hinder my legs and scrambled to stand beside Goronwy. I looped the fingers of one hand around Goronwy's sword belt and found Llywelyn's hand with the other. Llywelyn no longer protested. With a rush of terror, I realized he had lost consciousness. We had so little *time.*

"Mom! What are you doing?"

I looked back at my son who stood in the doorway to the balcony. *My beloved son.* I smiled, even as tears returned. "I love you. Give my love to Anna."

And with Goronwy at my side, and my arms around Llywelyn, I jumped.

2

15 November 1288

David

I threw myself forward, desperate to stop Mom and Goronwy. But even before I moved, I knew it was too late. They had jumped before I was halfway across the balcony. When I reached the wall from which they'd leapt, I leaned over the edge to gaze down at the rushing water. I prayed to see their heads bob up—and prayed that I wouldn't.

I wasn't a fool. I had asked Mom what was wrong with Dad, but it wasn't like I couldn't tell. Dad was having a heart attack and Mom had done what she felt she must in order to save him. I'd done the same for Ieuan three years ago. I could hardly blame her for trying it too. As the water rushed by, I continued to stare. Then Lili's arm slid around my waist. "What's going on? I heard you call for Aaron. Did someone fall?" she said.

I hugged her to me, and then Anna and Math appeared on my other side to peer over the wall with us.

No heads appeared; nobody sputtered to the surface. The water was moving so fast they might have been a quarter of a mile downstream by now anyway—if they'd hit the water at all. I turned around to see Aaron standing in the middle of the balcony. His face fell as he looked at me. I read sadness—and pity—in his eyes.

"You knew about this?" I said.

"Yes," Aaron said. "Or rather, your mother mentioned the possibility of-of—" he gestured helplessly towards the balustrade at my back, "—if the king's health didn't improve."

"I didn't even know he was sick." I turned to Anna. "Did you?"

"Are you talking about Papa?" Anna said. "He's been weaker than Mom and I like, but neither Aaron nor I have been able to put a finger on the problem. Why do you ask—?" Anna cut herself off, her face paling, and then she gazed over the edge of the wall again.

I looked past Aaron to the cluster of men-at-arms and servants who'd gathered at the entrance to the balcony. I lifted a hand to Evan, who came forward.

"Send a few men south along the river," I said. "Even better, go yourself."

"What am I looking for?" Evan matched my lowered tone.

"Bodies in the water."

Evan's jaw clenched. "My lord—"

I put a hand on his arm, gripping tightly as my father had gripped my shoulder before he'd fallen, and then eased up. For all that my mother had asked that I live more lightly, I had to contain

12

myself in front of these people. The Prince of Wales was not allowed to burst into tears, no matter what he felt inside. "I don't expect you to find anyone."

Evan's eyes narrowed, but he nodded, obedient because he couldn't *not* be. "Immediately, my lord." He turned away. When he reached the other onlookers, he made a shooing motion and they allowed themselves to be urged out of the wine cellar and up the stairs to the main part of the castle.

Then Math was at my side and clenched his fingers around my upper arm. "You sent Evan to look for bodies. *Who fell?*"

"Better if we discuss this elsewhere," I said.

"We know who, don't we?" Lili said.

"Not *here*." I wrapped one arm around Anna's shoulders and the other around Lili's. "Come with me."

I could feel Anna's silent protest at my refusal to talk, but how was I to say out loud that I'd seen Mom, Dad, and Goronwy jump into the river and disappear, whether into the water or the future? I ran over the events of the last few minutes in my mind and shook my head. They had to have made it. They *had* to—but I didn't know for sure.

Two minutes later, I herded everyone into my office. Math shut the door behind him and stood with his back to it, his fists on his hips. I hadn't let go of Anna, but now she pulled away and folded her arms across her chest. She glared at me with a mutinous expression. "Tell me."

"Dad was having a heart attack ..."

Anna dropped her arms, her anger gone in an instant. In two strides, Math reached her and put his arms around her waist so she could lean against him.

"... I ran for Aaron and by the time I got back to the balcony, Mom and Goronwy stood on the top of the wall, with Dad in Goronwy's arms." I tried to get my mouth to say the words *they jumped*, but couldn't get them out. I pinched the bridge of my nose and closed my eyes.

"Did anyone else see them go?" Anna said.

"No," I said, "not unless one of the guards noticed from the battlement above."

Math leaned over Anna's shoulder. "You're assuming they've gone to the future, and yet you sent Evan to look for them along the river?"

"I had to. We have to be sure," I said.

"They would have been carried quickly downstream," Math said. "The most likely spot for them to beach is at that sandbar, a mile to the south."

"Only if they'd actually entered the water." Anna was slowly recovering. She stared at me over hands clasped before her lips. "This is all my fault."

My jaw dropped. "How could this possibly be *your* fault?"

"I'm the one who thought about climbing to the top of a tower and jumping off it," Anna said. "Mom and I talked about it."

I barked a laugh. "I'm the one who actually *did* it!"

But Anna's eyes had filled with tears. She took a step towards me, Math loosened his grip, and I pulled her close. She wrapped her arms around my waist and sobbed into my shoulder. My own eyes were full of water too. I blinked back the tears. "They went, Anna," I said. "They made it."

Aaron cleared his throat. "My lord, as you guessed when we were outside, your mother discussed with me the possibility that this day might come."

"Why didn't you say something to any of us?" Anna said, her voice muffled in my shirt.

"Because she swore me to secrecy." Aaron raised his hands and then let them fall. "I'm sorry."

"The last thing she said to me was *love to Anna*," I said, which garnered another sob from my sister.

"So they really meant to go," Math said. "It couldn't have been an accident?"

"Nobody stands above the Wye River by accident," Lili said.

Anna released me and returned to Math. I paced to the window and back, running my hand through my hair and trying to *think*. "We need to discuss what we're going to do now, before any of us has to face everyone out there." I waved a hand towards the door, but I really meant *everyone*. The King of Wales couldn't disappear and have nobody notice.

Math nodded. "You'll have to tell the people something. I'm just not sure what."

"Let it be known to those here at Chepstow that your mother took your father to Avalon, for healing," Lili said, "as you did for Ieuan three years ago."

15

I stopped my pacing and resisted the desire to spit on the floor. *Arthur. Again.* The legend followed me everywhere. How could I shake it when even my own father talked about it as if it were true? Nobody understood that Arthur's boots were far too big for me. "We called it the Land of Madoc at that time and it was absurd then. They won't believe my mother has taken Dad to Avalo—"

"They will believe it because they want to," Lili said, "just as they accept you. They want to *believe*, so they do."

My father had said much the same thing. I pursed my lips and stared at the floor, warring with myself, not wanting to admit that what she said would work, and that she might be right.

"For those who come here inquiring after the King," Lili continued, "they will learn that he has headed north, to Aber."

Math coughed and laughed at the same time. "And those who ask at Aber will be told that he is at Caerphilly."

"Meanwhile ..." Anna said.

"Meanwhile, we must pretend that nothing is amiss," I said.

"We will have to alter our own plans too," Anna said. "Math and I can't go to England with you."

I looked over at her. "Why is that?"

"Because not only have we lost both our parents, but Gwenllian has too," Anna said.

I could have kicked myself for forgetting our half-sister. Thank goodness Anna could keep her head together. I seemed to have lost mine. Anna and Math had been planning to leave their three year old son, Cadell, with Mom, Dad, and Gwenllian while they rode with Lili and me to London. Up until now, I'd been thinking mostly of myself and how I felt. If that was my default under pressure, how could my father think me ready to rule England? First, I needed to rule myself.

Math nodded. "We can't leave them alone with only nannies. Think of what might happen!"

We all had a quiet laugh at that. Gwenllian was a reserved child under most circumstances, but bright. Lately, she'd been mouthing off to Mom in a way I never remembered doing. Mom claimed that Anna had been equally rebellious at this age. It wasn't as if Gwenllian got away with it, but without Mom around, and only Bronwen and a few servants to look after both her and the very boisterous Cadell, we might return to find Chepstow Castle in pieces.

"I want to argue with you, but I can't." I turned to Lili. "You don't have to come, either, if you think it might be better not to. You are pregnant, after all."

"As if that ever stopped any of us from traveling wherever we wished to go." Anna grinned. "She's in the first trimester and the pony you bought her is as placid as mine."

Lili smiled too and the light in her face made my heart ease, just a little. "I learned my lesson months ago," she said. "You aren't going anywhere without me."

3

15 November 2016

Meg

"What the hell, lady! Where'd you come from?"

Those words, said in perfect American English with the right amount of indignation, had me surging into consciousness. A man with a firm grip on my arm tugged me from the water.

I swept a hand over my eyes to clear them and found myself staring up at a fifty-something, overweight American in a baseball hat. His body was bare from the waist up and as I struggled to right myself, I understood why my legs had refused to move at first. I had fallen into a swimming pool, an indoor one within a cathedral-like glass atrium, in what appeared to be a fancy hotel. The man had his arm around my waist and was holding me upright.

The smell of chlorine was so strong it almost had me passing out again. I hadn't smelled a pool in years. "My husband—"

"Yeah, yeah, my buddy already called 911 or whatever they call it around here. Actually, I think these guys are always in the building."

These guys. How long had it been since I'd heard anyone say that?

While I struggled against the skirt which hampered my legs, the man dragged me towards the shallow end of the pool. By the time we reached the steps leading out of the water, I managed to get my feet under me and straighten. The water lapped around my thighs.

And then the urgency I'd felt at Chepstow came rushing back. I swung around, eyes searching. For all his exasperation, the man didn't waste words. He pointed to where bystanders had laid Llywelyn on his back beside the pool. Goronwy hovered over him. I could hear his sputters in Welsh and it sounded like he was trying to keep everyone away, when he really should be inviting their help.

"Goronwy! It's okay." I surged up the steps and out of the water, my legs moving awkwardly in my sopping wet dress. Contrary to my expectations (if this could have been something I would have expected) the expressions of the onlookers were more amused than stunned or horrified. Aside from the question of how we had appeared out of thin air above the pool, I was about as out of place among the scantily dressed crowd as it was possible to be.

I wore a long-sleeved gray kirtle, laced up the front, and my favorite deep red surcoat, now ruined by chlorine. Their eyes saw a frazzled, middle-aged-yet-pregnant woman in disarray.

"Llywelyn." I gasped his name and fell on my knees beside him. Llywelyn's eyes were closed, but he was breathing. I looked at Goronwy. "How long was he in the pool?"

"You mean *that*?" Goronwy waved a hand at the water. "Not long. It isn't deep and we only went under for a moment."

Three medical personnel burst through the double doors that led to the interior of the hotel and hustled towards Llywelyn. "What happened?" the first of them said as he reached us. He spoke in English, with the lilt of India in his accent. His nametag said, "Dr Raj". I'd once known a man who had Raj as his first name, but decided it wasn't the time to ask for clarification. I dearly hoped we hadn't ended up in New Delhi because that would mean a seriously long journey home.

"I think he's having a heart attack," I said.

The two other men set up the stretcher, while Dr Raj listened to Llywelyn's lungs and heart, and my own heart pounded in my throat.

"What are his symptoms?" Dr Raj said.

I swallowed. "Sorry." I had answered his first question completely wrong. I had tried to diagnose Llywelyn, rather than explaining what had happened. "He clutched his chest and felt like he couldn't breathe. Then he lost consciousness."

"Has he complained of feeling ill before this?" Dr Raj said.

"On and off for months," I said.

"Has he woken at all?" Dr Raj said.

I glanced at Goronwy, whose face was nearly as drawn and pale as Llywelyn's, and shook my head.

"How long has he been unconscious?"

"I—I—I'm not sure ..." I searched for words that wouldn't make me sound insane. "A few minutes? We all fell in the water. Goronwy got him out as fast as he could."

Dr Raj nodded. "We'll take care of him." One of the attendants had already put an oxygen mask on Llywelyn's face and the plastic clouded with every breath. Somehow, through all this, Llywelyn had managed to continue breathing. *Stay alive! Please keep breathing!*

Dr Raj nodded to his helpers, who loaded Llywelyn onto the stretcher. As they rolled it toward the doors, I trotted beside Llywelyn, holding his hand. The opening wasn't large enough for me to pass through it with him, so I had to move aside to let the men with the stretcher go ahead of me. Since I had to stop anyway, I took a moment to squeeze water from my dress so I wouldn't drip all over the interior of the hotel. The puddle I created headed for one of the drains in the concrete pool deck.

Goronwy had stayed close to me, even as his head swiveled from side to side, taking in his surroundings. His attention, like mine, always came back to Llywelyn, however. I nodded encouragingly to him, although I didn't feel particularly encouraged myself, before following Dr Raj through the double doors.

21

In a few strides, we caught up to the stretcher. We had entered a foyer, perhaps twenty-four by thirty-six feet, with three sets of double doors leading from it. The floor was comprised of white tile and the walls were painted a pale pink and decorated with Impressionist prints.

"Where are you taking him?" I said.

The attendants ignored me and rolled Llywelyn through the pair of doors to the left, heading down a tiled hallway which was decorated similarly to the foyer. Dr Raj stayed to answer, though his brow furrowed at the question. "To the infirmary, of course. Our facilities here are state of the art. We'll take good care of your father."

"Of—of course." I managed not to flush red. "But I must tell you that he's my husband, not my father."

Dr Raj glanced at me and then away again. "I'm sorry. My mistake. Forgive me." He jerked his head, indicating we should come with him, and hurried after Llywelyn. As I trotted beside Dr Raj, Goronwy stayed just to my left, silent as before and asking no questions I couldn't answer, for which I was grateful. I couldn't begin to imagine what he was thinking and feeling right now. I was carrying my emotions only a hair's-breadth below the surface and didn't know if I could handle his too, just now.

Thirty seconds later, we reached the medical clinic, accessed from the corridor through another set of wide double doors. Dr Raj pulled up, though he waved a hand to send the stretcher onward. The attendants bypassed the waiting room and the main desk and pushed Llywelyn into a wide hallway, more sterilely white than the first.

"If you will wait here," Dr Raj said, "we will attend to your husband."

"But—"

Dr Raj had already turned away, hustling in the wake of the two attendants. I stared after him, seeing nothing through the blur of tears that filled my eyes. Then the nurse who manned the desk came around from behind it and nudged my arm. "I'll need you to sign *here* and *here*." Pale-skinned like me, she spoke in English, with a fruity, upper-class English accent.

Blindly, I took the pen. I gazed at the form. It was in English but I couldn't make sense of it. I signed on the lines she indicated anyway. "What will they do to him?"

"Whatever he needs." The nurse tugged the clipboard from my hand and passed the forms to an orderly, who hurried down the hall after the doctor. "I have more papers that will need your signature, if you would step this way?"

"Of course."

The nurse handed the clipboard back to me, with four forms attached for me to fill out, front and back.

I took it. "Do you know how long it will be before we can see him?" I said.

"As long as it takes," the nurse said, back at her desk with her eyes on her computer screen.

I swallowed hard, bereft now. The urgency of our arrival in this world had passed and Llywelyn was getting the care he

23

needed. This was, of course, why I'd brought him here. Llywelyn had been fading for months, short of breath and suffering. I could hardly complain now that getting him treated meant I couldn't be with him.

Water drip-drip-dripped off my clothing into my shoes. I looked down. I was standing in a puddle. "Um."

The nurse didn't look at me.

"Do you by chance have a change of clothes we could borrow?" I gestured towards Goronwy who was equally soaked. He brushed a hand though his hair, shedding more water onto the floor.

The nurse looked up and bit her lip. "Let me see what I can do." She left her computer and walked down the hall. I took a step away from the desk so I could peer after her. She disappeared through a doorway to the left.

Still with the clipboard in my hand, I tucked my other hand into Goronwy's elbow. "Let's move over here."

I urged him towards a line of chairs which faced a picture window that looked over a garden and a green meadow beyond that. Mountains hovered in the distance. Late afternoon sun shone onto the grass lawn beyond the flagstone patio, reachable through French doors that opened from the waiting room. Clouds were moving in from the west, however, and soon it would be dark.

Thankfully, all the chairs were empty and nobody waited with us. Even if the nurse seemed imperturbable, I didn't think I could have handled more stares and curiosity. Now that we were here, now that jumping off the wall into the Wye River had 'worked', I was very near to hysterical laughter and/or unleashing my tears. I wouldn't have taken any bets as to which might fight their way out of my chest first.

I didn't dare sit down on one of the chairs, since my dress would soak it instantly. Goronwy, on the other hand, seemed oblivious to his drenched, temporally-out-of-place appearance. He stood in front of the big window and gazed out of it for a long minute. Then he turned back to me and asked his first question, though hundreds had to be crowding to the forefront of his mind. "Where are we?"

"I have no idea," I said, "other than that we're in my time. From the looks, this is a private clinic in the countryside, though I don't know in which country."

"You are speaking Welsh to me," Goronwy said, "but your words make no sense. What is *private clinic*?"

A smile quirked at the corner of my lips. Even after four years in Wales, I had fallen into speaking English for words that I couldn't find in Welsh. 'Private clinic' didn't translate very well into medieval Welsh. "People come from far away specifically to stay here. It's not anyone's home. It's like they are guests at a castle who pay for the privilege of spending the night. Likely, the residents are also very rich. Even better, I expect the doctors here are as skilled as any we'd find anywhere in the world."

"I'm glad for that," Goronwy said, "especially if what you've always said about your medicine is true. But I didn't mean that." He gestured towards the windows. "If I didn't know better, I'd say we're near Aberystwyth."

His observation caught me completely off guard. "What?" I moved to stand next to him.

"I know those mountains," Goronwy said. "They rise above the Abbey of Strata Florida."

"Really?" My heart leapt, and then I immediately squashed the emotion. It couldn't be true. Whenever we'd traveled in time before, we'd ended up in the United States, going into the future, and in the United Kingdom, going into the past. When I'd returned to the Middle Ages four years ago, I'd landed near Hadrian's Wall in the north of England, which had been a great disappointment. "Are you sure?"

"I can't be *sure*," Goronwy said, patience in his voice. "We've come more than seven hundred years into the future. With all the changes that have happened in that time, maybe the mountains don't exist anymore."

"They exist, I assure you." In all my years in Wales, both in the modern world and the medieval, I'd never made it to Strata Florida Abbey, but that at least I knew to be true.

Goronwy allowed himself a sigh and continued to stare out the window, watching the play of sun and shadow on the hills. I looked with him, stunned that they could be our mountains. The veil between Llywelyn's world and mine had never been so thin.

I hadn't heard anyone speaking Welsh yet, however. Admittedly, our doctor was of Indian descent and if Goronwy was right, if we were near Aberystwyth, the town was in western Wales, not in Gwynedd, so Welsh speakers with fluency were thinner on the ground here than in the north. But if Goronwy was right, if we

26

really were in Wales ... a wave of relief swept through me. Oddly, I hadn't wanted to go 'home' to the United States. I hadn't wanted the temptation of ending up in a place as familiar as that. I didn't know if I would have David's ability to walk away.

At the very least, finding ourselves in Wales would make life easier for Llywelyn and Goronwy. They knew the country; they knew the language up to a point. We could get by.

"You're taking this very well," I said.

"Am I?" Goronwy said, though I had the sense that his focus remained on the mountains, not on me. "How am I supposed to take it?"

"You could have behaved as I did. The first time I arrived in Wales, I didn't believe Llywelyn was who he said he was and I attacked him with a kitchen knife."

Goronwy laughed. "I know. He told me after we left Cricieth."

"*After* we left." I laughed too. "Smart man."

"Thank goodness he didn't tell me sooner or I would have made sure he left you behind."

I frowned at him. "That would have been a grave mistake."

"You would have been fair game for Dafydd."

"Which I was anyway."

Goronwy peered at me. "I have a hard time picturing you trying to stab Llywelyn."

I flushed. It wasn't my fondest memory of my initial trip to Wales. And yet my mistake had revealed Llywelyn's character to me in a way that little else could have. He'd been understanding and tolerant, even if he'd had a hard time getting his head around the fact that I didn't know—or believe—who he was. "I didn't know what I was doing, if that helps."

Goronwy grinned. "You did put my lord in a fine mood. Even at the time I was grateful for that, although I didn't yet trust you."

I smiled too. Really, our entire situation was so absurd as to invite amusement.

"Let's see if we can answer one question, at least." I spied a rack of pamphlets on the wall by the nurse's station and grabbed one. Sure enough, we were at a spa called *Healing Waters*, seemingly because of the aquifer over which the spa had been built. The pamphlet also told me that Aberystwyth received over forty inches of rain a year, spread out over two hundred days. I wasn't sure why this was a selling point, but maybe they meant to indicate that the healing waters would never run out.

I glanced from the pamphlet to the paperwork in my hand that I hadn't even started filling out. It asked all the usual questions—name, date of birth, address—all of which were plainly impossible to answer. I hadn't even asked what year it was, though if our parallel universes were still moving as they had, it should be November of 2016. I'd given birth to David twenty years ago tomorrow. How many different lifetimes had I lived since then?

I shook myself and tried to focus on the needs of the moment. Dr Raj was under the impression that we were staying at the spa, though hopefully even a private clinic would have a mandate to treat a man having a heart attack, regardless of whether or not he was in residence. I'd never had the kind of money necessary to stay in a place like this, but the pool into which we'd fallen indicated an extremely upscale resort, with state-of-the-art medical facilities.

Still, I had to think that the management would kick us out once they discovered that we had neither reservations in the hotel nor money. Unless ...

I plopped myself in one of the chairs behind Goronwy and picked up the hem of my gown. I hadn't sat earlier for fear of ruining the upholstery with my wet dress, but the nurse hadn't returned with new clothes, and I couldn't wait a minute longer.

"What are you doing?" Goronwy said.

"Saving us," I said.

Goronwy smiled. "I thought you already did that."

"Apparently, it's not a one-time thing." I glanced up at him. His eyes were twinkling. It had been a long time since I'd seen him so cheerful. David wasn't the only one who'd felt the burdens of the last few years, and hadn't been having enough fun. "You're happy about this?"

"How could I not be?" Goronwy said. "Is there any doubt that Llywelyn would have died, if not today then next week or next month if we hadn't brought him here?"

"He still might, you know," I said, expressing the fear that had roiled my stomach as I watched Dr Raj hurry off after Llywelyn.

Goronwy shook his head. "Not if everything you've told me about this world is true."

29

I swept tendrils of hair out of my face. The chignon at the back of my head had come loose and my hair was drying into a tangled mess. "But what if I made the wrong choice, Goronwy?" That, too, had been a concern I'd kept in the back of my mind—a secret one, which I hadn't dared voice to myself, much less to him.

"What do you mean?" he said.

"Our bodies break down," I said. "They're meant to. What if it turns out that Llywelyn had a stroke, or has a condition that isn't treatable? I may have condemned him to a long illness, or a lingering twilight, when if we'd stayed at home, he would have ... simply died."

"Did you do what you thought was right at the time?" Goronwy said. These were words I'd heard him speak to David when he'd questioned a course of action he'd chosen.

"Yes."

"Then leave it alone."

I took in a breath and let it out. *Leave it alone.* And yet, how could I not worry? I coughed a laugh. Hadn't I just asked David to try to live more lightly? That he shouldn't shoulder every burden life put in his path and dwell on what he couldn't control? Apparently, I needed to hear my advice as much as David did.

Goronwy glanced towards the empty nurse's station and then to the hallway beyond it. "Shouldn't we know something soon?"

I shrugged. "Maybe. These things always take longer than you think they should."

Goronwy snorted under his breath at my non-answer, but I'd spent enough time in hospitals, between my father's illness and my ex-husband's, to understand that news came when it did and you couldn't hurry it. Often, unless you were in the room with a patient at the exact moment a doctor made his rounds, you missed your chance to learn anything and would have no new information until the next day when that particular doctor returned.

"I have to ask again, how is it that you're taking this so well?" I said. "You can't understand a word anyone has said so far, you're dressed all wrong—not that anyone seems to care about that, not even that we're soaking wet—and we may be stuck here for the rest of our lives."

"I told you. My friend lives." Goronwy turned back to the window. "And those are my mountains."

I gazed at Goronwy's straightened shoulders for a second, and then went back to what I'd been about to do before we'd started talking. I studied the stitching along the three inch deep hem. Trying not to look as secretive as I felt, I shot a glance at the nurse's station. It was still empty.

I pulled my knife from its sheath at my waist and began to work at the stitching. When I'd separated enough of the hem so I could see inside, I sat back, a rush of relief flooding through me. This *was* the dress I'd put them in.

"What do you have there?" Goronwy said.

"My identity." I laid out my soaked passport (good until 2019), driver's license (good until April 2017, when I'd be forty-two), and a credit card. Plus four hundred very wet American

31

dollars. I had sewed a different credit card and another two hundred dollars into the seam of my every day dress, as well as scattered other pieces of my identity (including a thumb drive, which contained my entire digital life) throughout other pieces of clothing, all of which were (sadly) still in the Middle Ages.

Goronwy picked up the credit card and turned it over in his hands. "How is this your identity?"

"Actually, if that works, it's money." I took back the card. "It could allow us to stay here until Llywelyn gets well, depending on what all this costs."

"And if it doesn't work?"

"Then we'll start selling everything we own."

I stewed briefly about the ethical issue of running up charges on a card I would (probably) never pay back, and then put it aside. The first thing was for Llywelyn to live. I'd mail the credit card company a gold coin in payment if I had to.

I also decided I wouldn't mention how low my expectations were that the spa would accept my credit card. I'd been in Wales for four years. My sister could have—should have—cancelled the card as soon as I disappeared. It wasn't something I'd ever thought to mention or ask her in the years between my disappearances. I'd tried to tell her about my life in medieval Wales, and about Llywelyn, *so many times*. She'd always cut me off, never wanting to talk about him. Still, David's opinion was that part of her had always believed me—and certainly she'd believed me enough not to want any of us declared dead.

The moment I thought of Elisa, I felt a sharp punch to the gut. I honestly had no idea what kind of reception she would give me when I called her and told her I was here, in the twenty-first century, once again. But I had to call her, no matter how upset it made her.

David had related what had happened when he'd gone to her house. At first, Elisa had disbelieved who he was and that he could have been living in medieval Wales. Would she believe it was I on the phone, or simply hang up on me? Three years had passed since she'd seen David: a long time. While I'd had no way to contact her, humans weren't always rational beings. Could she forgive me for my silence?

At the very least, Elisa had to feel that I'd abandoned her. Certainly, David had made it clear when he left with Ieuan and Bronwen that I was happy in the Middle Ages and had no intention of returning to the modern world if I could help it. If it had been she who had told me that, how would it have made me feel? I had effectively chosen never to see her again.

Goronwy thumbed through the cash and then set it down on my lap in a deliberate motion such that his forefinger rested on the pile for a second longer than it had to. "You really did plan ahead."

He didn't speak the sentence as a question, but it was one. He was looking for answers. He had been the one to urge us to the top of that wall, but he could see now that I'd not told him everything I was thinking. "I wasn't planning for this, Goronwy, at least not specifically. I certainly hadn't planned on coming here today."

I looked up at him once and then down to my boots. Goronwy and I were friends, close friends, but Llywelyn had always been a part of our friendship. Goronwy and I had leagued together at times—most recently, in trying to get Llywelyn to consent to David's marriage to Lili—but we'd never gone anywhere together, or hung out as friends. Sitting with him here felt more intimate than he and I had ever been. It wasn't in a sexual way, but I found myself revealed to him. I'd never felt this way with any man but Llywelyn.

"I sewed my cards and my passport into this dress when I discovered I was pregnant," I said.

"Ah," Goronwy said. "You returned to this time at Dafydd's birth. You were afraid that it might happen again?"

I nodded.

"For good reason, I suppose," he said. "One would think that childbirth was difficult enough without adding time travel to it."

"It was twenty years ago to the day that I returned to this world the first time," I said. "That fact sends chills down my spine."

Goronwy massaged the back of his neck and stared at the floor. "I've never been comfortable with magic."

"And you think I am?" I said. "It's crazy! The whole thing is crazy."

"You've never talked about what happened to you all those years ago," Goronwy said. "I've only heard your story from Llywelyn."

"I can tell you now," I said. "Everyone was abed when Anna woke in the night, late on the 15th. I went to her and was holding her when my water broke. The next second, we had fallen onto my mother's lawn. David was born in the early hours of November 16th."

"By now, after three voyages to this world and back, you'd think we would understand why this happens and how it happens," he said.

"I've come to believe that there's something in me—in my children—that makes world-shifting possible." I held up my passport. "I may never know what that special something is, but I don't always have to be unprepared."

4

15 November 2016

Meg

I struggled with the forms for half an hour, before giving up on conveying anything close to the truth.

"Why are you smiling?" Goronwy eyed me as I bit the end of the pen.

"Because I'm making this up as I go along, and it's kind of amusing."

I'd made Llywelyn an American, given him my father's social security number (I'd memorized it before he died, when he was in and out of the hospital so much, and it stuck with me), and the address and phone number of my childhood home. In twenty minutes, I'd created an entire fake back story for him out of whole cloth.

By the time I finished, a new nurse had replaced the old one, who appeared only long enough to plop a pile of surgical scrubs on the chair next to me. She smelled of smoke, which she hadn't before, and I guessed that she'd taken my request for clothing as an opportunity to sneak a cigarette before going off-shift. I gave her a smile and thanks, which she didn't acknowledge. After she'd gone, I held up one of the shirts, pursing my lips as I studied it.

"What—what are those?" Goronwy said, looking truly discomfited for the first time.

"Dry clothes," I said. "Except now I'm having second thoughts." It wasn't that they wouldn't cover us adequately, but I couldn't see Goronwy willingly changing into the flimsy pants. And what would he do with his sword, which so far he'd kept well hidden under his cloak? Strap it around his waist? It would contrast badly with the lime green scrubs. Surely they would confiscate it.

For my part, at five and half months pregnant and *really* showing, especially in my wet dress, the pants might not even fit. I'd had my seamstress add to the seams of my dress only last week, and already it was tight. I'd meant to ask her to do it again in the morning.

I hated to think what the attendants who cared for Llywelyn had thought of his gear. He'd been wearing his armor and sword when we'd jumped from the wall, the same as Goronwy. It was part of his formal attire. After our talk on the balcony, we were to have feasted in the hall, as a proper send off for the kids' journey to London.

"I think I have a better idea," I said. "Come with me."

I took Goronwy's arm and headed towards the doors to the waiting room, though not before I passed off my falsified but completed forms to the nurse behind the desk. She took them without a word and didn't even glance up at us. Perhaps one of the hallmarks of the *Healing Waters* spa was that the staff didn't ask questions, no matter how odd their guests or patients appeared to be. If an individual had enough money to stay here, maybe he assumed he'd also bought discretion.

With my identification gripped tightly in my hand, I strolled with Goronwy towards the main lobby. As we walked down the pink hallway towards the doors through which we'd come initially, I felt like I was turning back the clock. How was it that we hadn't fallen into that pool a lifetime ago?

When we reached the foyer, instead of turning towards the atrium and the pool, we went through a different set of doors that opened into the lobby. And then we stopped short.

Goronwy laughed. "What is this place?" I couldn't blame him for laughing. He couldn't have ever seen anything like it, and I didn't know that I had either.

The hotel lobby was decorated to make the residents feel as if they'd entered the cavernous hall of a medieval castle. Gold and red tapestries covered the walls, thick beams held up the thirty foot high ceilings, and for all that the walls were comprised of grey stone and the floor was of highly polished hardwood, it had the effect of being luxurious and welcoming. The accoutrements were as plush as any fine hotel in New York or London.

A fire burned in an eight-foot-wide fireplace against the far wall, spreading a warm glow over the red and gold couches and chairs, which were arranged in conversational groups. Obviously, the designers had never been to the Middle Ages or they would have known that the chairs in that time were nothing if not uncomfortable. If my dress wasn't still dripping onto the wooden floor, I would have sat in one myself, to prove to myself that such softness existed.

"Come on." I tugged on Goronwy's arm.

He was still smiling. "I must speak to Llywelyn about making some changes to Caerphilly."

"I'll look forward to that." I'd already dismissed the decorations from my mind because I was focused on what needed to happen next, and I was nervous about it. We approached the front desk, and I smiled as brightly as I could at the young man who greeted us. He wore a perfectly pressed blue suit, with a stiff collar and a tie and the *Healing Waters* logo emblazoned on his pocket.

"May I help you?"

"I hope so," I said. "Do you have rooms available?"

"We have several." The man smiled at me but his expression faltered when his eyes skated to Goronwy and widened. It seemed my appearance was amusing, or at least non-threatening, but Goronwy's caused dismay. I glanced at my friend. He did look rather ferocious with his firm jaw, solid physique, and Stalinesque mustache, even if its growth wasn't as luxurious as Bevyn's.

Still, I ignored the man's surprise and continued to smile sweetly. "What are my choices?"

After another glance at Goronwy, the man looked determinedly away and peered at his computer. He tapped the keyboard. "I have three different suites available at this time."

"Could you tell me the cost?" I said. It was tacky, I was sure, but we were on a budget.

"The charge for the smallest is three hundred pounds a night. The largest is seven hundred and fifty."

I swallowed hard, though I shouldn't have been surprised at the cost. This wasn't a hotel, or even a bed and breakfast. Our accommodation had cost over a hundred pounds a night when my mom, Anna, David, and I had traveled through Wales after David's birth.

"We'll take the small one." If my card didn't work, we were stuck. Four hundred dollars was not the same as four hundred pounds and I doubted he'd take gold coin as collateral.

"Excellent choice," the man said. "Although not as expansive, they are quite comfortable. May I see your card?" He held out his hand to me.

I cleared my throat. "Certainly." It wasn't as if I hadn't expected to hand it over. Trying out the card was the whole point of this experiment. He shoved one end of my credit card into his charge machine and stared at the screen. Nothing appeared on it.

I bit my lip, but didn't say anything. Goronwy held his hand at the small of my back, pressing lightly and offering his silent moral support.

"Oh—you're American, aren't you? Is this a swipe card?" the man held the card up to the light and squinted.

"Yes," I said, though I would have thought all credit cards were swipe cards.

The man shook his head and mumbled something I didn't catch. He turned his machine ninety degrees so he could swipe the card down the side, then tapped something into the machine's keyboard and nodded. "How many nights may I reserve for you?"

"Let's start with three," I said. "Will that be a problem?"

"Not at all."

A minute later, we had a keycard to a suite, with no more questions asked. He didn't even want to see my ID. With some trepidation as to how Goronwy was taking all this, I led him to the elevator. "Hang on," I said. "You may not like this."

He eyed the panel of buttons as I pressed '5' for the fifth floor, and then his eyes drifted to the evergreen fabric on the walls, a velour shot with gold threads. "Oh, I'm fine," he said, though he clutched the handle on the wall as we began to rise.

The suite appeared exactly as advertised. Goronwy stood in the doorway, surveying it. He rubbed his boot on the plush carpeting. "Nice."

I gave him a brief tour, paying special attention to the bathroom. David still teased Ieuan about how much he'd enjoyed the bathroom during his trip to the twenty-first century. Goronwy went straight to the toilet and flushed it.

"How did you know to do that?" I said.

Goronwy grinned at me. "Ieuan described his experience." He pulled open the glass door that led to the shower and peered inside. "It's this I'm most interested in. Does water really come from that—" he was silent as he fought for the word "—pipe?"

"It does indeed," I said.

The suite consisted of a living room and two bedrooms, each with a massive, curtained four-poster bed, as befitted the pseudo-medieval decor. Goronwy stood with his hands on his hips in the center of the room, surveying it with a slow turn on his heel. "I like it," he said.

"I'm glad."

"I've also had a thought."

"Have you?" I said.

"I think we've had visitors from this world to ours in the past," Goronwy said.

This was unexpected. "How so?" I said.

"What if our ancient gods and goddesses weren't magic at all, but came from this world?" His eyes narrowed as he studied the forty-eight inch wide screen video panel on the wall. "What if *King Arthur* was a time traveler?"

"You're thinking that he could have come from this world to yours, just like the kids and I have?" I said.

"It would explain his extraordinary abilities." Goronwy rubbed his chin. "To the common folk, such a man would have been more than a hero, just as our Dafydd has renewed the legends of Arthur."

"It's an interesting thought, Goronwy," I said, glad that David wasn't here to hear that theory. Then again, maybe he would find it comforting to think that he wasn't alone.

"I wonder if the first Arthur was as uncomfortable with his authority as Dafydd is now," Goronwy said. "Perhaps he fled to Avalon—and by that, I mean this world—because he felt that he'd failed his people in the end."

I found myself laughing. In five minutes, Goronwy had created an explanation for the Arthurian legend out of thin air. And the odd thing was, I couldn't just dismiss it, not when I was standing in a luxurious suite with a man born in the thirteenth century.

"We must care for David such that he never feels the same way," Goronwy said.

"On that, we agree," I said.

After admiring the suite for a few more minutes, Goronwy and I returned to the lobby. Our next step was to sweep through the boutiques available at the spa. We had eight from which to choose.

When we'd passed through the lobby earlier, after acquiring our room key, I'd been surprised to find any of the stores open past five in the evening. But all of them had little 24/7 signs on their doors. The complex, if not the clinic itself, was as busy now as the pool had been when we arrived. It seemed we could have done our shopping at three in the morning. When the brochure said *round-the-clock service*, it meant it.

For Goronwy, I opted for the store specializing in travel wear, while I shopped in a different boutique which was well-stocked with maternity clothes. I had never been fond of elastic waistbands, but pregnancy was the one time in my life I viewed them as a necessity. I acquired new outfits for both of us, using my credit card with its $25,000 credit limit. I was still shaking my head over the fact that my sister hadn't cancelled it when I disappeared four years ago. It showed her love for me, and I was ashamed that I'd misjudged her. I also bought a cell phone.

We changed into our new clothes in the suite, leaving our old clothes to be cleaned (twenty-four-hour laundry!) and our gear stashed in a duffel bag I'd also bought. Then we returned to the waiting room.

Goronwy went to the window as he had before, although it had long since grown too dark to see anything but the garden and the road leading up to the clinic, both of which were lit by a dozen eight foot lamp posts. He shifted from one leg to another and I supposed that his new shoes felt awkward on his feet. Up until now, every pair of boots he'd owned had been made specifically for him, even if none of them had cushioned soles like the ones I'd bought him.

"Are you hungry?" I said. "We missed dinner."

Goronwy shook his head, but then stopped himself as he reconsidered. "I've seen several people pass by with white cups in their hands. What are they drinking?"

I guessed that he didn't mean the men laughing raucously down by the pool, who'd been drinking beer. "Most likely tea or coffee," I said.

"Could I try a cup?" Goronwy said. "Ieaun and Bronwen have both spoken of the taste as something to remember."

I smiled. "I would be happy to corrupt you." I rose to my feet, but before I had taken two steps towards the door, Dr Raj materialized near the nurse's station. "Your husband is awake. You can see him now."

"Thank you!"

Goronwy hadn't understood what Dr Raj had said, so I waved at him to come with me.

"Your husband—Llywelyn is his name, correct?—doesn't speak much English and all but one of the nurses had trouble with his Welsh. Perhaps you can explain to him better what has happened."

"Of course." For all that he wasn't from Wales, Dr Raj had pronounced Llywelyn's name correctly. Goronwy and I trotted down the hall after the doctor, who seemed to walk everywhere in triple-time. "What *did* happen?" I said.

"He has pericarditis," Dr. Raj said, "made acute by a pericardial effusion."

I waited through a couple of heartbeats for him to elaborate, but when he didn't offer up any more information, I said, "And that means ..."

"It's an infection of the tissue around the heart. While this condition is very serious, his coronary arteries are normal. It's odd." Dr Raj pulled up suddenly, causing me to stop abruptly too. "This type of infection is very rare, but it's the third case I've seen this month, which is why I recognized it so quickly. Often patients are misdiagnosed as having a myocardial infarction."

I had been fighting for breath, trying to encompass what the doctor was saying, but now had to ask, "A what?"

"A heart attack."

I nodded. I had heard that phrase before, even though I hadn't known exactly what it meant. I felt a bit like Goronwy must, swimming through a world of unfamiliar words and expectations. "Will ... will he be okay?"

"He's lucky to be here," Dr Raj said. "We're going to get him on the road to improved heart health."

I blinked. That sentence was right out of the pamphlet I'd flipped through in the waiting room. "Does he need surgery?"

"No. As I said, he is very lucky. We've drained off the fluid that was putting pressure on his heart, and the infection is bacterial, so it is treatable with antibiotics. He'll receive them via IV for the first forty-eight hours he's here, and then he'll take them orally. It is also a matter of making sure he maintains his fluids and nutrition. He has a good prognosis. I do have to ask you, however: how long has he been ill?"

"On and off for months," I said. What I didn't add was *ever since the battle at the Severn Estuary.*

"That's not uncommon with this type of illness. We've examined his blood." Now Dr Raj shook his head again. "We've never seen this particular bacterium before. Has he been to a foreign country recently?"

I swallowed hard. "Not really."

Dr Raj shrugged and didn't press me, even though *not really* was a non-answer. Either a person went to a foreign

46

country, or he didn't. "Even so," Dr Raj continued, "initial tests indicate that the antibiotic we're giving him is already working."

I allowed myself a sigh of relief.

"The one other thing I have to point out is that his cholesterol is very high—over three hundred." Dr Raj picked up the pace again. "That's very dangerous in a man his age, and unusual in someone as thin as he is who doesn't smoke. Does your husband have a stressful job?"

I swallowed a laugh. "Very."

"If you can afford it, you might talk him into retiring early."

"I would if I could," I said.

Dr Raj nodded. "Then maybe this incident will give him the push he needs." He gestured us into a room where my very pale and thin husband reclined in a bed. His hair had gone gray around the temples, and the scruff of his beard and mustache were nearly white. The other day when Gwenllian had rubbed his face and call him 'frosty', I'd laughed and dismissed the thought of him as old. But he looked it tonight.

I went to him, kissed his forehead, and caught his hand. He squeezed mine tightly, and the clamp around my heart eased a little more.

"I'll leave you three alone for a minute," Dr Raj said. "The nurse will be in soon because we're going to run a few more tests—" Dr Raj looked at his watch "—and then we'll need you to leave him so he can sleep."

"Leave him?" I continued to hold Llywelyn's hand but looked back to the doctor.

47

Dr Raj couldn't disguise his confusion. "Surely you would prefer the bed in your suite, Mrs. Gruffydd, to the recliner we provide here."

I nodded, but inside, my resolve hardened. While our change in circumstances had happened so fast I could hardly keep my feet, I wasn't leaving Llywelyn alone if I had any way to stay— not in the modern world in a modern hospital where he was helpless.

Dr Raj left the room, and I sat on the edge of Llywelyn's bed, rather than pulling up a chair. Goronwy picked up Llywelyn's sword in its sheath, which had been leaning against the wall in the corner. I scanned the room, concerned about what had happened to his clothes.

I needn't have worried.

Someone had carefully spread his armor over a chair in the corner and left his bracers on the seat to dry. Goronwy and I had even been gone long enough for the staff to clean and dry Llywelyn's clothes. They'd folded them and placed them neatly in a plastic bag, which hung on a hook near the door, next to his cloak. All Llywelyn wore was a blue-striped hospital gown.

Goronwy pulled out Llywelyn's sword and wiped down the blade with a cloth from the sink.

"Thank you. Wouldn't want it to rust." Llywelyn's voice creaked in the still room.

"My pleasure, my lord." Goronwy laid both sheath and sword on the counter by the sink and then pulled up a chair at Llywelyn's bedside. As Goronwy sat down, his eyes widened

48

slightly before he recovered. He cleared his throat. "It's softer than I thought it would be."

"I haven't yet found a comfortable chair in our Wales." I smiled at Goronwy, who smiled back, and then we both turned to Llywelyn.

"So this is the Land of Madoc," my husband said.

"We're calling it Avalon today," Goronwy said.

I ignored both comments and went to the heart of my concern. "I know you aren't okay, but are you with me, my love?"

"When I woke up, I thought I had died. Everything around me was white," Llywelyn said. "And then I saw one of the nurses."

Goronwy's lip twitched. "What did you think, then?"

"I knew where I was," Llywelyn said. "I find it remarkable that you could bear to live in my Wales for as long as you have, Meg. It's so clean here, and you have such marvelous—" he picked at the edge of his blanket with his free hand and then dropped it "—everything."

"It looks like heaven here," I said, "but we merely disguise the dirt better. Wait and see." I wasn't going to remind him this instant about the seven hundred years that filled the time between his world and this one, and what had happened to Wales in it.

Llywelyn leaned his head back to gaze at the ceiling, and then his eyes tracked to the IV drip running down his arm and to the machine beyond, with its blinking lights. "Ieuan and I spoke of this."

"Did you? I didn't know that." I glanced at Goronwy. "It seems you both did."

"I'm not blind. I knew what you two were planning." Again, Llywelyn lifted his hand and let it fall, as it seemed any gesture beyond that required too much effort. "I can't decide now if I am angry or grateful that you ignored my wishes."

"This is the way I see it," I said, feeling matter-of-fact all of a sudden, "if you died, we would have been left without you—and David would be king. On the other hand, if we took you to my time, he would still be king, but you might be alive, and there also remained the possibility of our return."

"We could have died in the river," Llywelyn said.

"Goronwy and I were willing to risk it," I said.

"The baby—" Llywelyn's throat worked.

"It's fine." I pressed his hand that I'd been holding to my belly. "It's kicking me now."

"And since you were dying anyway, it hardly seemed something we needed to ask your opinion about," Goronwy said. "It was our lives we were risking, not yours."

"How ill am I?" Llywelyn said. "I couldn't understand anything that brown man said to you."

"He spoke in English," I said. "You have an infection around your heart which all that–" I gestured to the IV drips and machines on the other side of the bed, "—is going to fix."

"That sounds hopeful, my lord," Goronwy said.

"It is hopeful," I said, finding myself more upbeat than I'd felt in months. "I'll need to ask about recovery time and how long you will have to stay here. A few days at least, would be my guess."

Llywelyn nodded, though he was looking paler than before, despite the overall positive news.

I leaned forward and put out my other hand to Goronwy. "By the way, Goronwy, it would be better if you didn't call him, *my lord*. We may be in Wales, but he is not its king, I'm sorry to say."

Llywelyn groaned and rested his head back against his pillow. "England won."

"It did." A nurse entered the room without knocking, though admittedly, Dr Raj hadn't closed the door. She spoke in Welsh, as had Llywelyn. "And my father is distraught."

I stared at her blankly—we all did—while I thought furiously about what else she might have heard us say. I was surprised that the nurse had understood Llywelyn at all, but on further consideration, that two word sentence sounded similar in any century. But what was she talking about? What did she mean by: *England won, and my father is distraught?*

"His only consolation is that they won by only one goal."

Relief coursed through me as I finally understood. The nurse wasn't talking about England's triumph over Wales militarily, but about soccer (or rather, *football*).

"Is Wales out?" I tried to calculate what event could be taking place in November. *The World Cup? No—too late in the year.*

"It was a *friendly*," the nurse said, "though don't tell that to my dad. It's never a *friendly* to him."

I laughed while Goronwy smiled and nodded, though he couldn't possibly have understood any of that exchange, whether or not he could piece together the words. I let go of Llywelyn's hand and moved aside so the nurse could listen to Llywelyn's heart, take his pulse, draw more blood, and check his machines. With a nod of encouragement, she left again.

After she'd gone, I went to the doorway, looked up and down the hall, and closed the door. "I'm feeling more and more uncomfortable about all the lies I've told the people here. We have a room in the–" I fought for the word in Welsh, "–*lodge*, for now, but–"

Goronwy stood up and began to pace at the end of the bed, looking down at his feet. The room was no more than fourteen feet wide and filled with furniture and medical equipment, so at most he got three steps before having to pause and turn.

"What is it?" I said. "What's bothering you?"

Llywelyn had closed his eyes, but now opened them to study his old friend. "It's these devices, isn't it?"

"It is indeed," Goronwy said. "You read my mind." He turned to me. "They're everywhere. Ieuan told me about Dafydd using your sister's *computer*," he rendered the word in English, "and the endless amounts of information stored in it. Whole books, whole histories, knowledge that it would take any one man a lifetime to master."

I nodded, though I wasn't sure where he was going with this. "I know. This world depends on electronics for everything."

Goronwy stopped his pacing and placed his hands on his hips. "You speak of the lies you have told and I ask—why would you feel the need to lie at all? Why can you not simply state who we are and why we're here?"

My brow furrowed. "Time travel isn't thought to be real, Goronwy. We wouldn't be believed. Worse, we'd be thought crazed."

"But—" Goronwy gestured to the machines at the head of Llywelyn's bed, "—people use these machines every day, for everything. You have lights in your ceilings that turn on with a touch of a finger." He flicked the light off and on, and then off and on again.

"The lights aren't magic, Goronwy," I said. "You've seen lightning in the sky. You've seen David generate electricity with that little water mill of his. All of this, here, is simply the water mill writ large, and these machines with their lights and their constant processing of information involve the same principle taken to its logical conclusion."

"So why wouldn't the people believe that the way you travel between worlds is possible, similar to electricity? You can't see it, but it's there."

"Because nobody has done it yet," I said.

"We have," Goronwy said.

"But nobody knows we've done it and I don't want them to find out," I said.

"Why not?" Goronwy said. "It would mean that you could rest easy with your lies."

I put a hand to my forehead, trying to think of a way to explain my dilemma to Goronwy so that he would understand. As far as we knew, time travel had never happened before and, deservedly or not, modern people didn't trust their government to do the right thing when it came to aliens or time travel. We'd read too many books, seen too many movies, embraced too many plotlines that involved rogue spies, secretive government agencies, and military solutions. Besides, Goronwy *was* the government in the Middle Ages. It would be like not trusting himself.

"Let me put it this way," I said. "Say we discovered that an Englishman had invented a better form of gunpowder. What would we do?"

"Try to find out what it was," Goronwy said, without hesitation.

"And if it happened that this same Englishman was visiting his cousin in Brecon?" I said.

"We would take him and his family into custody," Llywelyn said from behind me. His eyes were closed, but he'd been listening. "It would be our duty, for the good of our country. We would feel it was in our best interests to control him."

Goronwy was finally nodding. "You see the knowledge we have—your ability to travel to and from our time—in the same light."

"I don't know that I do," I said, "but the government, if it knew who you and Llywelyn were? Yes, I believe it would see it that way."

Goronwy gazed out the window of Llywelyn's room, though the darkness outside meant he couldn't see much beyond the bushes that grew underneath the window. Llywelyn had begun to breathe deeply, indicating imminent sleep. "I wish you didn't have to lie," Goronwy said softly.

"Me too," I said.

"This should be a joyous time for you," he said. "You've come home again."

I reached out a hand and touched his cheek. "I haven't, Goronwy. Like you, I'm as far from home as it's possible to be."

He looked down at his feet.

I pulled the credit card from my pocket.

"Do you need to buy something more?" Goronwy said.

I smiled. "How about coffee and a doughnut?"

5

15 November 1288

Bronwen

*B*eep, beep, b-beep, beep.

I woke with a start, shooting upright in bed. I gasped, unsure at first of where I was. The electronic sound still rang in my ears, but as my surroundings soaked in, I put a hand to my heart, forcing it to calm. I'd had an auditory hallucination, not uncommon for me. I'd gotten out of bed a few months ago, before Catrin was born, and reached the door to the bedroom before I realized I hadn't heard a phone ringing down the hall.

Thankfully, I hadn't woken the baby, who lay swaddled in the middle of the bed between Ieuan and me. Except Ieuan wasn't in bed. He stood before the fireplace, staring into it.

"What is it?" I said. "Why are you awake?" I checked the window. It felt like I'd slept for hours, but no daylight showed in the crack between the window shutters. Ieuan often woke up

56

before Catrin and me, but he usually reappeared later, after we were awake, rather than hovering as he was doing now.

"You fell asleep nursing. It's late afternoon still." Ieaun turned to me, a smile on his face, though it didn't reach his eyes. He came closer and pulled me up from the bed so he could kiss me. When we came up for air, instead of releasing me, he pulled me closer.

I held on for a second and then leaned back to search his face. "What's wrong?"

"Meg has taken Llywelyn and Goronwy back."

I gazed at him without speaking. I'd heard him. He didn't have to repeat what he'd said, but I was so stunned and scared for them I couldn't feel anything. His words rang hollowly in my head. "Are-are you sure—" I cut myself off. Of course he was sure. He would have made sure before he said anything to me. "When?"

"Just before sunset," Ieuan said.

I pressed both hands together and put them to my lips. "Where are Anna and David?"

"They've gone to the great hall, to put a good face on it. They're going to tell the people that Meg took Llywelyn to Avalon."

"That's one way to look at it," I said.

"Anna asked if you'd be coming to dinner. I think she'd like you to sit with her."

I could understand that. My heart hurt and Meg had been my substitute mom for only three years, ever since I'd come from the modern world with David and Ieuan. "I'll be out as soon as I nurse Catrin," I said.

"I'll let Anna know." He moved to leave, but then hesitated in the doorway. "It's going to be okay. Look what happened when Dafydd took me."

"The best thing ever," I said.

Ieuan smiled, as I hoped he would, and clapped a hand on the frame of the door. "Stop in and see Tudur before you go to the hall. He's flustered, and not just because of Llywelyn's departure."

"Okay." I settled Catrin in my arms, gently stroking her cheek so that she turned her head and latched onto my breast. I leaned back, grateful that the initial soreness and pain had finally passed. I don't know where I'd gotten the idea that having a baby was all sweetness and light. It was probably because I'd spent exactly zero time around babies since I stopped being one. Catrin was what Meg called *a high maintenance baby*, in that she cried more often than most babies and wanted to be held constantly. And she upchucked. A lot. David had laughed when I'd told him, but I'd narrowed my eyes at him and told him, *just you wait!*

I cuddled Catrin closer. I hadn't ever known such fierce love. Some historians have postulated that medieval people responded to the loss of so many of their children to disease by hardening their hearts and loving the ones they did have less, in order to more easily bear the pain of it.

But that wasn't what I saw at all, and certainly not what I felt. The losses made mothers love all the more strongly, because they knew they might have far too little time with any child—any person—whom they loved. The modern world, with its cribs and car seats and daycares, all designed to put distance between a

58

child and her mother, was stripped away here. It was only a mom and a nursing baby: child passed from arm to arm, from one person to another, until she fell asleep.

I huddled over Catrin, thinking of these babies we were having, all of whom were half-modern, half-medieval—and now Meg had gone back to the future. I hadn't asked Ieuan the reason she'd taken Llywelyn. I didn't have to. When David had arrived at Chepstow earlier in the week, Llywelyn had been having a good day. David had mentioned to me how glad he was that his father was healthy. I hadn't corrected David, figuring he'd see for himself soon enough. I just hoped this trip to the modern world would give Meg and Llywelyn what they were looking for.

And maybe, if I was lucky, Meg might remember me and bring me back a stick of lip balm.

After a while, Catrin finished eating, by which point my maid had arrived to help me dress. Twenty minutes later, with my hair arranged appropriately for the noblewoman I had become, I tucked Catrin into her sling and went to find Tudur, which wasn't hard because he was where he always was—in Llywelyn's office, stewing over piles of papers. In the Middle Ages, paper was made from linen rags and was much stronger and more durable than modern wood-pulp paper. It was going to last forever, as long as people didn't treat it as disposable or burn it. When I entered the office, Tudur was leaning forward, his hands in his hair and his elbows on the table, studying the material before him.

He looked up. "Bronwen! I need you!"

He spoke to me this way all the time. Somehow, in the last four months that I'd lived with Llywelyn and Meg, waiting through a difficult pregnancy for Catrin's birth, I'd become indispensible to the king's staff. It wasn't because I understood medieval law or had a fine hand, but because I knew how to organize. With no computers or filing cabinets, a busy office ended the day with papers scattered everywhere. Llywelyn—and Tudur as his surrogate at Chepstow—had come to rely on me to tidy it.

For a while, I'd even become Tudur's eyes. At first he'd refused to admit he had a problem, and then David's trip to England had overwhelmed all planning, so it was only last week that he'd told Llywelyn that he couldn't see to read anymore. Tudur's newly forged reading glasses perched on the end of his nose, confirming what I'd felt since I met him—that Tudur would have been more of a scholar than a soldier, had circumstances been different.

"What do you have there?" I said.

Tudur flicked the paper towards me. It wasn't out of disrespect, but because we'd grown used to each other and his lack of formality was a sign of trust, even friendship.

I picked it up. It was a monthly accounting report for the Abbey of St. Peter and St. Paul in Shrewsbury. The Abbey was almost entirely self-supporting. It held a weekly market fair and ran sheep for the wool trade. "I saw this on your desk earlier, made a note, and filed it." I said. "Why did you get it out again?"

"Because we both missed the significance of the words at the bottom—me because I couldn't see them, and you because you saw what the document was about and didn't read all the way down the page."

I peered at the words Tudur indicated. Someone had written them awfully small. "It's a list of herbs." I looked up at Tudur. "Are you going to tell me why we care?"

Tudur lifted his chin. "Read it over carefully. What does it say?"

No paper ever came out of Shrewsbury Abbey written in anything but Latin, which is why I had only skimmed it in the first place. My knowledge of the language wasn't great, but it had gotten better in the last three years and I did my best: "*Conium, Somniferum, Mandragora, Aconitum* ... wait a minute. *Aconite.* This is a list of poisons!"

"It is indeed." Tudur leaned back in his chair. "They've been sent to London."

I gaped at him. "To where in London?" I flipped the paper over to look at the back. It was blank. "The document doesn't say."

"It doesn't, does it?" Tudur said. "The man who brought that list here asked the carter, however, and he said that the cargo was destined for Westminster Palace."

"Are you telling me that Humphrey de Bohun ordered a batch of poisons?" I said.

"We don't know," Tudur said. "We do know that our beloved prince will be residing at Westminster as long as he is in London," Tudur said.

"When did the shipment leave Shrewsbury?" I said.

61

"Last month," Tudur said. "That paper arrived here four days ago."

"The poisons could be anywhere by now," I said. "Used already, for that matter. Have you told David?"

Tudur took in a deep breath through his nose. "At the moment, the Prince is in no condition to be told anything."

I pursed my lips. "I'll tell him. Or I'll tell Lili. It might be nothing, but ..."

"Alphonse of Toulouse was murdered by poison," Tudur said.

"As was Baldwin of Jerusalem," I said, "not to mention old King Henry I himself."

"Henry died from eating too many lampreys," Tudur said.

"Who dies from eating too much fish?" I shivered. "Lampreys are disgusting creatures, I admit, but that's a fairy tale the Normans have told themselves."

Catrin stirred in her sling and whimpered. "You'd better go," Tudur said. "Urge caution on our young prince, would you?"

That sounded unlikely to be successful. "I'll do my best," I said.

I turned to go but Tudur coughed, causing me to pause in the doorway. "I fear for him," Tudur said. "This mantle of Arthur that burdens him ..."

I looked back. Tudur was resting his head in his hands again, staring at the papers before him, though this time I didn't think he was seeing them.

"You are the first to imply in my hearing that David isn't the return of Arthur," I said. "You don't believe it?"

"What?" Tudur scoffed. "Believe it? Of course I believe it. I just don't trust what the English may do with the legend. They think Arthur belongs to *them*, when really, David is one of us."

I swallowed hard. It was absurd and I would never say as much to David, but every year that passed, I found myself agreeing more and more with Tudur.

6

15 November 1288

David

I wasn't getting any closer to accepting that Mom and Dad had gone 'Back to the Future' on me. Sure—I'd done it to them, and I understood why Mom had jumped, but I didn't have to like it.

I glanced down the table at my family, eating the evening meal as if this was business as usual. I couldn't do it. I could hear Mom's parting words to me again, about living lighter, but I found myself growing more and more angry with every minute that passed. It was probably good that nobody was paying any attention to me, because my face had flushed and in another moment steam would start coming out of my ears. Even as I tried to damp it down, my anger grew all the more intense because I didn't have a right to it, nor was there anybody at whom I could direct it.

Worse, Lili had spent the meal eyeing me carefully, though without admonishing me in the way I deserved. She had kept a gentle hand on my left thigh, even as I reached for the flagon to pour myself another cup of mead. Instead, it was Bevyn's lips that thinned into a line. He was here because I'd asked him to come to England with me, as an advisor I personally trusted. He had a wife and child on Anglesey, but I was selfish enough to keep him from them for what would probably turn out to be over a month.

"That'll be your seventh," he said. "How much more self-loathing are you going to inflict upon yourself?"

I stopped in the act of pouring the mead and set down the flagon. My fingers tightened on my cup and I almost swore at him. He'd read my mind as easily as fishermen read the weather.

"I am aware of that," I said.

"Are you really?" Bevyn said.

Yes, Goddamn it! And what gives you the right to tell me what I should or shouldn't do? I glared at Bevyn, teeth gritted, and resisted the temptation to sweep the table clear of food and drink.

I took in a deep breath through my nose and let it out slowly.

I knew it was my seventh cup. I'd been looking forward to drinking at least seven more, too, until I fell asleep right at the table, rather than face the future that confronted me. Did no one realize that if Dad didn't return, *I* would be the King of Wales? That at twenty, I would suddenly be responsible for the welfare of an entire country, and if I followed his suggestion, threw my name into the hat as he wanted, I'd rule the people of England as well?

Looking into Bevyn's eyes, I warred with myself as to how to answer him, but my answer was never in doubt. His warning had created the desired effect in me. I couldn't upbraid Bevyn any more than I could castigate my father.

Bevyn rose to his feet. "Come with me."

Reluctantly, I rose to match him. Everyone was looking at me now, leading me to believe that I hadn't been as unnoticed as I'd thought. Ever since we'd come to Wales alone and had only each other to rely on, Anna, at least, had been attuned to my emotions, whether I wanted her to be or not. Her eyes fastened on mine, and I read pity there. I pressed my lips together. I didn't want anyone's pity and hardly deserved it.

With great effort, I said, "Continue the meal. Bevyn and I are going to take a little walk." I leaned down to kiss the top of Lili's head. "I apologize for my behavior, *cariad*. I'll be back."

Lili slipped her hand around the back of my neck to keep my face close to hers. "I love you."

"I know," I said, "though I imagine you might be reconsidering the decision to marry me about now."

That got me the smile I wanted and she released me. I straightened, only to find that the change in altitude had flown every cup of mead I'd consumed straight to my head. I was a big man—two inches over six feet and two hundred pounds—but the brewer at Chepstow was a master and made a potent drink.

"I got you, boy." Bevyn was one of the few, out of all my acquaintances, who could get away with calling me that. He knew it, of course, which was why he felt free to say it—and why he'd decided that he was the one companion best suited to recall me to my senses.

I put an arm across Bevyn's shoulder and left the hall with him. Upon leaving the shelter of the building, we entered the lower bailey of the castle—and walked into a rainstorm. After only two steps, my boot found a puddle. Water splashed all the way to my knee. "Where are we going?" I said.

"Out."

I didn't say *really?* even though that would have been a reasonable response. I never went anywhere without my *teulu*, but I sensed that Bevyn wasn't feeling very reasonable right now, any more than I was. He urged me across the bailey, navigating the puddles that had formed at low spots in the packed earth the best we could, and underneath the portcullis. Bevyn waved at the man who stood sentry at the entrance to the castle. His brow furrowed in response, until I lifted a hand to him, too. He couldn't know that I was drunk and in no condition to be going anywhere.

I glanced at Bevyn's profile. Could this be ... betrayal? Even as the thought passed through my mind, I shook my head, sending my senses flying all over the place. It couldn't. Not from Bevyn. Sure of that, if of nothing else, I allowed Bevyn to lead me to the barbican and the lower gate. Before we'd gone ten yards, however, hurrying feet sounded behind us.

"My lord!"

Bevyn stopped before the great wooden door that was the first line of defense for the castle. I tottered around to face the man who'd come. Whether Bevyn wanted company or not, Evan and a contingent of my men weren't going to let me leave the castle unattended.

"Tell them to stay back," Bevyn said. "There's something you should see—but only you."

A dozen of my men crowded into the barbican. I crooked a finger at Evan. "What is it, my lord?" Evan stepped forward.

"Bevyn and I must see to something," I said. "You may follow, but give us some space to be alone."

"Yes, my lord." Evan bowed.

Even as he turned back to my men, however, he glanced at Bevyn, who nodded. The need for Bevyn's approval brought the same acid taste to my mouth that I'd been feeling earlier. During my conversation with Mom and Dad, and all through dinner, I'd been bemoaning the constraints on my life. I was a Prince of Wales, and while that sounded like an awesome thing to be, it wasn't nearly as cool in practice when one had to live it every day.

A wash of rain and darkness greeted us as we entered the clearing to the south of the castle. We walked out of reach of the torchlight at the gate, heading west along the road towards the town of Chepstow, a hundred yards away.

Rain rat-tat-tatted on the helmets of the men behind us. That same steady rain soaked my hair and streamed down my face. It was like standing in a cold shower. I pulled up my hood, coming more to my senses with every yard I walked, and no longer in need of Bevyn's assistance.

I didn't ask where we were going either—I didn't really care. With our departure from the hall and the coolness of the evening, my rush of fury had dissipated to a more manageable discontent, and even that was easing. We passed through the town gate, admitted by the guard at another simple lift of my hand, and turned down a side street. Bevyn stopped at a small house halfway along the block. He made a *halt* motion with his hand at Evan, who held his men a few paces away. Then Bevyn knocked at the door.

A tall man opened it. "Yes?" And then his face cleared as he recognized Bevyn. "My lord! I'd heard you were in Chepstow, but didn't expect you to honor us with your presence tonight."

"I'm here with the Prince." Bevyn gestured to me. I'd been standing behind him in the shadows and now showed my face.

Even with the introduction, however, I didn't step into the house because I'd recognized the townsman as Aeddan, the man who had sheltered me when I was sixteen. I'd been abducted by several of my own men and subsequently escaped. Behind Aeddan, a lanky young man who could only be Huw, his son, straightened from a squat in front of the fire. He was the same age now that I'd been then.

The slow fire in me that the rain had dampened threatened to rise again. I knew in an instant why Bevyn had brought me here: he wanted me to see—and to understand—and to remember—why I carried the burdens I did. And to accept them again. I could have been rude, turned away from the unwanted lesson, but at Huw's expansive smile, I thanked Aeddan for his hospitality and crossed the threshold into his house.

"I am honored to welcome you here, too, my lord," Aeddan said.

His addendum had a genuine laugh rising in my chest. Aeddan had been awestruck over Bevyn's appearance. Me, he could take or leave. I stopped in front of Huw. At the sight of his bright eyes and smile, I let the laughter show. I ruffled Huw's hair as I had when I'd seen him last. But then I dropped my hand as I acknowledged that he was nearly as tall as I was, and two years a man. "What are you doing here at Chepstow?" I said.

"We're merchants now, selling our wool at the market in the village," Aeddan said, with obvious pride. "This is my uncle's house."

"He's out visiting," Huw said.

I turned to look at Bevyn. "How did you know they were here?"

"We've kept in touch ever since your abduction when you were sixteen," Bevyn said.

His words made me suddenly ashamed. I hadn't asked about Aeddan and his family, not once. I'd hardly thought of them again after that summer, except vaguely in passing, and only then because the memory of my vulnerability still ate at me. Aeddan must have read regret in my face because he bowed his head. "You've had many things on your mind, my lord."

Which was true, but not necessarily an excuse. How many others had I left behind in the last six years? How many had I used and then forgotten in the immediacy of daily life as a Prince of Wales? Rather than my rescuers, it was Dai, my surviving abductor, whom I'd later tracked down, only to find that he'd lost his leg below the knee as the result of a riding accident. I'd left him as he was, unable to find it in me to punish him more than fate already had.

Bevyn clapped me on the shoulder. "No use going from an angry drunk to a maudlin one. I didn't bring you here for that."

I blinked at him, my head clearing. "Then for what?"

"Let's settle in first." Bevyn nudged me towards a stool near the central fire and when I sat, Huw handed me a bowl of broth. I sipped it, feeling the salty warmth fill my stomach and glad to have it inside me instead of mead. Bevyn went to the doorway, spoke a few words to Evan, who had remained in the street, and then closed the door. He approached the fire. "The men stand guard and the town is quiet. We may speak freely now."

I took another sip, studying Bevyn over the rim of my bowl. I raised my eyebrows in expectation of an explanation for all this. So far, I'd done everything he'd asked. It was time he enlightened me.

But now that it came to it, he seemed to have trouble knowing where to begin. He opened his mouth, closed it, glanced at Aeddan, who nodded, and then tried again. "There have been ... some complications with this journey we're taking tomorrow," Bevyn said.

I really wished I hadn't drunk all that mead. Between it and the heat from the fire, I was having a hard time focusing and I could tell from Bevyn's hesitation that this was important. I rested my elbows on my knees and took another sip of broth. "Tell me."

It was Huw who spoke, after a glance and a nod from his father. "It was only this afternoon that the message from London reached us. Bevyn was to speak to the king this evening, but ..."

"He is not available," I said. "You'll have to make do with me. What is it?"

"Our contacts in England are worried," Bevyn said. "Everyone knows that you are coming to England for the wedding of William and Joan, and many believe it is a ruse to draw you out of Wales. To draw you to your death."

This was more like the Bevyn I knew. I rubbed my chin. "Do you believe that it is Humphrey de Bohun himself who plays us false, or someone else?"

"Not Bohun," Aeddan said. "In fact, we haven't heard anything from that quarter other than that he welcomes you to England. Others, however, do not wish you well. For example, the son of Owain Goch, Hywel, still plots with Valence to unseat your father."

Owain Goch was my father's older brother, whom he'd imprisoned for most of his life and who died in 1282, before I came to Wales. Valence had trotted Hywel out as a challenge to us last summer, because under Welsh law, Hywel should have a right to lands in Wales comparable to my father's. "That I knew—"

Bevyn held up a hand. "Let him finish."

"Meanwhile, Valence has allied with Alfonso of Aragon, who seeks a quick marriage to Princess Eleanor," Huw said.

"Eleanor is the eldest daughter and has first claim to succeed her father, were the barons to consent to that," I said.

"She's nineteen now. How long can the barons deny her right to rule?"

"As long as they can," Bevyn said. "Both Valence and Alfonso are in London and will attend William's wedding."

"Thus, Alfonso strives for the throne, even if no baron wants to see a Spaniard with the crown of England on his brow," I said. "It would be as horrifying to them as a Frenchman."

"Alfonso has made no secret of his intention," Bevyn said. "Whether he thinks he can control Valence instead of the other way around isn't clear. Valence views Alfonso as his puppet."

"Valence prefers to work behind the scenes. That's been his pattern." I studied my companions. "What is the nature of the threat against me?"

"Ambush on the road," Aeddan said.

Delightful. "As if I haven't had enough of those," I said.

"We are looking into it, my lord, but without specifics of time and place, only rumor ..." Aeddan said.

I nudged Bevyn, who'd come to sit beside me. "Then you'll just have to keep me safe."

Bevyn bowed his head. "As always, of course."

"You spoke of news from London," I said to Aeddan. "I hope you have more. We've had some difficulty distilling truth from falsehood these last few weeks. What of Kirby, the other regent?"

"He didn't support Valence's attack on Wales, and is working to reform the Treasury," Aeddan said.

I almost said, *borrrring,* but didn't. I understood the power Kirby wielded. Edward had appointed him Lord Treasurer in 1284, making him upon Edward's death the nobleman with the highest standing. Now, in addition to regent, he was also the Bishop of Ely. Although his demeanor was mild, he had stepped into the middle of difficult disputes with aplomb. For example, before King Edward's death, he'd summoned the mayor of London and his alderman to the Tower of London to discuss disorder in the city. When the mayor had resigned in protest of the summons, Kirby had refused to appoint another and had ruled London himself since then.

"Okay. What else?"

Aeddan cleared his throat. "Questions have been raised as to whether or not the death of Prince Edward, the last remaining son of King Edward's body, was a natural consequence of disease, or he was ... helped along the path to Heaven."

"London is rife with rumor and suspicion," Huw said. "The barons are reluctant to crown anyone in Edward's stead, for fear that the one they choose committed regicide to get there."

Bevyn scoffed. "Such a man wouldn't be the first king to murder his predecessor. Still, there's more to it than that. Right now, we have two rivals to the throne: Alfonso and William, with their respective betrothed princesses, Eleanor and Joan. However, neither Alfonso—or rather, Valence—nor the Bohuns have the support of enough barons to actually *take* the throne. Everyone wants a third candidate and they're all jostling among themselves to determine who that's going to be."

"Gilbert de Clare has my vote, though if he ultimately betrays us and turns against Wales, he would prove as difficult an enemy to counter as King Edward," I said. "Still, none of this touches on me. I pose no threat to anyone but Hywel."

"Perhaps," Bevyn said. "You have power in your own right, however, and the Norman lords know it. Whichever side you come down on could influence other barons. Wars have been started for less."

"Are we really talking civil war?" I said. Dad had said as much earlier in the day. "Has it gotten that bad?"

"We fear it," Bevyn said. "War in England can be good for Wales, but much depends upon who wins."

"So we're back to Valence again?" I said. "Or is it Vere or Bigod's heir who most concerns you?"

Bevyn growled. "All of them."

"Roger Mortimer has been freed from the Tower," Huw said.

That wasn't good news. "Edmund Mortimer remains in London, doesn't he?" I said. "He is still our ally, along with Clare?"

"Yes," Aeddan said. "That is true as far as we know. We've not heard differently."

I eyed the shepherd-turned-trader, finally taking note of Aeddan's continual use of the word 'we'. In the three years since Wales had declared itself independent from England, Math, my father, and I had cultivated circles of informants—spies—to help us make sense of what was happening in England as well as in our own country, listening to anyone high and low who had news to give us. We wanted to know of a threat to Wales *before* it happened. The survival of Wales was a problem my father and I faced every day. It was immediate, constant, and distracted us from more important things—like improving the daily lives of our people—or a working telegraph, for that matter.

And yet what kind of life would they have if we failed and Wales fell under the Norman boot?

Despite our efforts, we'd failed to hear of the gathering of Bigod's forces at Bristol in preparation for his attack on our southern coast last August. That we'd learned of it first from Humphrey de Bohun still galled me.

Even with that failure, Tudur, in particular, had become skilled in weighing one bit of information against another. His seat at Chepstow was a gathering place for information from the whole of south and mid-Wales, and the March. Aaron's Jewish connections had given us another network of information; Math's connections with the Welsh in England provided yet a third. I looked from Aeddan to Huw to Bevyn. Was this a fourth source I hadn't known about?

"What do you mean by *we*?" I said.

The three men looked down at their feet. Their instinctive and unintentional sign of uncertainty let me know that this was something I didn't know, that they didn't necessarily want to talk about it, and that Aeddan's 'we' included Bevyn.

Bevyn cleared his throat. "The Order of the Pendragon."

I licked my lips. I was already sure I wasn't going to like this. "Why have I never heard of it?"

"You weren't meant to," Bevyn said.

"Am I to understand that the Order of the Pendragon is ... a secret society?"

"I'm not sure what you mean by that, exactly," Bevyn said, "but if you are asking if we are a group of like-minded men who seek to protect you in any way we can—who are willing to give our lives for you, then yes. That is the Order of the Pendragon."

I found myself torn between anger, awe, and laughter, and was tempted to check my forehead for a lightening-shaped scar. "How many of you are there?"

"Nearly one hundred, at present," Bevyn said.

One hundred! Sweet Jesus. "How long has this been going on?"

"Since your father acknowledged you as his heir," Bevyn said.

"Six years, you mean? You've been part of this group for six years?" I couldn't have been more stunned if he'd hit me on the head with a cast iron pan. "Who are they? Where do they come from?"

"From all walks of life," Bevyn said, "and from all over England and Wales, the better to serve and protect you."

I let the silence drag out as I considered the implications and the planning required to pull something like this off. "You trust every man in the Order?"

"Yes," Bevyn said.

"That means you know each and every one of them?" I said.

"Yes, my lord," Bevyn said. "Every man was either personally recruited by me or by someone well known to me."

"You did this yourself, you mean?" I said. "You're the leader?"

"Leadership in the Order is more fluid than that," Bevyn said. "More complicated."

"Is it, now?" The question had come out dry and semi-sarcastic. I couldn't help it.

Bevyn closed his mouth.

I eyed him for a long moment before prodding him, even though it was clear he didn't want to say more. "Meaning what?"

"We have no status, no titles, no fixed station for any member in our Order," Aeddan said. "Each member is his own man, but we all look to Bevyn for guidance."

"Lord Carew joined us very recently," Huw said. "He's proven his worth in your service many times over."

I couldn't argue with that. It was no less than the truth, which was why Dad and I had included him in the party traveling to England tomorrow.

I scrubbed at my hair with both hands and didn't say what I really thought, which was that they'd all run completely amok. They had stated point blank that my life was more important than theirs, and had backed up their belief by creating a secret society whose sole purpose was to protect me. I found myself growing angry again. I wanted to tell them that they had no right to lay this burden on me, no right to build their lives around *me*. But I didn't chastise them—*God help me, I couldn't.*

"We're putting every man we have on full alert during your trip," Huw said. "You will be well protected, and if you need anything at any time, we'll see to it."

I closed my eyes for a second, and then opened them. I was defeated. "Thank you." What else could I say?

We spoke among ourselves for another few minutes, small talk mostly. I asked about Aeddan's wife and other children, and tried not to convey to them anything but my gratefulness. It would do no good to complain, and as I sat by the fire, I wasn't sure I had a right to my discontent. *Live more lightly*, Mom had said. To which I could only reply, *How*?

Bevyn and I said our goodbyes, and I promised Aeddan that his family would be welcome in any castle in which I was staying, anywhere in Wales. Bevyn and I walked back to the castle through another cloudburst. Evan kept his men ten paces behind us as he had on the way to Aeddan's house.

"Why did you bring me to them?" I said, once we left the village behind.

"To sober you up."

"I'm sober, believe me," I said. "I've been sober every day since I was fourteen years old and my sister drove my aunt's van into that clearing and saved Dad's life. I've been nothing *but* sober."

"I know it."

"Thus, I'm asking you again—*why*?" I said. "You could have told me what was happening in England and what we might face in London without all this—" I gestured expansively with one hand, meaning the rain, the walk, even the world at large, "—without letting me in on the secret of your Order."

Bevyn halted in the middle of the road, within range of the torch lights from the gate, and turned to face me. "You needed to know."

I folded my arms across my chest. "Why?"

Bevyn's jaw worked. "Did you know that it was I who was the first to go to your father, back at Castell y Bere, after you came to us? It was I who told him what he had."

A coldness spread throughout my belly. "Go on."

"I told your father that he had to be very careful with you, that you were no ordinary boy. You were far more than he could ever have hoped for in a son, but you were untrained—woefully untrained—and that meant handling—on his part and on mine—with soft gloves."

I thought back to those first days in Wales, when my life had narrowed to sword play, languages my mind had refused to encompass, and meals that by the end of the day I was too tired to eat. Bevyn had been right in his understanding of me. "But all that changed, didn't it?" I said. "It was the boar hunt."

Bevyn nodded. "Up until then, you were all raw potential. At the boar hunt, the kind of man you were became clear. We knew for certain then."

"My father treated me differently after that." I said, knowing it for truth, though I'd never understood the chain of events before. I eyed my old friend warily. "Before that day, he considered *not* claiming me as his son, didn't he?"

80

Bevyn barked a laugh. "Never that. He would have claimed you even had you sported a limp and a twisted shoulder, so desperate was he for an heir. But he had to acknowledge that you had been raised in a different world, one he didn't understand and never could. You were strong, intelligent, and well-fed, but innocent. He didn't want to undermine the foundation your mother had given you while building in you what you needed to survive here. To rule here." Bevyn slapped a gloved fist into the palm of his other hand.

A chill settled on my shoulders at Bevyn's last words. "What you're telling me without saying it aloud is that my father knew of your Order, isn't that right?"

Bevyn nodded.

"You chose to tell me now, not because you thought *I* should know, but because my father is absent."

"You are Wales, my lord," Bevyn said. "You cannot run from it, nor afford any more drunken evenings."

"No," I said. "I can't."

And then without warning, a bloom of laughter rose in my chest, along with something else—something like hope. I tipped back my head and let the laughter out. It grew and grew until I was laughing so hard I had to hold onto Bevyn's shoulder lest I lose my balance. Tears streamed down my cheeks, mixing with the falling rain, and I wiped at the water with the back of my hands.

"I am delighted at your change of humor, my lord, but what is it that you find so amusing?" Bevyn smiled, but his eyes reflected puzzlement.

I held my belly, swallowing down a few last chuckles. "A secret society exists solely to protect me. I have my own personal Order." It was strange and hilarious—and beyond insane. I laughed again, and this time Bevyn joined me, even if he still didn't fully understand.

Live lightly indeed.

7

15 November 1288

David

I lay in bed with Lili in my arms, listening to her breathe and unable to sleep myself. Something about the night's events had sparked a change in me. I didn't know yet if it was real change or the mead talking, but I wasn't nearly as morose as I'd been. The black cloud that had followed me—maybe for years—was fading to gray.

It was both comforting and terrifying to know that the Order of the Pendragon existed: comforting because someone beyond my father was looking out for me; terrifying because I hadn't known about it and Dad hadn't seen fit to tell me. He had sought to train me to be king, and yet had kept secrets—important secrets. What else would I discover about ruling Wales now that he was gone?

And that was another problem. I'd never felt like the boy lion in *The Lion King*, singing about how he couldn't wait to be king, without acknowledging that for this to happen, his father had to die. My father was somewhere around sixty—he'd always been vague on the exact year he'd been born. Regardless of the specifics, he was twenty years older than Mom. It was my impression that he felt those years more now than he had even a few years ago when I first came to Wales. Sixty was *old* for the Middle Ages. Mom had said that the median life expectancy for males who survived childhood was forty-eight. I was twenty—and of course would live forever—but even I was daunted by the idea that I had fewer than thirty years to live. Dad had to feel he was living on borrowed time.

Mostly that didn't bear thinking about. It was only at times like these, when I held Lili in the middle of the night as she slept and I stewed in my own juices, unable to turn off my brain, that I allowed myself to truly contemplate what I'd done when I'd returned to Wales three years ago. It had been my *choice*, far more than my duty. Why was I seeing only now how heavily that choice had weighed on me? I'd known at the time, and said out loud, that I was willing to trade security and longevity for the possibility of becoming someone who mattered. I still believed it. It was more that I hadn't truly understood what it meant until today.

With Dad gone, I had to face the fact that I mattered *now*. The future of Wales rested on my shoulders. Despite my training, despite the number of people who supported me and might die for me—literally—now that it came to it, I knew down to the deepest core of my being that my back wasn't broad enough to carry the burden.

A rumbling began again in my chest, a laughter I couldn't swallow or hide. Did nobody realize how inadequate I was? I had people referring to me openly as the return of Arthur. Couldn't they see how absurd that was?

As I chuckled to myself, trying not to wake Lili, the last of my tension oozed away into the bedcovers.

"You're not sleeping," Lili said.

"You're not supposed to know that." I pulled her closer.

"I always know when you're not sleeping," Lili said. "The thoughts start spinning in your head so fast I can hear them. What were you thinking that made you laugh?"

"That I have a task before me that I can't possibly manage, even with help, but I'm going to attempt it anyway."

"And that's funny?" Lili said.

"It's freeing," I said.

She rolled over so she faced me, snuggling closer. "You're not going to fail."

"Of course I am, Lili," I said. "And it's okay. Why aren't you asleep?"

"I was thinking about the Order of the Pendragon, and the wedding, and the poisonous herbs from Shrewsbury, and who is going to win the throne of England," she said. "It's all a jumble in my head, the same as you."

I threw a hand over my eyes. "You really did read my mind. My life will never be the same again."

"You're silly." Lili poked me in the side.

85

I grabbed her hand. "I am having second, third, and fourth thoughts about attending William's wedding."

"We have to go. You said as much to the others and nothing has changed," Lili said. "We can't let people know that your father and mother have disappeared—not yet—not until our people have become accustomed to your rule."

"But that's exactly it," I said. "I won't be ruling Wales. Nobody will. That was one reason Dad wasn't going to come with us in the first place."

"That, and he has as much of a price on his head as you do," Lili said.

"Now that's comforting—"

"We'll have gone and come back by the end of the month," Lili said. "If your parents haven't returned by then, we may have to address the people, but until then ..."

"Until then, we pretend that nothing has happened, which means that I have to put on finery and make small talk with men who would just as soon run me through as look at me," I said.

"And here I thought, when you first spoke of traveling to England, that it might be fun."

"We can't lower our guard, not for one second," I said. "They'll all be there—Alfonso, Mortimer, Valence, my cousin, Hywel—every one of them eyeing my throat and possibly each other's, which is actually the only good news. They hate each other as much as they hate me. Maybe more, since they know each other so well." I rubbed my eyes. "From the moment we set foot in

England, we must assume the worst of all but our closest companions."

"Then you'd better get some sleep, husband," Lili said, curling into my arm and putting her hand on my chest. "On top of everything else, it's your birthday in a few hours."

I listened as her breath quieted and thought that she was asleep, but then she said, "I've been thinking about my father."

I rubbed her shoulder. "I know." I'd been thinking about Cynan too, worried that he'd try to use his connection to her to either hurt her, or influence me. Admittedly, he had confessed hatred for my father, and by extension, me, but greed did strange things to people.

"Have you ever heard Bohun mention him? Do you know where he is?" she said.

My stomach clenched at the hitch in her voice. Cynan had abandoned her and Ieuan when she was very young. She hadn't seen her father in years, not even at our wedding, since we hadn't invited him. Ieuan and I had encountered Cynan three years ago, when he had helped Humphrey de Bohun capture us and kill our men, before we managed to gain the advantage. Cynan had been released with Bohun at the signing of the treaty.

He served Humphrey de Bohun now, and it was Humphrey de Bohun we were going to see.

"No," I said. "But I will find out."

A few minutes later, she was asleep, despite her insistence that she never slept when I didn't. Now that she was pregnant, she slept more hours than she was awake. This journey would wear her out—it was a hundred and ten miles to London—and it wasn't a trip we could make by car.

Because my plan was to travel lightly, without much in the way of baggage, we should reach Westminster Palace by the 19th of November. That was cutting it very close to William's wedding, which would take place on the 20th. If the Bohuns viewed our abbreviated trip as an insult, so be it.

I was betting that Humphrey not only understood our hesitation in riding into England, but also approved of our caution and didn't mind sharing the limelight with me for as little time as possible. If anyone asked me to my face, I would say that I trusted our new allies, these Norman barons who'd pledged their allegiance ... but I didn't. I couldn't afford to, especially now. We would stay a week and then return, provided everything went well.

Ha. When had everything gone well? I wished I had a plan, beyond mere attendance at the wedding and the hope of keeping the poisonous politics of the English court at bay.

Dad and I had spent the last six years reacting to the actions of others. Some English lord would make a move, and we'd counter it. In August, we'd come out on top yet again, but the odds were against holding off Norman designs on Wales forever. Luck had played a role in everything we'd managed to accomplish so far, but I couldn't count on it always being on our side. You made your own luck, yes, but sometimes you were just plain lucky. Particularly after we'd run into Clare and he'd turned out to be an ally, I'd had a vision of Valence running around behind the scenes, patching his plan together with duct tape. It hadn't held, but that wasn't to say it wouldn't next time.

For once, why couldn't it be our side that *acted* instead of *reacted*?

I'd mentioned this to my father, and he'd given me a hard look. And then Dad had said the same words to me that he'd spoken on the balcony this afternoon: *You know what you need to do.*

Was that it? Was he right? I shook my head. I couldn't see it.

* * * * *

Arising to face the day, having fallen asleep in the early hours of the morning, I was no closer to any conclusion apart from the thought that some motion was better than no motion. I put my fears about the future of the United Kingdom aside because my first concern was getting us to London in one piece. I was very much aware that, whatever our strength of arms, we had women among us, and noncombatants. We would be vulnerable the whole time we were on the road, and we had no idea when and where our enemies might plan an ambush.

My squire, Tomos, waited for me as Lili and I headed out of our solar, where we'd breakfasted. I stopped in front of him with my arms outstretched so he could adjust my sword belt, armor, and surcoat to his satisfaction. He was as bad as my manservant in wanting me to look perfect, but I'd learned that a good boss identified people who had the skills and qualities they needed, and then got out of the way to let them do their job. Tomos made my life easier in both the short and the long run.

A few paces on, Anna stepped into my path. "You need to wait a second."

I pulled up short. "Why?"

"They're not ready for you," she said.

I glanced at Lili, who gave me a rueful smile. "You are the King of Wales for now, my love. You can't simply stroll out of your rooms and mount your horse. Everyone else has to be ready first."

"Don't be ridic—" I began a protest, and then stopped. Lili and Anna were right. Six years ago at Castell y Bere, I'd noticed that Dad would appear at the start of whatever journey was planned for the day—whether hunting a boar or riding to war—at the very moment everyone else was ready to go. He wouldn't keep us waiting, but at the same time, never had to wait outside himself. At the time, I'd marveled at his impeccable timing. As I grew in experience, I realized that his counselors stage-managed him, just as Anna was stage-managing me today.

Evan hurried through the main door that would take us into the great hall. "It's time, my lord."

"Thank you." I held out an arm to Lili, who took it. We entered the hall and walked down the aisle between the tables, under the eyes of the castle residents who would remain behind. In the bailey, a small escort of my men sat at attention in their saddles. I nodded to them, helped Lili onto her horse, and mounted mine.

Spurring Cadfarch, I led the way through the barbican. Once outside, we collected the rest of my men and the servants, who were clustered to one side, mounted and leading pack horses. Our entourage would not include drawn carts for this journey because they were too slow. All in all, we had a force of one hundred fighting men and twenty retainers. Hard to think about so few of us facing three million English.

We crossed the Wye River at Tintern Abbey and headed northeast. The rain from the night before had ended, which made the ride more pleasant, though a chill wind whipped the air. The countryside was lush and beautiful, even in late fall. To my eyes, England and Wales were nothing less than a country-sized park and I never tired of the green.

One half of my brain constantly scanned the road on either side looking for threats, even though my scouts were well-trained. The other half maintained my conversation with Lili. The coming baby occupied our thoughts and we were a long way from settling on a name that was acceptable to both of us.

"My lord!"

The entire company jerked at the shout. Ahead of us, the road went straight for a mile, before climbing into hills on the other side of the valley below us. At the crest of the opposite hill, visible amongst the leafless trees, a company of men waited. Sunlight glinted off their armor and the points of their pikes.

"They've at least, fifty, my lord," Evan said. "The Mortimer banner flies above them."

That I could see for myself. I didn't rebuke my captain for stating the obvious, though. Instead, I gritted my teeth and acknowledged my disappointment. We hadn't gotten even a day into England and already Roger Mortimer, or at least his men, rode against us? Clare and Bohun had insisted they would see to our safety from the moment we crossed the border into England. It seemed they had underestimated the hatred of those who opposed us. Roger Bigod was dead, but William de Valence and Roger Mortimer were very much alive. As Bevyn had pointed out, they would prefer that I vanish from the face of the earth.

"Formation!" Evan barked the order, but my men were already moving; the instruction was hardly necessary. The men with pikes went to the front and would lead the charge. I'd reconciled myself to the knowledge that in this kind of skirmish, my men would insist on keeping me to the back.

I didn't object. I had Lili to protect and had no interest in dying on an Englishman's sword, today or any day. I had no need to prove my manhood by giving them the chance to kill me.

I glanced at Bevyn out of the corner of my eye. He had moved closer to Lili and we sandwiched her between us. We fell to the rear of the fighting force, with our servants even farther back—twenty yards farther now and losing ground—with only three men to protect them. That left the soldiers in the company free to focus on our enemy ahead.

They weren't exactly rusty, either. It had only been a few months since August and the fight in the Estuary. Nobody had forgotten how to fight, or what it felt like. Blood pounded in my ears and I clenched Cadfarch's reins in my left hand and the hilt of my sword in my right. With our greater numbers, we had the advantage. We would find the perfect spot on the heights to defend, forcing them to ride through the valley and charge up our hill to reach us.

"They've stopped." Lili stood in her stirrups, straining to see the company ahead.

She was right. As we watched, three riders broke away from the bulk of the Mortimer force. One held the Mortimer flag, which streamed behind them.

"It's Edmund Mortimer himself," I said.

"Christ on the cross," Bevyn said. "Give us a little warning next time."

I would have smirked if Lili hadn't held a hand to her heart. My own heart beat so fast I could barely hear Bevyn's curse.

"After last summer, I hoped never to participate in a cavalry charge again," Lili said. "I'm glad I won't have to see one today."

I put a hand on her arm and squeezed. "Me too." Shaking my head at how long it was taking my pulse to slow, I spurred my horse. My men parted to allow me to pass through them, and I picked up Evan and Carew on the way to the front of the line. Once the three of us were in the lead, the rest of my men followed us into the valley. Near the central and lowest point between the hills, we met Edmund and his two men.

"My lord." Edmund bowed his head.

"You surprised us," I said, seeing no reason to hide the fact. "I hadn't realized you planned to meet us on the road today."

"I *hadn't* planned to meet you on the road," Edmund said. "I intended for you to find us waiting at the ford of the Wye so we could escort you into England. We were—" his chin firmed "—delayed."

I didn't like the sound of that. "What happened?" I matched his flat tone and matter-of-factness.

"Before we set out this morning, we had word of an ambush prepared for you." Edmund gestured to the east. "Further into England."

My hands clenched around the reins, and then I forced myself to relax. "Was the information accurate?"

"Five miles to the east, enemy archers squatted in a roost," Edmund said. "They loosed arrows at my men when they approached, and then they fled. My men are combing the woods for them now, but—"

"But you don't expect to capture them," I said, as aware as Edmund that woodsmen who knew the ground could easily disappear into their own forest. Edmund wouldn't discover their identity unless one of the archers' own betrayed them.

"How are your men?" I said.

"Two are dead, another gravely wounded," Edmund said. "The deaths and the difficulty in approaching the blind held my men back and allowed the cowards to escape."

I nodded. As in the modern world, a committed assassin was the most difficult threat against which to defend. Short of hiding in my castle and never leaving, I had no recourse but to be as unpredictable in my movements as I possibly could. Unfortunately, this trip into England was the most predictable journey I had ever made.

"I'm sorry for your losses." I held out a hand to Edmund and he took my forearm. "Thank you."

"It was no more than our duty, but I appreciate your thanks," Edmund said.

"Do you know which lord might have ordered the attack?" I said.

"How can I say for sure, when my own brother is a prime suspect," Edmund said, "and Valence's castle at Goodrich is a stone's throw from here?"

He had a point. "Are your men prepared to join mine?" I said.

"Of course." Edmund turned his horse's head and we rode up the hill to where his men waited. I helped Lili off her horse and we rested while our men sorted themselves into a combined company. When we set off down the road again, Lili and I were in the center of the riders as before, but now Edmund rode on my right. It was the position usually reserved for the most trusted man in a lord's company, because it was Edmund's shield, held in his left hand, that would protect my right side if I was beset.

"We should ride as quickly as our horses allow," Carew said from a few paces ahead.

Edmund glanced at me. "I imagine that is your plan for the next three days."

"How many men scout the fields on either side of us?" I said.

"A dozen," Edmund said.

"Good," I said. "Mind they don't see the bows on the backs of my scouts and take them for the enemy."

"They won't."

I had meant what I said as something of a joke, but Edmund was deadly serious. He had lost two men today and my jaunt into England was looking more perilous by the hour. Now, England didn't appear as much like a park as county fair, and this road was the shooting gallery.

With fifty more riders than before, and able to ride only four abreast on the narrow road, we were vulnerable all along our length. Evan shared leadership with Edmund's captain, riding side by side at the head of the company. He had been working on his English (as had Bevyn), and spoke it well enough to communicate, albeit with a strong Welsh accent.

We kept going, past noon and into the afternoon. "It would have been better if William had married Joan in any other town but London," Bevyn said. He rode on my left, on the other side of Lili.

"Better for whom?" I said. "Other than us, that is."

"Everyone," Bevyn said. "London is too big a city in which to protect you—or anyone else—properly. We may be staying at Westminster Palace, but the moment we leave the grounds, we're too exposed."

"Though inside, we're too enclosed," Carew said. "Do you realize how many servants and court attendants enter and leave the palace every day? It's impossible to inspect, or even begin to control, all of them. On top of which, you will have only a handful of us around you there."

Bohun had invited Lili and me to stay at Westminster, which Dad and I had decided was an invitation we couldn't refuse. Clare was housing the rest of my people at his castle of Baynard. "Given that we own no property in London—an oversight I will remedy as soon as possible—we couldn't have asked for a better situation than the one we're in. Neither the Palace nor Baynard's Castle is far from St. Paul's Cathedral, and to have the wedding anywhere else would send the wrong message. Bohun knows that. It is where kings marry, and Bohun wants his son to be a king."

"You should be the king instead, my lord," Bevyn said.

I glanced at Edmund. We were speaking in Welsh, but he understood the language. Even so, his face remained impassive and he acted as if he hadn't heard what Bevyn had said. I leaned across Lili and lowered my voice so only she and Bevyn could hear me. "Even if I wanted the throne, the people of England would never accept me. And what's with the *my lords* all of a sudden, Bevyn? Usually you don't use my title more than once every three days."

"We aren't in Wales anymore, my lord," Bevyn said. "And I think you're wrong about how the English feel about you. Did you notice how many people came out to see us pass through that village a mile back?"

97

"I noticed," Edmund said, indicating that my attempt at whispering had done no good. "It is only your due, my lord."

I straightened in my seat and bit my tongue on the words, *not you too?* The village had been a solidly English one, and yet we'd been greeted at the green by a delegation of townspeople, including the local burgesses. Instead of riding through without stopping as I'd intended, we'd stayed for half an hour. A girl had come forward and offered Lili a bouquet of dried flowers, while the headman of the village had personally brought me a cup of beer to drink and water for Cadfarch. Ironically, I was far more surprised by their hospitality than I'd been at the sight of Mortimer's men. Fighting Englishmen was normal. Homage from them was not.

"You say that, Edmund, and it's all very well and good not to be hated, but I'm having a hard time understanding why they would they treat me this way," I said. "Isn't it odd to have Englishmen bowing and scraping as if I wasn't a Welsh rebel and upstart? Their king died because of me, for God's sake."

"Dafydd—" Lili said, objecting (as my father did) to me taking the name of the Lord in vain.

I put out a hand to her. "Sorry. But it's not normal. Something isn't right."

"They love you here, too," Bevyn said, "the ambush notwithstanding."

"How have they even *heard* of me?" I said.

Bevyn shook his head. "It doesn't have to be only bad news that travels quickly. There may be more of this as we get closer to London. You must prepare yourself for it."

I coughed a laugh. "I find that highly unlikely."

"Sir Bevyn is right, my lord," Edmund said. "You have made an impression on the people of England, and not just because of the battles you've won. While a military victory makes for a fine tale around the fire in the evening, it isn't skill on the battlefield that makes a great leader."

"I do know that—" I said.

Edmund ignored the interruption. "In fact, if a man is forced to resort to violence to achieve his ends, whether in his own household, his estates, or his country, it's an outward manifestation of how little power he wields and how tenuous is his hold over his people."

"Edmund speaks the truth, my love," Lili said. "Back at that village, they admired you before you arrived, but when you spoke to them in their own language, and honored their leaders, though you are a prince and they are common folk, they began to love you."

Edmund nodded. "You have won the loyalty of the Welsh not through fear, but through love, wouldn't you say?"

He was right (or I hoped he was right), but even so, I didn't know how to answer him. A certain sector of the nobility would argue against Edmund's assertion, insisting that love made a ruler weak.

"Lord Mortimer," Lili said, "did you tell the people in that village that we were coming through today? Is that how they were prepared?"

"They already knew," Edmund said. "Don't ask me how. And I would add, my lord David, that to speak openly of your distrust of my people would offend many."

Although Edmund spoke calmly, I was suitably chastised. "I apologize, Edmund. It won't happen again."

"We have only ever experienced grief from England," Lili said. "Please understand that it may take time for us to accept adoration instead."

"The English are practical folk and no more blind to the truth than any men. We can see your husband's nobility as well as any Welshman," Edmund said.

I'd apologized, but I had offended Edmund. I cleared my throat, anxious to move on from this topic. "We're going to London, we're attending the wedding, and we're coming home." I gazed fixedly ahead, trying not to see the knowing looks that passed among my companions. "Nothing more. Is that clear?"

"And if the succession becomes a topic of conversation, in private or in council?" Bevyn said.

"Or in Parliament?" Edmund added.

"We have no comment," I said.

"Yes, my lord," Bevyn said.

It was only after Bevyn eyed me and his lip twitched so that his moustache danced, that I realized that he would see *no comment* as a step up from simply *no*.

8

16 November 1288

Lili

We rode all day, taking the road that led to Gloucester, and finally reached the castle where we were to spend the night. It had been in the hands of the English crown since the time of William Rufus, and now Thomas de Berkeley was the custodian. Thomas was a contemporary of Bohun and Clare, and like Humphrey de Bohun, had stood by a father who'd fought and lost at Evesham. Like Bohun, too, he'd reconciled with Clare in the intervening years.

Clare had said that he would join our party there. Between Clare and Edmund Mortimer, Dafydd would be traveling with the power of the March personified at his side.

If someone had told me a year ago that any of these men—Bohun, Clare, or Mortimer—would ever ally with Wales again, I never would have believed it. Taking Humphrey de Bohun as an example, Ieuan had spent his life *hating* the Earls of Hereford, and taught me to hate them too. But here we were, riding to William's wedding.

Then again, perhaps it wasn't so unlikely as all that. The Marcher barons cared more for their own power than for anything else. Clare's first wife had been Alice de Lusignan, the niece of our current mutual enemy, William de Valence. One might have thought that the marriage would have been a reason for Clare to have supported Valence in August, and indeed, Valence and Clare had intended for the marriage to bring them closer together.

However, their relations had soured when King Edward had made Alice his mistress. The fact that Edward and Alice were cousins hadn't seemed to matter to either of them. To appease Clare for the loss of his wife, Edward had promised him a wedding to Edward's daughter, Joan, but Edward had died before anything formal might be arranged.

And now Joan was marrying William de Bohun. It wasn't clear to me why Clare chose to support Bohun's rise to power, since it was a loss for him. Perhaps Clare believed that England wouldn't accept him as King—that he had too many ghosts in his cupboard—and believed he could consolidate his power under William.

Edmund Mortimer pulled up to allow Dafydd and me to draw abreast. "Clare tells me that Thomas de Berkeley has plans to dine with you tonight. He's riding in from his estates to the south for that purpose."

Dafydd shot a look of surprise at Edmund. "Why?"

"He wants to meet you," Edmund said, but didn't elaborate.

We'd come a long way for our first day and had long way left to go to reach London. I could feel Dafydd eyeing me. He worried about my welfare all the time, but these last few miles even I could tell that I'd gone pale.

"Are you well?" Dafydd said.

"A little queasy," I said, unwilling to admit more than that.

"Perhaps it would be better—"

"Don't even say it," I said. "It's been one day. I want to keep going. It's a simple upset stomach and the need to get off this horse."

Dafydd nodded to Edmund, who spurred his mount, and soon we reached the gatehouse. Gloucester Castle and its defenses covered almost the entire southwestern portion of the town of Gloucester. The Severn defended it on the west, and the rest of the castle was surrounded by a moat. Though a number of people came into the street to see us pass by, we rode through the town without stopping and arrived at the north-eastern entrance, with its inner and outer gatehouses and drawbridge over the moat.

Dafydd helped me from my horse and by the time I landed on the ground, Clare himself had hastened across the bailey towards us, followed by Lord Thomas de Berkeley. Both were handsome men in their forties with a regal bearing—though Berkeley's hair was dark brown and Clare's was red.

"My lord!" Clare stopped three paces from us and bowed. At first glance, this Gilbert de Clare was a very different man from the one we'd found shimmying down a rope outside of Clifford Castle in August, in that his demeanor was precise and his clothing perfect. His red hair still stood on end, however, and his eyes were as clear and glittering as ever.

"Clare," Dafydd said and tipped his head. I gave him a weak smile. I really didn't want to lose control of my stomach at the Norman baron's feet. He might become somewhat less accommodating towards us if I ruined his boots.

"If the steward is prepared, my wife needs a bed," Dafydd said.

"At once." Clare gestured towards the entrance to the great hall. It was built in stone, as most castles were these days. The need for defense, and the protection stone offered, proved of greater merit than the desire for less draft and cold. We'd begun the day under sunshine, but the wind had picked up over the last hour and the clouds to the west spoke of rain.

Sir Thomas himself showed us to our rooms. "My lady," he said, with a smile and a bow. "I hope you find your accommodations to your liking."

Our rooms turned out to be adjacent to his own and as richly appointed. While it made Dafydd uncomfortable, I knew this kind of reverence was no less than he deserved. Dafydd pulled the curtains back from the big four-poster bed, revealing a soft mattress and down pillows. A fire burned in the grate. The chimney appeared to work well, too, since the room wasn't full of smoke. Dafydd turned to me. "A bed fit for a princess," he said.

"I don't care what it looks like, as long as I can lie down on it." I moaned as I sank into the bed and tucked a pillow under my head. Dafydd found a second pillow to put between my knees and stroked the hair off my face.

"Thank you, Lord Thomas," Dafydd said. "Would it be possible for broth and bread to be brought here? I doubt my wife will want to join us for dinner."

Sir Thomas nodded. "At once. As to yourself, please come to the hall at your leisure." He left.

My maid, Branwen, hovered in the doorway. "I'll see to your food, my lady."

"Thank you." I smiled. She'd see to the food, and those moments in the kitchen would supply me with all the relevant gossip in the castle. In her late forties, having lost her husband some years ago, she was far more fluent in English and French than I, and had one of those personalities that invited confidences. I didn't know how she did it, but she hadn't failed me yet.

In her absence, Dafydd untied both my boots and dropped them to the floor. "Thank you, Dafydd, now go away," I said.

He slid his hand over mine. "Are you sure? I can stay if you need me."

I waved my other hand at him. "People want to talk to you. I'm going to lie here and drink some soup. I'll feel better if you're not watching."

I didn't play games with him and usually meant what I said. If I told him to go away, it wasn't a cry for attention but my genuine wish. So, he said, "Okay."

105

"You should dress in your finery first," I said.

He stopped, halfway to the door, and turned back. "I'm sure that's not necessary, Lili—"

"They'll expect it."

Dafydd sighed, but he knew I was right. We'd planned for it, even. Seamstresses had spent a hurried few days sewing new articles of clothing for both Dafydd and me, so that we would look like the prince and princess we were. Anna had consulted Maud de Bohun as to what was fashionable in London right now, so I would fit in. Dafydd would be out of place in an English castle no matter what he wore, but had bowed to their greater fashion sense.

"My lord?" Dafydd's manservant held a cloak in one hand and a brush for his boots in the other.

"Make it quick, Jeeves."

Though the man's real name was Rhun, Dafydd had started calling him Jeeves, with Rhun's permission, the day after I'd hired him. It was a jest, one that only he understood (though he'd tried to explain it to both of us). What I did understand was that even after six years, Dafydd was uncomfortable with having a personal servant. I hadn't had my own dedicated maid before either, not until I'd married Dafydd. But I had to agree that life was easier with someone to assist me.

Dafydd's first manservant had been Hywel, Anna's companion from Castell y Bere. After the fiasco at Lancaster, Dafydd had sent him to Math at Dinas Bran, and there he'd stayed. Three years on, he was a retainer at the castle, married and expecting a child of his own.

Jeeves would have made a good captain of Dafydd's guard, but weak eyes had made warfare impossible for him as a youth, and by the time Dafydd returned from the Land of Madoc—or Avalon, as I'd found myself calling it of late—with directions for crafting eye glasses, it was too late for him to change professions.

Dafydd sat and stuck out both feet while Jeeves quickly brushed the dirt off his boots and then whipped out a rag to polish them. Dafydd had changed his tunic and shrugged into the cloak I wanted him to wear—one that was a deep blue and a perfect match for his eyes. It also wasn't travel-stained like the one he'd worn all day.

"Don't eat anything that another hasn't already tried," Dafydd said.

"I won't." Neither of us had forgotten about the poisons from Shrewsbury. Dafydd gave me a last kiss and a long look, and then departed.

I sighed.

"He means well, my lady," Jeeves said.

"Of course, he does," I said. "But I am his wife and carrying his first child so he worries about everything."

I closed my eyes and managed a short nap before Branwen returned with soup and bread. "I tasted it first," she said. "It's good and salty." She helped me to sit with my back to the headboard and fluffed the pillows behind me.

"So," I said, after taking a sip of the hot broth. "What have you heard?"

Branwen gave a slight cough. "My lady, I don't listen at keyholes—"

"We've been here for nearly an hour, Branwen. That's more than enough time. Please tell me what you've heard."

Branwen gave up the pretense of misunderstanding. "Nothing unusual, my lady. Bohun and Kirby aren't speaking to each other but aren't actively at each other's throats either; the wedding plans progress; and it is said that the Bishop of London himself will marry William and Joan." She looked away, a smile playing around her lips.

"What?"

"As the wine steward tells it, Joan is a reluctant bride," Branwen said. "Before King Edward's death, her heart was set on the Church."

"She wanted to be a nun?" I laughed. "Don't tell that to Humphrey de Bohun. He wants a grandson to be King of England after William, not a cold bed for William to come home to."

"Oh—and Lord Roger Mortimer has been released from the Tower of London."

I nodded. I already knew that, thanks to the Order of the Pendragon, but didn't mention it since I didn't want to discourage Branwen's quest for information.

"Thank you," I said.

Branwen handed me a cup of water. "They have a deep well here." She didn't understand why I had to abstain from wine, but Dafydd had explained quite clearly why the ban was important, and when Anna, Bronwen, and Meg had supported what he'd said, she'd backed down.

She had protested similarly when we'd ridden to Chepstow from Rhuddlan after I discovered my pregnancy. Once we arrived, Meg had assured her that riding was no more harmful than walking, particularly in the first trimester. As with the wine, Branwen didn't necessarily believe I'd made the right decision, but I was her mistress, and she was nothing if not loyal. I'd even heard her chastising one of the kitchen staff back at Chepstow who'd questioned my decision to ride into England with Dafydd.

For my part, I accepted what Dafydd told me, as I had to accept so much of what was unusual about him. I loved him, and I trusted him, and if wine was bad and riding good, I believed him. So often it was I who understood the politics or attitudes of this time and place more than he and had to explain it to him so he could accept it. It was only fair that I listened to him sometimes and accepted what he said, even when I didn't understand the reasoning behind what he believed.

I took a sip of the water and sighed. "I should get up. It's Dafydd's birthday, and I'm missing it."

"The kitchen already knew of it," Branwen said. "Lord Clare has everything arranged, just as you hoped."

"You're too good to me, Branwen," I said.

"Nonsense," Branwen said. And then she hesitated such that I looked into her face.

"You have something more to add?" I said.

"I have heard that your father will be at Westminster," she said.

I swallowed hard at this not-unexpected news and nodded, trying to get a grip on my emotions. *So be it.* I was a grown woman, a married woman, and a princess of Wales. What could my father say to me that could hurt me more than he already had?

I was glad I had been able to rest and felt better as Branwen helped me into my gown and fixed my hair. Because nobody was expecting me to attend the dinner, I made my own way to the hall. I peered through the doorway, just as Sir Thomas snapped his fingers and stood, with Clare rising beside him. Clare held his hands behind his back and wore a disconcerting smirk on his face, as if life couldn't have pleased him more.

"Now!" Thomas rapped the handle of his belt knife on the edge of the table, calling for quiet, which he got nearly instantly. "Today is a celebration!" He spread his arms wide. "Not only has Prince David of Wales honored us with his presence, but today is also the day of his birth!"

Dafydd gaped at Thomas, and then looked down the table at his companions. He thought one of them had talked. Later, I'd tell him that I was the culprit, and he'd be forgiving.

Clare leaned into Dafydd. "If you could say a few words, my lord?"

Dafydd stood and lifted a hand to the crowd, to applause he richly deserved. He was so *good* at this, even if he refused to admit it.

"Thank you very much for your hospitality and your birthday wishes," he said, speaking first in English, and then in French. "Your land is rich and lovely, your people are just and loyal—" he broke off as he spied me in the doorway. He smiled and then finished his speech without stumbling: "I am honored to be with you tonight."

He reached me in three strides, kissed my cheek, and took my hand to lead me to the dais. "Are you okay?"

"I didn't want to miss your birthday celebration," I said.

The crowd applauded some more as four servants brought out a layer cake the size of a boulder.

"I can't believe this is all for me," Dafydd said.

"Happy birthday, my love," I said as he seated me in a chair beside him, one that Edmund Mortimer had vacated at my approach. "You did very well, especially when your wife went behind your back to ensure the day was memorable."

Dafydd had lifted his goblet to his lips, but now he laughed and sputtered, almost spewing his wine across the table. "This is your doing? I am betrayed!"

Clare laughed, having overheard, took my hand, and kissed the back of it. "I am honored that you trusted me with your secret."

And then to Dafydd, he added, "Your legend grows."

Neither Dafydd nor I had to ask what Clare meant.

9

17 November 2016

Meg

Lywelyn spent all of November sixteenth alternately asleep and awake, but by noon on the seventeenth, he was more bright-eyed than I'd seen him in months. At that point, I couldn't put off calling my sister any longer. It had been wrong of me to wait this long, but I hadn't wanted to throw myself on her mercy. I'd been hiding, not wanting to deal with her suspicion and skepticism. After David's birth, she had refused ever to mention his father, refused to hear anything about him. How would she feel about seeing Llywelyn in the flesh?

I had to wait until mid-day to call because of the time difference between Wales and Pennsylvania. By seven in the morning their time, she and Ted would be awake, but not quite out the door for work.

I'd bought the best cell phone the woman who sold it to me had in stock. I wished I could have reached Bronwen at Chepstow instead. And really, it wasn't fair that I couldn't call her. It was the same planet, right? Just a little twisted to one side? Why didn't cell phones work in our medieval world?

David had been working on generating electricity ever since he'd come back from the twenty-first century with his reams of directions for modern inventions. He'd built a little plant associated with a water wheel that powered Caerphilly's flour mill, tapping into the energy the water created. Not that he'd had anything to use it for, other than powering useless electronics.

I knew he'd tried to work my phone, after he'd spliced together wires from Elisa's minivan. I'd caught him flipping it open and had so wanted to hear him say, *I have three bars!* But he had nothing.

Thus, calling my sister in the United States would have to do. I curled up on the sofa in our suite. My fingers trembled as I dialed Elisa's number.

Ring, ring, ring.

"Hello?" Ted's voice came down the line, a little sleepy.

"Ted. It's Meg."

Silence. And then he let out a whoop that had me pulling the phone away from my ear before he deafened me. "You're back? You're really back?"

"For the moment," I said. To my horror, I found my throat closing over tears instead of laughter.

"Where are you?" The authority in Ted's voice came through loud and clear. He was an organizer and a doer. The day

113

Elisa had brought him home had been a good day in our household.

"Near Aberystwyth," I said.

"You're really in Wales? Right now?"

At the incredulity in his voice, I lost it. I'd worked hard to contain myself for the last two days and just when I wanted to come across as reasonable and not needy, I fell apart on the phone to my brother-in-law.

"Yes!" I sobbed the word into the speaker.

"It's okay, Meg." Ted repeated the words several times until I was able to speak again. "Do you have a place to stay?"

"We're at a clinic."

"Are you okay?" His voice was urgent.

"Yes. But I brought Llywelyn here because I was afraid he was going to die."

"You brought Llywel—" He stopped and then tried again. "You mean you brought Llywelyn, *your* Llywelyn, to the twenty-first century?"

"I did." My tears were abating. "It's mind-boggling, I know."

"Do you have money?"

"For now. I sewed one of my credit cards into my dress, so we have that," I said.

That earned me another moment of silence. "I knew it was the right decision not to cancel them," he said. "So you've been planning this for a while?"

"I've had to, Ted. I'm pregnant again."

Ted coughed and laughed at the same time. "Oh, Meg. The world is turned upside down."

Laughter bubbled up in my chest. "You're not kidding."

"All right." Papers rustled in the background. "Consider me on a plane to Wales. Into what city should I fly—?" He stopped again. "Never mind. I'll figure it out."

I gave him the address to the spa that was written on the brochure and he said he'd get a map off the internet. "What about ... Elisa? And the kids? If they could come too ..." My breath caught in my throat at the thought of seeing them again.

A sigh. "All three have the chicken pox."

"What?" I choked on a laugh. "Surely they were vaccinated."

"They were. I know. Crazy, isn't it?" Ted said. "My mom was planning to arrive today to help out, so they won't miss me if I leave."

"Can I talk to Elisa?" I said. "Will she want to talk to me, do you think?"

"Of course, she will," Ted said. "Just a sec."

Ted must have had the phone pressed to his chest, because the sound of his voice came to me muffled. I got a *who is it* and a *what*? from Elisa. Then some more silence before she came on the line.

"God, Meg!" Elisa said. "I can't believe it's you!"

"Hi, Elisa," I said.

"Are you like ... back for good or ... um ...?"

"That's not the plan." I spoke as gently as I could. "Llywelyn has been ill for months and we took the risk of coming here in the hope that someone could help him."

"Ted said that you're in Wales?"

"Apparently."

"How—how—why? Last time David came to Pennsylvania."

I laughed. "You're asking me? We're talking about time travel here, right?"

"I thought David said that you went to an alternate universe?" Elisa said.

I managed not to grind my teeth. "Yes. Yes. You're right. Regardless, we're here now, at Aberystwyth."

"Ted has bought himself a ticket. I'm not feeling well, Meg. I'll give him the phone again." Elisa passed me off to her husband.

"I arrive at Heathrow tomorrow morning at nine," he said. "That'll be the eighteenth."

"You really don't have to—"

"Of course I do. Don't even say it. Besides, I've been meaning to check on some of our overseas assets and this will give me a chance to do that."

I realized that Ted must have changed jobs, which shouldn't have surprised me. It wasn't unusual to move from the political realm to the business world and back again. "Are you sure? If Elisa needs you—"

"As I said, my mother's coming and the airline wouldn't even let Elisa or the kids on the plane," Ted said. "I've made my return for the Tuesday before Thanksgiving. It'll be fine."

116

"Okay," I said. "Thank you. I can't possibly thank you enough."

A low rumble of laughter flowed down the line to me. "Are you kidding? I get to meet the last Prince of Wales! The real one! From the Middle Ages!"

"I do love you, Ted," I said. "And he's the King now, not the Prince. We're no longer under England's yoke."

Ted guffawed. "I need to go now. I'll see you tomorrow afternoon, at the latest. Can I call you on this phone?"

"Yes, I'll buy more minutes—"

But Ted had hung up. I stared at the phone. I hadn't spoken more than a few sentences to Elisa. I almost called her back, but I didn't. She didn't want to talk to me. Or, if that wasn't completely fair—couldn't. I hadn't allowed myself to hope, but it would have been fun if Elisa could have been as excited to talk to me, and to meet Llywelyn, as Ted was.

Although I looked longingly at the bed and its plush softness, I left the suite and returned to the hospital wing. I poked my head into the room to find both Llywelyn and Goronwy asleep. Llywelyn's chest rose and fell rhythmically, while Goronwy reclined in one of the chairs which, despite Dr Raj's belief that they were uncomfortable, was designed to allow a guest to sleep in the room with a patient.

I watched them silently. We'd arrived almost two days ago now. Llywelyn's color was better and he should be switching to oral antibiotics soon. A discarded tray sat on the table next to his bed, with every dish empty. A few more meals like that and

Llywelyn really might get well. My stomach clenched and then I forced myself to relax. It had been a long couple of months, knowing how ill he had become and being unable to do a thing about it. I wasn't going to get over my worry for him just like that.

Goronwy stirred, and I entered the room to pull up a chair on the other side of Llywelyn's bed. Llywelyn turned his head to look at me, and his eyes were completely clear.

"Your medicine is like magic," he said.

I shook my head and smiled. "The nurse told me as I passed her desk that she's never seen anyone recover as quickly from pericarditis as you."

Llywelyn's eyes glittered. "Maybe nobody has ever needed to recover as quickly as I did."

"With no scientific evidence whatsoever, I'm guessing that it's because you've never had any medical treatment in your life, so your body has no previous experience with antibiotics. The medicine is probably curing infections in every nook and cranny, ones which we didn't even know you had."

"How soon can we go home?" Llywelyn said.

"You're ready to leave?" I said. "You've already seen enough?"

"I want to see that memorial you talked about," Llywelyn said. "At Cilmeri."

I shook my head. "I don't want to take you there."

"Why not?"

"It's morbid," I said. "And ... well ... I just think you're not going to like it."

Llywelyn's eyes narrowed as if he were angry, but his mouth twitched, even as he said, "You've been keeping secrets from me?"

"I didn't think you needed to know that right next to the memorial is a water source called "Llywelyn's Well' where the English soldier who cut off your head washed it of your blood."

Llywelyn choked. "You jest!"

"I do not jest." I thought a moment. "If you really want to see the sights, I could take you to Aberystwyth Castle, the one Edward built after you died. It's a complete ruin now, covered with graffiti."

Llywelyn relaxed against his pillows. "I might like to see that."

I didn't have to explain to him what graffiti was. Ancient people wrote on things they shouldn't all the time. I leaned forward to put my arms around him and he pulled me close so he could kiss me without having to move. "I'm glad you didn't die," I said.

He smiled. "So am I." His brows came together. "I'm worried about Dafydd."

I sat back. "I hope he had a good birthday."

"We should have been there to celebrate it with him," Llywelyn said.

"He would have spent it journeying into England, whether we were there or not." I managed to say this matter-of-factly, but barely. "He's twenty now. A grown man for six years. He'll be fine."

"Do you really believe that?" Llywelyn said.

"He is your son," I said. "What do you think?"

"When I was his age, my uncle died and I stepped into his shoes as Prince of Wales," Llywelyn said. "You're right. It is wrong of me to think our son capable of less than I. He's less damaged than I, and sometimes that comes across as weakness, when really he's stronger inside and has less need to prove himself."

"Speaking of sons," I said, "I've arranged for someone to come and have a look at me."

"At you?" Llywelyn's eyes widened. "What's wrong with you—" And then he broke off and nodded. "The baby."

"The midwife should be here any minute," I said.

"Well, then." Goronwy got to his feet. "I'll see about some more coffee. And maybe a doughnut."

Both Llywelyn and I grinned at Goronwy, who left the room, jingling coins in his pocket. I moved closer to Llywelyn and he scooted over so I could sit on the bed beside him. We wound our hands together and he put his other hand on my belly. "I never thought I'd say this, but I'd prefer a daughter, Meg."

"It would be easier for David," I said. "How could you not prefer that, given the warfare within your family?"

"I'm going to live," he said. "So you won't have to raise her all on your own."

"You'd better live," I said. "Did you know that we could find out if it's a boy or a girl right now? Today?"

Llywelyn's brow furrowed. "How?"

"They have a machine here that looks inside a woman's womb," I said, using the medieval term. "We could at least be

120

prepared." I rubbed my stomach. "Whatever it is, it's going to be huge."

"I know I shouldn't comment until I've examined you, but you do look rather larger than I would expect for a woman who's only five months pregnant."

Goronwy had left the door ajar after he'd gone through it, and the midwife stood in the doorway, smiling at us and speaking in Welsh. Like the nurse, she understood our speech well enough. To my ear, medieval Welsh and modern Welsh sounded quite different at times, but I hadn't been raised on them either.

"I'm five and a half months," I said, trying not to sound defensive. I turned sideways so she could see my belly better. "If that makes a difference."

She tipped her head back and forth in a *maybe* motion, then held out her hand to me. "I'm Audrey. Would you like to come with me?"

"Meg." I shook her hand. "This is my husband, Llywelyn."

Audrey shook Llywelyn's hand too. In medieval Wales, men clasped forearms in greeting, and women might touch fingers, so he didn't have any experience with a full handshake. Still, he managed a credible one with what looked like a firm grip. "I hear you're going to be just fine," she said to him.

"I plan on it," he said.

Audrey nodded and gestured for me to come with her. I shot a look at Llywelyn who said, "Find out."

"Okay," I said.

We went to a different part of the clinic and Audrey gave me the kind of medical exam I hadn't had since I'd been pregnant with Anna. She weighed and measured me and asked about various womanly issues. All was well until she put her stethoscope to my belly. She moved it here and there as she listened, but didn't comment. One minute became two.

I watched her, my heart in my mouth. "Is everything okay?" I said, finally. The longer she didn't talk, the more uncomfortable I had become.

Audrey took the buds away from her ears. "Any history of twins in your family?"

I shook my head slowly, while my heart raced and my stomach slowly sank into my shoes.

"Because I hear two heartbeats."

10

17 November 1288

Bronwen

"Two ladies are here to see you, Madam." Dai, one of Chepstow Castle's permanent retainers, hovered in the doorway to the women's solar.

I looked up from the journal entry I was writing. "To see me?" Nobody ever wanted to see me, not while I was at Chepstow. As lady of the manor for Ieuan's holdings in the north—at Buellt or Aberedw—I led a busy life. Here, Tudur was Llywelyn's castellan, and he had an army of servants and household workers to run things for him. That's how I'd gotten involved in the office work in the first place—to find something to do. Nobody had been more surprised than I that I was good at it.

"Surely they're looking for Anna," I said. "Please tell them she left this morning for Dinas Bran with Math and the children." We'd thought it best to split up, to spread our influence across Wales more broadly in case trouble arose. For his part, Ieuan had left with a company of riders to patrol the southern coastline and wouldn't return until tomorrow.

"I asked them already. They insist on seeing you."

"Who is it?"

"They wouldn't leave their names."

I laughed. "Please send them in."

For once, Catrin wasn't attached to me. We'd had a long day of pacing and crying while I tried not to scream along with her, followed most recently by an hour-long nursing session. She'd fallen asleep ten minutes ago and her nanny, Elen, had begged to be allowed to wander off with her. Soon enough, Catrin would wake up, start crying, and they'd both be back.

Two women entered the room and curtseyed. I nodded at Dai, who closed the door behind them. "How may I help you?" I said.

The older of the two women hastened forward. "My lady, I have some disturbing information for you." She spoke in French.

"First, please tell me who you are."

The woman put a gloved hand to her mouth in a dainty gesture. Her behavior was far more refined than mine, for all that she called me *my lady*. "This is my daughter, Anne. I am Jenet, lady in waiting to Lucy, the wife of Roger Mortimer."

My eyes widened. "The wife of—" I cut myself off at the sharp look she sent in my direction, belying the outward delicacy of her manners.

"We have something to tell you ... to-to-to help Prince David," Anne said.

124

I gestured that they should seat themselves and they did, though they perched on the edge of the bench as if it would break if they put their full weight on it. The two women exchanged a glance and it was Jenet who spoke again. "My lady, I fear that we have knowledge of a plot against the Prince."

They'd had my full attention since they entered the room, but now my heart quickened. "What is the plot and how do you know?" I said. "And at what risk have you brought the information to me?"

"I have no fear for myself," Jenet said. "Lady Mortimer resides currently at her estate in Lydney and since we were so close, I asked permission to visit my ill sister in Chepstow. A ferryman rowed us across the Wye yesterday."

"Lady Mortimer chose not to travel to London for the wedding of William and Joan?" I said.

"She is pregnant again, and as she miscarried her most recent child, she didn't want to risk travel in these early months."

"I see," I said.

Everyone knew that Lucy and Roger did not have a happy marriage. His imprisonment in the Tower of London aside, they normally spent most of their time apart. She endeavored to spend her time in the country, while Roger stayed in the city. Given that he'd once tried to murder Llywelyn, I had never been disposed to think well of him, but I'd since learned that he was a philanderer and mercurially violent.

"I'm sorry your sister is ill," I said, "but very thankful you chose to see me."

Jenet looked down at her hands. "I almost didn't, but when Anne heard at the market that you were in residence ...."

"It is at my urging that she's here." Anne took her mother's hand in hers.

"Please tell me what you know," I said.

"It has many pieces, my lady." Jenet took in a deep breath and let it out. "I know for certain that Lord Valence arranged for an attempt on Prince David's life two days ago, while his company rode through Gloucestershire."

I pressed a hand to my heart. "You say *attempt*. It failed? It has to have failed or I would have heard!"

"Roger Mortimer's brother, Edmund, discovered the plot before it could succeed," Anne said. "We wouldn't have come all this way to tell you if that were all the information we had. We have more."

I went cold all through. "What more?"

"Please," Jenet said, "if we tell you, you must promise not to reveal where you heard it."

"I promise," I said. "Of course, I promise."

"There is a baron, a fine lord that Lord Roger refers to only as *the churchman*. In public, he supports Prince David, even going so far as to welcome his bid for the English throne, but in secret, he plots against him."

"He intends to kill him?" I said, letting her mistaken comment about David's desire to be the King of England go for now. "How?"

"Not murder," Jenet said, "but a plan to discredit him. Lord Roger's exact words were: *When the time is right, we will unveil the truth, and the upstart Prince will find himself in Hell's deepest pit. He will have only himself to blame for his presence there.*"

"To whom was he speaking?" I said.

"To his wife." Jenet cast her eyes down.

I stood. "You must return to your sister. Your lives might be forfeit if you were discovered here. It is very brave of you to have come."

"We had to," Anne said.

"I will ensure that Prince David gets this information," I said.

Jenet and Anne rose to their feet too. "Thank you for seeing us," Anne said. "You aren't nearly as strange as we've heard."

"Anne!" Jenet slapped her hand lightly on Anne's arm.

"Well she's not! And your baby is beautiful," Anne said. "We saw her as we passed through the hall."

I gaped at her, and then I laughed. "Thank you. And thank you for coming. You are Welsh, I gather?"

Jenet frowned. "No, of course not."

"Then why—?"

"Prince David is King Arthur returned. It is wrong of Lord Roger to harm him in any way," Jenet said, "and Valence is a despicable man. Lord Roger should not aid him."

I clasped my hands in front of my lips and looked over them at the two women. "Again, I thank you for your loyalty. Prince David thanks you too."

They smiled, curtseyed, and departed. As soon as they'd gone, I swept up my cloak and hurried from the room. I passed Elen and Catrin, who was still asleep, on the stairs.

"My lady! Are you all right—"

"I'll be right back, Elen," I said. "Keep Catrin happy until I return."

I flew through the lower bailey. Nobody stopped me until I attempted to leave the castle without an attendant. The guard at the door warred with himself for a count of five as I stood in front of him, hopping from one foot to the other in my impatience. I sighed with relief as one of the younger members of the garrison hurried into the barbican. "My lady Bronwen, what is it?"

"I must visit the town," I said. "You may come, but please don't hinder me."

"Yes, my lady."

We hurried down the road and through the town gate. I turned down the side street that David had told me about and fetched up at Aeddan's door. Before he left Wales, David had mentioned his visit and the Order of the Pendragon, knowing I'd commiserate and laugh. Although I hadn't known who he was at the time, I'd actually met Huw a few days before at the market. When David described him, I knew instantly that the young man at the market stall, wheeling and dealing to sell his wool at the best price, was Huw. I knocked on the door.

128

Huw's father, Aeddan, opened the door. "My lady!"

"Hi." Being Ieuan's wife meant I never had to introduce myself. "May I come in?"

"Of course," Aeddan said.

I left the guard on the doorstep and entered the house. Huw straightened from his seat by the fire. "My lady, what is it?"

"I need you to ride to Prince David immediately," I said without preamble. "He is in danger."

11

17 November 2016

Meg

"Did you see the vid?"

I heard the question as I stood in the guests' kitchen at nearly midnight, fixing Goronwy another cup of coffee with too much sugar and cream (he took it exactly the way Bronwen did, which I thought was funny). At the rate he was drinking it, the man was going to become addicted in a week. I wasn't going to tell him that the last two cups I poured for him had no caffeine in them. What he didn't know wouldn't hurt him. Besides, the lateness of the hour meant we all needed sleep.

"I heard about it."

The second voice belonged to our nurse, whose name I didn't remember (Deb, I thought), but I didn't recognize the first speaker.

"My boyfriend had just come on when they arrived. There was a flash which whited out the video, and then the three of them fell in the pool."

"Did they fall through the skylight?" my nurse said.

"You mean as if from a plane?" the first voice said.

"I hear it was open, so it could have happened that way."

The first speaker scoffed. "Rubbish. What kind of sense would that make?"

"Then what?"

"I hear they're part of a secret government study to travel from one place to another by scrambling our atoms, like in Star Trek or Dr. Who."

"Don't be daft. How likely is it that one of them just happened to have a heart event and drop into our pool, while another is up the duff?" the nurse said.

I wasn't attuned to British slang, but I'd heard the phrase in reference to me earlier. The nurse meant I was pregnant.

"What then?"

"I don't know. But I like them. And the woman is having twins."

"I heard. I'm going to see Danny later if you want to come with me and have a look ..."

Their voices faded down the hall, along with their footsteps. I looked down to realize that as I listened, I'd shredded a Styrofoam cup into fifty pieces. Before I could convince myself that the impulse was stupid, I followed the two nurses back to the waiting room. They took the elevator to the second floor, but I kept going to the opposite end of the building, to where the administrative offices lay. Although I hadn't explored very far, I had poked my head through the door on the main floor, just to see what was there. During normal business hours, which wasn't now, a secretary at the front desk guarded the entrance.

I peered through the window in the door. At this hour, a security guard reclined in the secretary's chair, watching a show on a mini-television. I pulled back after a quick glance. He hadn't looked up. I went to the main elevators. Our suite lay on the fifth floor, but the complex had a basement too. I wanted to see that footage and I guessed that the *Healing Waters* spa hadn't wasted a view on their security guards, who were supposed to be watching the cameras anyway.

Down I went, all by myself, and the elevator doors opened to reveal a brightly lit—albeit empty—basement corridor.

"Hey! What are you doing down here?"

I'd hardly stepped off the elevator when a man in a blue uniform came around the left-hand corner.

"I was looking for a bathroom," I said, with a hand to my belly as if I was a desperate pregnant woman.

The man's brow furrowed. "You have one in your room."

"It's occupied." I stated this flatly, and got a smile. He tipped his head in the direction he'd come. "You really shouldn't be down here, but if it's urgent, it's the first door on the right as you walk down the hall."

"Thank you!"

I hurried down the corridor. As I turned the corner, I glanced back. He lifted a hand to me and I waved before ducking into the bathroom. After thirty seconds, I edged open the door and peered through the crack. When I didn't see anyone, I slipped out and continued down the hall. The corridor jagged to the left again and I realized I must be under the administrative offices, which is exactly where I hoped to be. Three doors down on the left, a sign said, "audio-visual". I turned the handle.

It was locked.

And then the door opened to reveal a slender man, a little taller than I, with dark hair and eyes, wearing the same blue uniform as the man I'd spoken to by the elevators. "May I help you?"

"Hi!" I said, as brightly as I could, and trying to turn on the charm. "I was wondering if I could see the video that shows me falling into the pool?"

The man's head jutted forward as he stared at me. "What? How do you know about that?"

"I heard a nurse talking about it. You're Danny, right? She said you showed it to her and I'd really like to see it too." I almost added *please* but decided I didn't want to come on too strong.

"Ma'am, you aren't supposed to be here. I can't show you—"

"I know you're not supposed to," I said. "But since you already showed one of the nurses ..."

He gaped at me, seemingly too stunned to reply.

"Really, I'm the only person you *should* show it to, since you violated my privacy by showing it to anyone at all."

I had no idea if Wales had privacy laws, and certainly a business and its cameras were a gray area. Still, Danny swallowed such that his Adam's apple bobbed up and down. He leaned into the hallway, looked both ways, and then caught my arm to pull me into the office. "Let's make this quick."

His desk sat before a bank of twenty screens, showing all portions of the spa, including the pool, elevator, hallways, lobby, and waiting room where I'd sat with Goronwy. Thankfully, no cameras appeared to be running in the suites themselves, nor in the patients' rooms. The man pushed at a rolling office chair with his foot, indicating that I should sit, while he tapped a few strokes on the keyboard. Ten seconds later, the screen in front of him filled with the pool atrium.

He fast-forwarded, and then stopped. I leaned forward. The paunchy American with the ball cap swam the breast stroke at the near end of the pool, and then ...

FLASH!

Light blew out the picture on the screen and when it came back into focus, Goronwy, Llywelyn, and I were struggling in the water. I watched the man lift me up while two or three other swimmers helped Goronwy get Llywelyn out of the pool.

Danny stopped the video and rubbed his hands together. "So that's it."

"Who else has seen this?" I said.

"Er ... a few people. I left a note for my boss this morning to check it out, since I knew he hadn't seen it yet, but he's been out sick the last three days."

I could hardly believe my good luck. "You mean, the manager of the hotel doesn't know about this?"

"No." He gestured towards the screen. "Care to tell me what this is all about?"

I studied the screen, thinking furiously, and decided I'd do best with some version of the truth. "You know, I really can't. How about you? Have you ever seen anything like it?"

Danny shook his head. "I can't explain it at all. I've been taking some courses in physics at the University of Aberystwyth, and if my instructor told me that you were part of an experiment with multi-faceted anacamptic LED photometrics, I'd nod and agree, but I wouldn't even know what he meant."

I laughed. Danny had hidden depths. "Thanks for showing me, Danny." I stood and put a hand on his shoulder. "What about your boss? Will he be mad? Do you think we'll get in trouble or anything?"

Danny glanced up at me. "I can't see why." He gestured to the screen, which was stopped on the image of Goronwy helping Llywelyn out of the pool. "It's not like it's your fault our camera blew out."

"Okay." I went to the door, but paused to look back. "Do you know when your boss is getting back?"

"He's got the flu." Danny tapped into his keyboard, focused on his screens. It was like he'd forgotten me already. "It'll be another day at least."

"Thanks." Once in the hall, I couldn't stop my hands from shaking. I had a day's grace, maybe two, before I needed to think about getting Llywelyn out of here. I was grateful to the spa for taking care of him, but if Danny's boss saw that video, he was going to ask questions.

I hurried back to the elevator. As it rose one floor, I closed my eyes and breathed deeply, resting my head against the walls. And then I pressed the button for the fifth floor. I needed a moment before going back to Llywelyn and Goronwy. I'd felt the closeness of the Middle Ages time and again since we arrived in the twenty-first century, but it was incidents like these that showed that the veil between their world and mine wasn't a veil at all, but a brick wall.

12

18 November 2016

Meg

As it turned out, it was the spa that decided they'd had enough of us—not because of our abrupt arrival, but because we'd run out of money. After three days in the clinic, we'd maxed out my credit card: $25,000 and they were going to boot us out the door. Not all of that money had been spent on health care, admittedly, what with the suite, food and clothing for Goronwy and me, and a new phone. The administrator who brought the bad news looked at Llywelyn over the top of her electronic tablet. "We'll have to transfer you to the hospital in Aberystwyth."

"Can you wait a few more hours? Please?" I said. "My brother-in-law is coming from the States. I think he'll be able to help us out."

The woman bit her lip and gazed down at her screen. I could see the wheels spinning in her head. While the spa was relatively full, they still had empty rooms. A paying guest was a paying guest. "And there are these other irregularities ..."

I didn't want her to talk about the surveillance camera, if she knew about it. "I know, I know. We'll fix it. Give us until this evening. Please."

She nodded curtly. "I'll speak to my supervisor."

I heaved a sigh. This was just what I needed to make the day perfect. I'd told Llywelyn and Goronwy about my encounter with Danny. It didn't mean much to either of them, even having seen a television now, though they could see that it worried me. I still wasn't sure what I had actually *seen*. Why the flash of light as we penetrated the space/time continuum? From our experience, it looked like the exact opposite—a black hole.

Of much greater import was the news that Llywelyn and I were having twins. His response had been the same as mine, passing through surprise, joy, and resignation in turn. We were having a boy and a girl and had progressed out of our shock far enough to start thinking about logistics. When the administrator had arrived, we were in the middle of an argument about whether or not we should be thinking about returning to medieval Wales at all. If birthing one child was dangerous in the Middle Ages, birthing two could be exponentially worse.

We hadn't even gotten to the part where I went into labor and found myself in a different time. To give birth to twins after leaving Llywelyn behind, either here or there, was my worst nightmare—and what had prompted me to sew my credit card and identity into my dress in the first place.

If I hadn't been pregnant, I would have drowned my emotions in Bronwen's foods of choice—chocolate, onion rings, and diet Coke—because that was all I wanted, but I forced down a sandwich and milk instead. Llywelyn, on the other hand, had eaten three meals yesterday, breakfast and lunch today, and the hospital staff had begun to look upon him favorably. I knew better. Another day here and he was going to become very grumpy about still being abed and would begin to make everyone else's life miserable.

I walked the attendant out the door, making small talk and trying to butter her up a bit, and then paced around the lobby, trying to calm myself. I got another cup of milk from the snack bar and then returned to the clinic. Llywelyn looked up as I returned to his room. "Are we going?"

"We're not leaving until they forcibly wheel you out of here," I said. "But I think I managed to stall them for another day at least. It may be that's all the time you really need."

Llywelyn plucked at the sheet. "The longer I stay in this bed, the weaker I'll become."

"You're stronger than you were when we left Chepstow," Goronwy said from the recliner. "Far stronger."

Llywelyn raised one leg and then the other. He could get to the bathroom by himself now, especially since he was no longer attached to an IV. His last session with the therapist had been spent speed walking the corridor, far better than what he'd managed on his first attempt two days ago.

Llywelyn pointed his chin at Goronwy. "Where did you get those clothes? If I'm to leave here soon, I can't wear what I wore into the pool."

Goronwy smiled and smoothed the lapels on the black leather jacket I'd bought him, since I wouldn't let him wear his cloak in the hospital. "As soon as you are able, I'll walk you to the lobby. You can see some of these magical items Meg has been keeping from us all these years."

I rolled my eyes. I had $400 in cash left. That would be about enough to buy a jacket to match Goronwy's. None of the clothes had sported price tags when we'd shopped initially. At the time, I hadn't cared what they cost.

I was glad, however, that we'd done the ultrasound yesterday when we still had money.

In the middle of his banter with Goronwy, Llywelyn's eyes tracked to the door. I turned. Ted stood in the doorway, smiling, though with no Welsh—or medieval Welsh for that matter—he couldn't have understood our conversation.

"Hi, Meg." He wasn't looking at me as much as he was observing Goronwy and Llywelyn.

I got to my feet and went to him. "Hi, yourself."

He was tall and lanky and had to bend to hug me. "You look great!"

"Thanks." I rubbed my hand down my belly, revealing the curve beneath my outsized shirt.

"Oh, wow."

"You'll be an uncle for the third—and fourth—time."

140

"I'm staggered," Ted said, "but glad nonetheless."

I tipped my head to the bed. "Come meet my husband." I made the introductions, switching back and forth from English to Welsh so all the men could understand.

Llywelyn held out his hand and shook Ted's, medieval style, grasping forearms instead of hands. Ted shook and then bowed at the waist, and then did the same towards Goronwy. I didn't bother to mention that it wasn't necessary and simply patted him on the arm. For someone who'd never bowed to anyone in his life, except perhaps to an Asian client, he did it well.

"Go on, Marged," Llywelyn said, his eyes on Ted as he spoke. "The more you let him help us, the quicker we can get home."

I looked up at Ted. "Thank you for coming. At this point, we do need your assistance."

"You need my credit card," he said, though with a grin. "Always my pleasure to serve the King of Wales."

He bowed towards Llywelyn again, I kissed Llywelyn's forehead, and we left the room. Rain beat against the windows in the atrium as I took Ted to the front desk to do what he did best, which was to take care of things. He had the desk clerk refund all the money I'd spent on my card and transfer the full amount to his, but with the assurance that he would continue to pay for whatever we needed until we left the spa.

"You need to sleep," I said. "I can see it. Why don't you go up to our room and we can talk more in the morning." Ted hadn't wanted to cancel our suite, even though Goronwy and I had used it only sporadically, taking turns napping on one of the great beds.

"We need to talk now," Ted said.

I eyed him, suddenly concerned that something wasn't right in his life. "About something other than the enormous debt I owe you?"

"Just—" he stopped, seemingly at a loss to articulate what he was feeling.

I took pity on him. "Come with me." I brought him to the clinic's waiting room. It was still deserted, as it had been every time I'd passed through it in the last three days. Ted collapsed onto one of the couches and gestured for me to sit across from him.

I sat.

"Elisa and I have money," he said. "I can't imagine spending it on anything more important than Llywelyn's health." He shook his head. "It's not that. It's you. How are you, and what is your plan? Do you really intend to go back? And if so, how?"

I looked away. The rain glistened on the picture window. The sun had gone down while we were at the front desk and the light from the lamp posts lit the driveway as it had every night, though I hadn't noticed it particularly since that first evening. "We have to go back, Ted. David and Anna are there. My grandchildren are there."

"Grandchildren?" he said. "David told me about Cadell, but ...."

"Cadell is three now, and Anna is pregnant again. Bronwen has her little Catrin, and David's Lili is pregnant with their first."

Ted sputtered. "*David* is married? He's only nineteen—"

"He turned twenty two days ago." I smiled. "We live in the Middle Ages, Ted. Life is too short to wait on love."

Ted held up his hand. "Okay. I guess I can understand that. But *how* are you going to get back? Between you and David, you've sacrificed two cars for this endeavor. Are you going for a third?"

"I don't know." I wrapped my arms around my middle, imagining the rental car bill he'd be stuck with if we drove it into the Middle Ages. No wonder he was concerned. He and Elisa were wealthier than anyone I knew (or had known), but they weren't made of money. "I'm scared, actually. Scared to try."

"You came here okay," he said.

"I know. But at the time, I didn't feel like I had a choice. Llywelyn was *dying*. But now ..." My voice trailed off as I tried to find the words to explain what I was feeling. It was true that I didn't want to stay in the twenty-first century, but it would be *easier*.

"What did you do to come here?" Ted said.

"We jumped off the wall at Chepstow Castle, into the Wye River."

Ted gaped at me. "That's a sixty foot drop!"

I was impressed that he knew that. It occurred to me that even though he'd been married to my sister for nearly twenty years, I didn't know him quite as well as I thought I did. "Less, since the water was running high, but you're right," I said. "If I'd had more time to think about it, I would have been terrified."

"Good Lord." Ted threw back his head and gazed at the ceiling. "If Elisa hadn't had David standing in her kitchen three years ago, I think she still wouldn't believe where you live, where you went." His head came down. "Part of me wants to go back with you. I took a trip around Wales after David's visit, in the hope of gaining a better idea of what your life was like."

"Ted—"

"I know, I know. I can't go with you. I can't leave Elisa and the kids, but Meg ... my God. Have you considered, you know, telling anyone?"

"About who we are?"

"And what you've done," Ted said.

"Who would I tell?"

"I don't know ... a scientist? One of those famous physicists?" Ted said.

I stared at him. I did not want to get involved in this. I'd already said as much to Llywelyn and Goronwy. "That's David's department, not mine. Besides, how could we possibly convince anyone here that what I said was true? Llywelyn is the *King* of Wales. Who's going to believe that?"

Ted raised a hand and let it drop. "I don't know. Just an idea." He studied me for a moment. "What if you're not alone, though? What if other people have shifted worlds like you have? What if it's not just you?"

144

Anna, David, Bronwen, and I were officially *missing persons* according to the police. "I hadn't ever considered it at all until Goronwy brought up the idea that Wales might have been the recipient of travelers in the past." I had to laugh. "I don't want to think about running into someone else from the twenty-first century in medieval Wales."

"I can see how that would be awkward," Ted said. "Yet we can't ever understand *why* you travel in time unless you talk with someone who might know more than you."

"Do you have someone in mind? Someone you trust?"

He took in a deep breath and let it out. "I have a friend. He's a guy I went to college with. He teaches here in the UK, at Cambridge."

I eyed my brother-in-law, suspicion rising in my chest. "You already called him, didn't you?" My face flushed and I leaned forward. "You told him about us?"

Ted didn't even have the grace to look abashed. "I did."

"What? When? What if he tells someone else?" I leapt to my feet and paced to the picture window beside the French doors. The rain continued to fall against the pane. "What if someone from the government finds out?" Coming hard on the heels of the revelation about the camera image, Ted's idea was not at all welcome.

"That's ridiculous." Ted waved a hand dismissively. "Why should you be afraid of the government?"

"Why should I be—" I broke off as three dark SUVs swept up the driveway and stopped in the roundabout by the front door to the spa.

"What is it?" Ted rose to his feet and came to stand beside me. Six men dressed in black protective gear—maybe it was armor, even, though I couldn't be sure in the low light—stepped from the front two vehicles. They didn't head straight for the front door of the spa, however. They hovered by the back of the second SUV, talking to each other and looking towards the third vehicle.

"Oh, Ted." I felt in my pocket for the key to our suite. "Take this. Go get our stuff."

"What?"

I pointed at the trucks. "If they're not here for us, that's fine, but what if they are? Goronwy needs his sword." Llywelyn's sword was still propped against the wall in his room, where he'd insisted I leave it, along with the rest of his gear.

"Meg." Ted kept his tone reasonable, like he was trying to convince a child that vanilla ice cream was just as good as chocolate. "You're overreacting."

"Am I?" I was already heading down the hall to Llywelyn's room. "Call me when you're safe and we'll meet up." I threw the words over my shoulder and didn't look back. I needed Ted to do as I asked and not argue with me, which he would continue to do if I gave him a chance.

As I burst into the room, Llywelyn was awake, sitting up and smiling. I eyed him. He looked bulkier under his hospital gown than he had even this morning.

146

"We're going now," I said.

Goronwy fixed his eyes on my face. "Something's gone wrong, hasn't it? What?"

"I don't know for sure, but we need to get Llywelyn out of here. Immediately."

Llywelyn didn't wait to be told twice. He swung his legs over the edge of the bed, stood, and ripped off his hospital gown. Then I understood why he'd been smiling. He'd put on his shirt and breeches and then worn the gown over the top. I could have kissed him, but it would have taken too much time.

Meanwhile, Goronwy reached for Llywelyn's sword and strapped it to his own waist. With the black leather jacket, he looked more like a pirate than a medieval man. Either way, the sword was terribly conspicuous. It wasn't as if we could leave it, however. In the Middle Ages, a man's sword defined him. I helped Llywelyn shove his feet into his boots, which the pool water had neither shrunk after they'd dried nor destroyed with chlorine. Of course, his manservant had been coating them with lanolin, a natural waterproofing, every week since they were made.

I thought about returning to the waiting room and leaving the building via the patio, but I didn't dare pass by the nurse at the desk. I wished I could see if the men in black were still in the driveway or if they'd entered the spa. In my head, I traced the path they would take to reach Llywelyn's room. It wasn't far. They could be here any second.

"This way." With Llywelyn's cloak over my arm and his armor in the plastic bag that had held his clothes, I led the way out of Llywelyn's room. He'd gotten dressed because he was feeling perverse and stubborn (which would have driven the nurses mad if we'd stayed through tomorrow), but I was glad for it now. He moved well for a man who'd been happy to have used the toilet by himself for the first time thirty-six hours ago.

"I'm really okay," Llywelyn said.

"You probably won't be *okay* for a few months," I said. "Not if what the doctor said about what happened to your heart is true. But you look pretty good, I admit."

Llywelyn grinned and stood taller. As we turned the corner of the hallway, however, Goronwy put a hand on my arm. "They're coming!"

I listened. Worse, they were coming from the wrong direction. I'd expected them to reach us by going through the lobby, but booted feet rapped in the corridor ahead of us. Without giving myself time to think too hard about it, I pulled Llywelyn and Goronwy into a room on the right with its door ajar. Once inside, I left the door open slightly so I could peer through the crack between the door and the frame. Four men in black tromped past the room and then turned the corner. I didn't doubt they were headed for Llywelyn's room.

I'd been too distracted when we first entered the room to worry about who was in it with us, but now looked towards the window. A very startled elderly woman sat up in her bed. The staff had turned off the lights in the room everywhere but on the headboard. They shone on her permed, white-pink hair.

"I apologize for disturbing you," I said in Welsh.

"You should have knocked," she said in the same language.

"I know. I'm sorry. We're merely passing through," I said.

I went to the window, a metal and single-paned glass affair with hinges along the left side. I undid the latch, but I couldn't get it to swing outward. It was two feet wide and three tall, set at waist height above the radiator. One edge of the metal frame was bent. I banged on it with my fist, frustrated.

We could escape into the gardens beyond if we could just get through it.

"It's stuck," the woman said, though I clearly already knew that. Her eyes were on Llywelyn. As if it were the most natural thing in the world, he had undone the laces on his breeches so he could tuck in his shirt, and then laced them up again. He also pulled out the needle the nurse had left in his arm in case she needed to reinsert his IV. Goronwy slapped a cloth over it.

"I need you, Goronwy," I said.

"Hold this to the wound while I help Meg," Goronwy said.

Llywelyn pressed on his vein while Goronwy put his shoulder into the window. It popped open, and its momentum crashed it against the outside wall.

More boots sounded in the corridor. I hated to think they (that ubiquitous, and yet unspecified 'they') had raised a spa-wide alarm already. I was hoping they'd assume we'd taken Llywelyn for a walk. While Goronwy climbed awkwardly through the window, I wrapped Llywelyn's cloak around his shoulders. He looked at me with bright eyes. "I haven't had this much fun in a long time."

I pressed a hand to his chest. "Hush. Tell me the moment you need to rest. You moved more quickly tonight than you have in weeks." I held his hand to steady him while he clambered out of the window after Goronwy, and then I scrambled out myself, ending up in a rhododendron. Bent double, Goronwy and Llywelyn set off across the grass. Before I closed the window, I leaned through it to speak to the woman in the room. "That was the true Prince of Wales."

The woman's eyes widened. "It was?"

I pointed towards the door. "There are men here now who want to lock him up to prevent him from claiming the throne. If you could—"

"They won't get anything out of me!" The woman pulled her covers up to her chin and glared at me, defiant.

"Thank you." I closed the window. I couldn't latch it, but I shoved at it hard and it caught, as it had before we'd opened it. Then I turned and followed Llywelyn into the night.

13

18 November 1288

David

We spent the last night before we were to reach London at Windsor Castle, only twenty miles from the city. All we had left was a morning's ride that we could complete before noon. That we were staying tonight at such a famous estate (thanks to a special dispensation from Humphrey de Bohun, who controlled it due to his station as regent) had prompted giggles from Lili. Since it had become my quest to find more joy in my life, it made me laugh to hear her.

At the same time, the closer we got to the village that surrounded the castle, the more solemn we all became. "It starts now, doesn't it?" Lili said.

"What does?" I said.

"Being careful," she said, "of everyone and everything."

"I think it actually started the moment we set foot in England," I said.

Dong ... dong ... dong.

"What am I hearing?" I reined in. "Church bells?"

I'd long since shed the habit of checking my left wrist for my watch, but this time I couldn't figure out what hour the bells were chiming. Sunset wasn't for another hour and there wasn't a monastery here anyway, though Windsor did have its own leper hospital.

"It seems so, my lord," Clare said.

The town was situated on the southern side of the Thames River, which we'd cross tomorrow morning before continuing to London. We had to pass through the town to reach the castle. The western gate lay ahead of us, wide open.

Lili put a hand on my arm. "Dafydd—Look at the people."

"They're kind of hard to miss," I said, though I couldn't figure out what was exciting enough about the arrival of our company that the townspeople of Windsor would feel the need to crowd the battlements of the town wall. Below, those who couldn't fit on the heights jostled one another as they passed through the gate and lined both sides of the road. The people we'd encountered in England so far had treated us well and hundreds had greeted us throughout our entire journey, not just at the first village, or at Gloucester Castle. However, this took it to a new level.

"What do we do?" Lili said.

"Keep riding," said Carew.

"A smile and a wave wouldn't go amiss," Clare added.

Lili obeyed, raising her hand in greeting to the first people we passed. Her smile was a little sick, but the crowd cheered anyway. She shot me a wide-eyed look but I had no answers for her. With people crowding the horses on both sides, this was about as far from being careful as it was possible to get. Still, I smiled too, and held up my hand to the onlookers as we passed under the gate. More cheers. Instead of lifting my spirits, this got me really worried. Did they have me confused with someone else?

Once inside the town walls, we rode along the main road until we reached the town center, at which point a gathering of men greeted us. Windsor had received a royal charter from Edward in 1277 and was one of the most important towns in all of England, with a vibrant and active merchant class. I was looking at a dozen of the town's most upstanding citizens.

I could read Bevyn's face. Back at Chepstow, he'd been optimistic as to how welcoming the English would be to us, but now that it came to it, he couldn't stop his eyes from flicking to the left and right, looking for threats.

"My lord—" Bevyn said.

I held out a hand to him, which the crowd seemed to interpret as another wave because they cheered again. "It's okay. Nothing's going to happen to us today."

Trying to portray a confidence I didn't feel, under the principle of *fake it 'til you make it*, I dismounted. That meant everyone else had to dismount too. It was a matter of convention and a sign of respect to me, at least in their eyes. One of the townsmen stepped forward. He wore a large floppy hat, which he swept off his head, revealing thick white hair and blue eyes. His beard matched his hair and if he'd been wearing red, he would have been a dead ringer for Santa Claus.

The man bowed to me and the men behind him followed suit. "Welcome to Windsor, my lord David," he said. "I am James, the headman of our town."

"Thank you," I said in English. "You honor me with your kind welcome." The heads of the rest of the men popped up. Their expressions showed surprise, and then relief that I could not only understand them, but could respond in kind.

I stuck out a hand to James, who started at the sight of it, but I left my hand there, and after a moment he tentatively took it and shook with a credibly firm grasp as if he was a modern person instead of a medieval one. I worked my way through the rest of the men, shaking hands with each one. When I finished, I turned back to James. He held out a key on a thick chain. "The key to our fair city, my lord."

I took it and put it around my neck, as gravely as I could, though internally the whole scene had me thinking *what the hell*? If James hadn't referred to me as David, I would have been even more convinced he had the wrong man. Even so, it was nice to see that they'd thought of Lili too. Bevyn had helped her from her horse, so as to allow a group of four girls to give her a handmade doll (admittedly, all dolls in the Middle Ages were handmade). The doll's blue eyes, black hair, and green dress bore a surprising resemblance to Lili herself, and I wondered if they'd known in advance what Lili looked like. Of all the things that had happened today, I found that most hard to believe, and yet, likely.

154

Lili took the doll with a smile which didn't falter when a group of boys approached and handed her a wooden sword. She stood there, with a toy in each hand and a bemused expression on her face. Then James said, by way of explanation, "For the coming child, of course."

"Of course," I said, though inwardly I ground my teeth. That Lili was pregnant had been the least well-kept secret in Wales, but that the news had spread so quickly all the way to Windsor shocked me. "We thank you again."

Carew had stayed nearby throughout the small ceremony, and now he gestured that Lili and I should remount our horses. I thought about it for half a second, and then gave a quick shake of my head. If we were going to do this, we might as well do it right. I took the gifted sword from Lili and slipped my other hand into hers. "I think we should walk."

"That would be wonderful." Lili's voice held relief.

Hand in hand, we left the green. The headman of the town immediately understood that we planned to walk and hustled after us. "Talk to me," I said. "I'd like to hear about your city."

"Of course, my lord." He came abreast and immediately launched into a discussion of his livelihood (he was a wool merchant) and the history of Windsor, a subject about which I was, in fact, interested. I smiled down at Lili, who held the doll tucked under her arm. She seemed at ease for the first time today, though maybe that was merely relief at not having to ride her horse again until tomorrow.

155

The rest of the delegation sorted themselves out behind us and were followed by my people, leading their horses (along with mine and Lili's). As the townspeople realized what we were doing, they loosed a roar of excitement and people hurried to follow us or to run ahead so they would be in a good position when we passed them.

Lili and I strolled towards the castle. The towers showed above the town to the east so it would have been easy to navigate towards it even if the road didn't go that way and the town headman wasn't there to direct me.

We passed two dozen houses and shops before it came—that one word which I couldn't escape and which sent a chill through me any time anyone said it—or in this case, shouted it: "*Arthur!*"

Lili's step faltered. "Did I hear what I think I heard—?"

I gripped her hand more tightly. "Yes, you did."

Others among the crowd took up the cry and surged towards us. Evan appeared to Lili's left, boxing her in, while Carew, who'd managed to push through the crush of people, elbowed James out of the way on my right.

"This is mad, my lord," Evan said.

"I would have to agree. I am no Arthur," I said.

Evan glanced at me, his expression puzzled. "I didn't mean that, of course. I meant that you shouldn't be exposing yourself in this way."

"They love him," Carew said, "and mean him no harm." Even so, his eyes scanned the crowd and a hardness had come into his tone, matched by his downturned mouth and the grim lines around his eyes.

"My people mean well, my lord." James hurried to keep up with Carew's long strides.

"I believe you." I took a deep breath and slowed, allowing James to catch up. People pressed us on every side, but here was my chance to speak to a genuine Englishman. "I would be pleased if you could explain to me, James, why your people are so accepting of me. King Arthur was a Welshman. He defeated the Saxons at Mt. Badon ..." My voice trailed off at James' raised eyebrows.

"Is that what your legends say?" James said. "I suppose those French ones do as well, but our people remember Arthur differently."

"Perhaps you would be so kind as to speak to us of those tales," Lili said, gracefully interceding. "We don't know enough of them."

James blushed and bowed, even while walking. "My lady, you honor me," he said. "My lord, it may be that King Arthur defeated an army of Saxons that had invaded Wales, but did he lead his forces into England and overrun it, burning and pillaging everything in his path?"

"No." Lili glanced at me. "No, he didn't."

"Did he enslave our people, force them to bow to him, or to give up our laws and lands in favor of his own?" James said.

"He did not," I said.

James dipped his head. "You know, of course, that the monks at Glastonbury discovered the graves of King Arthur and Guinevere at their Abbey."

"We heard that," I said.

"King Arthur brought peace to this island; he protected the Cup of Christ and His memory," James said. "Are you saying that you would do less than he?"

My teeth were clenched so tightly I could barely speak the words around them. "I would do all of those things."

James' eyes lit and he faced forward, a smile on his lips. Neither of us spoke again. What was there to say?

We passed the last house in the village and, still unscathed, entered a grassy expanse the size of a football field in front of the gatehouse of the castle. Like many castles in England, its original motte and bailey construction had given way to a grander design, most recently paid for by King Edward himself, before his death. Two round towers defended the gateway that greeted us and bore a marked resemblance to Rhuddlan Castle in Wales. Perhaps that shouldn't have been surprising, considering Edward had ordered the building of both of them.

The castellan, a Sir George something or other, waited underneath the gatehouse, having left the portcullis up and the doors wide open, just as the town gate had been.

He strode forward to greet us and bowed. When he looked up, he had *tears* in his eyes. I would have laughed at the absurdity of it, but he was serious, and I couldn't mock or belittle his beliefs—or the beliefs of any of these people.

"They really think you're Arthur returned," Lili said, as we followed Sir George into the bailey.

"So it seems," I said.

In the middle of this century, Windsor Castle had withstood a siege from Simon de Montfort's forces, and afterwards King Henry had a built a luxurious palace to replace what Montfort had burned. The lower ward consisted of a chapel, great hall, and the apartments of the king, which as regent, Humphrey de Bohun had put to his own use. Sir George took us through the lower ward to the more private upper ward, where our suite was located. Henry had built these apartments for the use of his wife and children.

I had decided not to say anything negative to Sir George about our elaborate reception. By this point, it was too late to stop what was going on. But when Sir George flung open the door to our suite, Carew turned on him: "What in the name of St. Mark is going on? You weren't supposed to tell anyone that Prince David was coming here—for his own safety!"

"I apologize, my lord," Sir George said, "but we had no way to keep it secret. The people of Windsor knew of his journey almost as soon as I did."

Carew glared at him, clearly not buying his excuse. He flung out a hand to point towards the city. "Is tomorrow's departure going to look like that? How can I protect him with that crush?"

Sir George's eyes were wide and he was anxious to appease us. "I'm doing my best, my lord, but the people want to see Prince

David. I could no more keep them back than reverse the course of the Thames." Sir George pointed at me. "Only *he* can do that."

Sir George was referring to one of the legends about King Arthur, one that said a sign of his return was the Thames River flowing upstream.

"It's just this Arthur nonsense," I said, trying to calm Carew. "Perhaps it will be better before dawn."

Sir George looked from Carew to me. "But aren't you King Arth—?"

"Of course n—" I began.

Carew spun on his heel to glare at me while at the same time Lili grabbed my arm, their disapproval forcing me to reconsider my words. While they didn't expect me to accept Arthur's mantle, they did expect me not to deny it outright.

Clare and Edmund had followed us from the bailey and now entered the room. Edmund closed the door to the suite. "You would be wise to lower your voices," he said.

I nodded. It was time to mend some fences. "All is well. Carew is rightfully concerned that if word of my arrival in England preceded me to this point, then those who plot against me have had equal warning." I clapped a hand on Sir George's shoulder. "Thank you for your welcome. I am honored to have had such a fine reception." I felt like I'd said that a hundred times already this trip, and we hadn't even arrived in London yet.

"My lord." Sir George bowed, somewhat appeased.

"If you would excuse us, we would wash before we eat," I said.

"Of course, my lord," Sir George said.

As Sir George departed, Bevyn, who'd been waiting outside, stepped through the doorway. "Branwen is coming, along with Jeeves. Evan and I will see to our people."

"Thank you," I said.

Bevyn bowed and followed Sir George.

Lili rubbed her eyes. "I don't know about you, but I could lie down." She disappeared through a far archway that led to the stairs up to our bedroom, one floor above. As promised, Branwen and Jeeves hurried in a moment later, with Tomos on their heels. I pointed to the stairs. Branwen and Jeeves went up them, while Tomos settled himself on the second step as an out of the way place to await my pleasure.

I turned to look at my three Norman advisors, and as I did so, realized that I no longer knew how much I could trust any of them. Or rather, it wasn't that I couldn't trust them, but I didn't know if I could rely on them to do what *I* said, as opposed to what they thought was right. They would guard me with their lives, but all of them, and in this I included Bevyn, would filter information or withhold it if they thought it would serve me better.

"This King Arthur thing," I said. "I'm guessing that it hasn't caught you all entirely by surprise like it has me?"

The men wore the same expression on their faces, as if my question had sparked the identical response in all three of them: that for once, maybe, they would tell me the truth. "That men here believe you are—or at least might be—the return of Arthur is not news to us," Edmund said. "Rumors of your nobility spread to England years ago."

"What do you mean, *years ago*?" I said.

Clare looked at me sideways. "You didn't know?"

"No."

"It was one of the reasons King Edward hated you so much," Clare said. "One Christmas, he paced around his solar, raging at me and Roger for not taking care of you sooner—"

"Murdering me, you mean—"

"—or at the very least, for not killing your father when we had the chance."

"My brother and I did try to kill your father." Edmund bowed. "My regrets, my lord."

"Thank goodness you bollixed it up," Carew said.

Clare laughed.

I was pleased that all three men sounded pleased about that.

"Why do you think I didn't hesitate to throw in my lot with you three years ago?" Carew said. "I knew then who you were. Your people have known from the day you saved your father's life."

Ack. I scrubbed at my hair with both hands. "Okay. I understand that you believe the legend, or whatever. But why does my presence here mean anything to the people of Windsor?"

The three men exchanged a glance. "They believe you to be Arthur returned too," Carew said.

I managed to contain my sigh. "I realize that. But it would be helpful to discover exactly what that *means*. I tried to get it out of James, the headman of the town, but it's still not clear to me. Who is Arthur to them? What are the details of the legend? Who do they think me to *be*?"

They stared at me blankly. It was like I'd asked them to explain why one plus one equaled two. They *knew* the answer and couldn't believe something so simple needed an explanation. "You are the savior of Britain, of course," Clare said. "You are the one who will rise up in our hour of need and lead us to victory over our enemies."

And then Edmund recited, with sentiment and without irony, the poem I by now knew well, albeit stripped of its references to Wales:

He will come,
No longer hiding,
The dragon banner raised high,
The land will be red
With battle and strife.
None will stand against him.
All will fall to their knees before him.
When Arthur returns.

* * * * *

Later that night, I lay beside Lili, who had survived yet another state dinner without throwing up. I was close to drifting off to sleep when she said, "I had Tomos do some inquiring for you."

My eyes popped open. "Tomos? What did he do?"

"He speaks English and French, you know."

"I do know. That's one reason I picked him to be my squire," I said. "But he's meant to be my eyes and ears, not yours."

"You were too busy tonight to think of it," she said. "Near the end of the meal, he walked into Windsor with Carew's squire, Gwilym, to inquire about a beer."

"They went to a tavern?"

In the dark, I felt Lili's nod. "As soon as the patrons learned he was your squire, he and Gwilym had as much free beer as they could drink."

I had to smile. "Good thing he hasn't tried this before, then, or he'd have been rolling home every night we've been in England."

"He admits he was tempted to stay longer, but left after a short while, not wanting to be locked out of the castle when you might have need of him," she said. "But he talked to a dozen townspeople. They confirmed what you heard: everyone believes you are the return of Arthur."

"Again, I don't even know what that means," I said. "It's silly."

"Ssshhh!" Lili slapped me (gently) on the shoulder. "Don't say that out loud. It's not nice to mock."

I rolled onto my side, trying to make out her expression by the light coming through the cracks in the window shutters. "You

164

are right, of course, as always. From the first, you warned me that I couldn't stop the legend. How many times have I denied it? It does no good."

"I told you not to bother," Lili said. "The moment you unfurled that banner—maybe even the moment you drove into that clearing at Cilmeri and saved your father's life—it was too late."

"So does this make you Gwenhwyfar?"

Lili wiggled uncomfortably. "Don't be ridiculous."

"If I have to be Arthur, I don't see why you can't be Gwenhwyfar. It's only fair," I said. "Though ... Anna truly doesn't want the mantle of Morgane on her shoulders."

"Your mother told me that the French invented the unpleasant aspect of her story," Lili said complacently. "We can ignore it."

"Did Tomos learn anything else?" I said.

Lili's pressed her lips together, suddenly far less forthcoming, even if what she had to tell me next was the real point of this conversation.

"Is it something I don't want to hear?" I said.

Lili plumped her pillow. "One of the townspeople described how you saved your father at Cilmeri. It wasn't the real story, of course, but it was close—in that you and Anna charged into the fray and killed the attackers who besieged him."

"Admittedly, I am thankful they didn't mention my aunt's minivan, but how could they possibly know about that?" I said.

"They know because one of your father's men talked. Or his wife did. Or a man-at-arms was drunk and embellished the details—"

"Lied, you mean."

"—and then it spread," Lili continued, ignoring me. "Everyone in Wales talks about you all the time. You know this, right?"

"But for the story to reach Windsor?" I said. "That's crazy."

"Is it?" Lili said. "Why? People love heroes. They tell stories in the hall and to their children at bedtime. But that's not the part you won't like."

I could just make out the shadow of a smile on her face. She had tucked both hands between her cheek and the pillow.

"You might as well tell me the rest," I said.

"The man ended his story by relating the tale of the last time Edward attacked Wales, when the rivers flooded. You stood on the bluff overlooking the debacle, and as it became clear that Edward's men were routed, you held up your sword and shouted, *God wills it!*"

"I did not—"

"And then, Tomos says, as the man finished his story, everyone in the bar lifted their right hand and said it too—not as a shout, but solemnly."

I closed my eyes. Gotten out of hand? This was so far beyond *out of hand* that I had no idea how I was going to reel it in again, and what I would do if I couldn't.

14

18 November 2016

Meg

We ended up in a ramshackle shed full of rusting gardening implements, on the far side of the spa's property. It was November. It was cold and raining. After such an auspicious beginning, it came as a shock to be fleeing what I had thought was a haven.

"We have to keep moving," Goronwy said.

"Llywelyn needs to rest," I said.

"I'm fine—"

"You're not and I have to call Ted," I said.

"Ted is the one who betrayed us!" Goronwy said. "He's as bad as Dafydd!"

I knew without asking that Goronwy didn't mean my son, but Llywelyn's brother. Given that he had betrayed Llywelyn four times and tried to assassinate him once, it was something of an exaggeration to compare him to Ted, but I got the point. Still, I thought Ted's problem was ignorance, rather than malice.

"I know, Goronwy, but I don't think he meant to." I dialed Ted's number and didn't quail under Goronwy's glare.

"Where the hell are you?" Ted's voice came over the line an octave higher than normal and twice as loud.

"Where are you?" I said.

"I don't know. Some road, about a mile and a half from the spa. I almost got hit by an SUV squealing into the parking lot as I was leaving," he said. "Let me come get you."

"Listen, Ted. You need to tell me what you told your friend."

"I told him everything!" he said. "I told you that I came to the UK after David chose to return to the Middle Ages, right? During that trip, I had drinks with my friend. He and I have talked often since then. I called him as soon as I arrived at Heathrow. My friend was very excited and wanted to know everything."

I pressed a hand to my forehead and closed my eyes. "What's weird is that he believed you," I said. "Did he ever say why?"

"He had independent confirmation," Ted said. "He knows people who know people and he could trace your other disappearances and returns. Something about satellites and the Norad tracking system."

I moaned. "Ted—"

"Don't you see how *exciting* this is?" he said. "We're *this* close to figuring out what's really going on!"

168

"Who's *we*, Ted?"

Pause. And now Ted sounded defensive. "It's not like he pumped me for information or anything, and I never asked him what he was doing with what I told him. I assumed he wasn't doing anything with it—that he was just as curious and excited as I was."

"Oh, Ted."

"Do you really think he could have called the cops down on you?"

"He works at the University of Cambridge, right?" I said. "Does he have ties to the military?"

"No!" Ted said, but then his voice became very small. "But his wife works—" he cleared his throat, "—for the government. MI5, I always thought."

I gazed down at my wet feet. While MI6 was the British equivalent of the CIA, MI5 was the government agency tasked with internal spying. "I'm hanging up right now," I said.

"No—wait! What should I do with your stuff?"

"Are you near a crossroads?" I said.

Scuffling sounds came from Ted's side of the line. "Yes. Looks like there's a sign—Yswyth is the name of the village—and my God—there's an actual telephone booth."

"You mean a call box?" I said. "Is it big and red?"

"Got to love the English and their antiquated phones," Ted said. "We're so isolated out here we're lucky to have cell phone reception at all."

"The people who live here are Welsh, Ted," I said, automatically. "Leave our duffel by the box. We'll pick it up. *You* get out of there now."

"Why?" he said. "Why can't we go wherever you're going together?"

"Who paid for our room?" I said, and then answered my own question: "You did. This has gone way beyond your friend. If they don't already have all your contact information, they will in a minute. They'll be on the lookout for your rental car, and at the very least, they'll trace your cell phone—and then mine—if they haven't already."

"*They*, Meg? Seriously?"

"I'm hanging up, Ted. Thank you for everything. Give my love to Elisa and the kids."

I snapped the phone shut, flipped it over, and removed the battery. I stood in the darkness of the shed, not speaking, trying to think. The rain pounded on the metal roof and dripped through unsealed cracks, forming puddles on the wooden floor that was so filthy, it was indistinguishable from the mud outside. Goronwy eyed me from beside Llywelyn, who'd found a seat on an overturned bucket and sat with his head in his hands.

"Can we go home, Meg?" Goronwy said.

"That's the best idea I've heard all day," I said. "The question is—how?"

And that was something I didn't have an answer to. Regardless, we had to get out of this shed and to a place where Llywelyn could lie down. My memory of the spy movies I'd

170

watched in the past had me casting around for all the ways those men could track us.

I had a little money. I couldn't use my credit cards anymore, but when Ted had straightened things out with the spa, he'd handed me two hundred pounds in cash, too. I still had my four hundred American dollars. If we could find a place to stay where they wouldn't ask questions, we could pay.

"I knew it was too good to be true," Goronwy said.

"I told you that the cracks and the dirt of our world would reveal themselves, given time," I said. "It takes a while sometimes to see it—though in this case, not as long as I had hoped."

"Then let's go." Goronwy poked Llywelyn who rose to his feet. The two men ducked under the low lintel above the doorway of the shed and straightened. Llywelyn stretched and tipped back his head to allow the rain to fall onto his face.

"I feel great," he said.

I eyed him sourly and pulled up the collar of my jacket so the rain wouldn't drip down my neck. We set off. If I'd been leading us, we would have been stumbling around in the dark, but the difference in my men between the environment of the hospital and the countryside was tangible. They knew who they were out here. They liked being outside.

Within a few minutes of leaving the shed, Goronwy found a makeshift road across the field, which allowed us to keep moving. Beside me, Llywelyn breathed in through his nose and out through his mouth as he strode along, as if nothing at all was the matter with him. I feared that he might really have a heart attack if he had to exert himself too much, but he kept pace.

I used the other half of my brain to worry about the men chasing us. Any moment, a spotlight from one of the SUVs could find us. But after twenty minutes of walking, we came out on one of those typically narrow Welsh roads that were big enough for one car, even though a map might claim two could fit. I took comfort that any SUV that attempted to come down it would find it impossible to maintain any rate of speed.

At the same time, the stone wall on one side and the hedge on the other had my nerves even more on edge because if an SUV followed us, we'd have nowhere to run.

"What are we walking on?" Goronwy said. "This material covered the road that led up to the spa too."

"It's called *asphalt*," I said, using the English word since the Welsh equivalent wouldn't make sense to him anyway.

"A cart would ride very smoothly on this, but it doesn't seem like it would be healthy for a horse's hooves," he said.

"You're right," I said. "It's not. These roads were made for cars, which you haven't really seen up close yet. It's our method of transportation."

"I know about them, Meg," Goronwy said, gently. "I saw yours, and your son's, and Bronwen's, even."

"Sorry," I said. "I forgot." And maybe that was why he was taking this trip to the modern world so well. In addition to knowledge of the vehicles, after David had rescued my suitcase from its hiding place in Scotland and Aaron had brought it back to me, I had been able to show him and Llywelyn pictures of the modern world. They'd handled my phone and my laptop, and felt the fabric in my rain jacket.

We'd gone another half mile when the road straightened out, allowing us to see the lights of the village twinkling in front of us. That call box couldn't come soon enough. Without an umbrella, Goronwy and I were soaked through. Llywelyn was probably in the best shape, since he had his thick wool cloak with a hood. My cloak was in the duffel bag that we were hoping Ted had left us.

We hugged the side of the road as we approached the town. The call box sat on the corner where our little road and the main one (which admittedly was hardly any wider) intersected. At the start of a hedge that circled one of the houses, we hesitated. Llywelyn and Goronwy stayed close on either side of me, pressed into the bush, surveying the road from a crouch. Now that we'd left the darkness of the field and were in Stwyth, a string of streetlamps lit the street, the call box, and the stores and houses that made up the small town center.

I caught my breath. Ted leaned against his car, which he'd parked in the narrow, graveled parking lot of a convenience store on the other side of the street. He was clearly keeping an eye on the call box, which was on our side of the road, only fifty feet from me.

"What's he doing?" Llywelyn said, low in my ear.

"Is he thinking that if he watches for us, we'll let him come with us?" Goronwy said. "If so, he's in for a rude awakening." Goronwy remained unforgiving.

I knew what Goronwy and Llywelyn were thinking: if they'd known the rules, they would have done better. The implication was that Ted—who did live here and did know the rules—should have watched the backs of those who didn't. I studied Ted and his surroundings. Perhaps he sensed my eyes on him. Before I could draw back, he looked in my direction. Our eyes locked. He straightened and took a step toward me.

I couldn't let him do that. "Wait here," I said to Llywelyn and Goronwy.

I broke from our hiding place, dashed to the rear of the call box where Ted had left our duffel, threw it over my shoulder, and ran back to where Goronwy and Llywelyn waited, the heavy bag bouncing awkwardly against my body. When I reached the men, I looked back. Ted was staring at me, his mouth open, and I waved a hand at him in a *go away* motion.

I was preparing to shout the words at him, to make myself completely clear, when two black SUVs screamed through the intersection. They pulled to the side of the road—on the wrong side of the road—where Ted waited. The vehicles blocked more than half the road, big enough that cars coming both ways would have to squeeze between the parked cars on the left and the SUVs on the right.

"That can't be good." Llywelyn backed away, burrowing deeper into the hedge.

174

I turned to look at him. He had a wry smile on his face—maybe the first I'd seen in a long while—and had made a deadpan joke. I wanted to hug him. "Sorry about this. I can't believe anybody really cares who we are, but—" I gestured to the SUVs, "—obviously someone does."

We couldn't hear the conversation between the men in black and Ted, but it went on for a few minutes. Then one of the men led Ted around the back of one of the vehicles. To his credit, Ted didn't look towards us. One of the soldiers opened the back passenger door and urged Ted inside with a hand on his shoulder and another to the back of his head. Ten seconds later, both SUVs pulled back into their lane and headed north. Goronwy stirred, but I put a hand on his arm. "Wait."

Sure enough, thirty seconds later, both SUVs roared through the intersection going the other way, back to the spa. A spray of water flew up as the right wheels of the following vehicle hit a puddle. I caught sight of Ted's face, illumined in the rear passenger window—and then he was gone.

Once the tail lights had disappeared into the distance, we rose to our feet. The rain continued to pour down. "Come on," I said.

We trotted across the street, me in the lead and Llywelyn and Goronwy following, carrying the duffel bag between them. When I reached the car, I bent to look under it. Relief washed through me. I *had* seen what I'd thought I'd seen: when the first SUV had appeared from the south, Ted had closed his mouth, looked at me for a split-second, and nodded. He then dropped his car key to the ground and kicked it under the car with his foot. It lay in a small puddle behind the right front tire.

I grabbed it, unlocked the car, and pulled open the driver's side door. I waved Llywelyn around to the other side. "Get in, gentlemen."

"I thought you said we couldn't ride in Ted's vehicle because those men could track it?" Llywelyn said.

"However it is they might do that," Goronwy added.

"They can, but—" I popped the trunk and felt around for anything metal. I came up with a tire jack. I stepped back, took a deep breath, and swung it at the little light that lit the rear license plate. The jack rebounded off the plate with a thunk. I'd missed the light. I aimed a little better, swung, and the light went out. "I don't think they'll be looking for his car at the moment, now that they have Ted. I'm thinking we have a little time before they begin to wonder if they should have brought in the car, too."

Neither Llywelyn nor Goronwy objected further. Once in the car, I bent to show Llywelyn how to buckle his seat belt, but he brushed aside my hand. "Who do you think took you from your chariot at Cricieth?"

I smiled. "You did."

"Besides, I drove with Dafydd at Buellt a few years ago."

It was odd, with all the advances in technology, how little seatbelts had changed in the twenty years since I'd driven into Wales the first time. I adjusted my seat and when I put my hands on the wheel, I swallowed hard. I was sitting on the right side of the car, what was to me the 'wrong' side compared to how I might drive in the United States. I would have to drive on the left side of the road, too. Thankfully, Ted had rented an automatic, not a stick shift. I drove out of the parking lot and pulled onto the road, heading north and all the while reciting, *stay to the left, stay to the left.*

"Where are you taking us?" Llywelyn said after we'd left Stwyth behind us. I had yet to overtake another car, or have one pass me on the right. *Small blessings.*

"I don't know," I said.

"I don't have any holdings this far south," Llywelyn said.

"I know," I said. "Even if you did, it's not like any of your castles are still habitable. We can't camp out at Castell y Bere. The walls are only a few feet high in most places and none of the buildings have a roof anymore. Dolwyddelan is the only one that's been semi-rebuilt, but it's far away, and I can't see the point of going there."

We drove in silence for two more miles. I glanced at Llywelyn. He gazed stonily ahead. Rain continued to pour down and I set the wipers on a higher speed, so they flicked back and forth at a constant interval. I checked the speedometer. I was driving forty miles an hour. Neither man had ever traveled this fast before. Llywelyn clenched his fingers around the handle on the door and Goronwy's face was pale in the rearview mirror.

A turn out appeared up ahead, so I slowed and pulled into it. After turning off the car, I twisted in my seat so I could see both of them at the same time. "I need your help figuring out what to do, because I don't have all the answers—or maybe any answers. I am from this time, but I've never experienced anything like this either. We all want to go home, right?"

"Yes," Llywelyn said. "Though I have my concerns about the trip."

"I guess I knew that," I said. "What concerns you, specifically?"

"The last time you were pregnant, when it came time to deliver Dafydd, what happened?" Llywelyn said.

I took in a deep breath and let it out. "I took Anna back to my mother's house. I know. I've thought about that too."

"In addition, it almost happened to Anna before she gave birth to Cadell," Llywelyn said.

A rueful expression crossed Goronwy's face. "Could we ... wait? Wait until you are ready to deliver the babies?"

"And then what? What are the odds that at the moment my water breaks, you two are holding on to me?" I said. "I disappear into the Middle Ages, leaving you here alone? No." I shook my head. "If it happens, it happens, but I won't risk you two spending the rest of your lives in the modern world without me."

Llywelyn pursed his lips and looked out the window. "When you put it that way, it does sound like a poor choice." He reached out a hand and took mine. "I'm worried."

"I don't want you to worry," I said, "but I do feel that it's better to go home now, safely, without new babies in my arms. When my time comes, we'll deal with whatever happens."

"We need a plan," Goronwy said.

"We need to feel like we have a plan anyway," I said. "If we do manage to get back to the Middle Ages, I don't know where we'll end up. I'm open to your thoughts—and honestly, just because you're from another time doesn't disqualify you from having a better idea than I have at the moment, since I don't have any."

"How far can this vehicle take us?" Goronwy said.

"As far as we want to go," I said. "We can be anywhere in Wales or England before morning."

"You're telling me that Chepstow, which is at least a hundred miles from Aberystwyth, is reachable tonight?" Llywelyn said.

I checked the clock on the dashboard. It said 10 pm. It felt like it had to be two in the morning by now, but it wasn't. "We could be in Chepstow in three hours. We could easily be in London by dawn."

Llywelyn allowed that to sink in. "What kind of condition is Chepstow Castle in? You said that Aberystwyth is a ruin, as are all of my—" Llywelyn swallowed his words without finishing the sentence, his earlier amusement gone.

"Chepstow is in pretty good shape for a ruin," I said. "The balcony is still there, if that's what you're thinking."

"We could go there—jump off it again?" Goronwy leaned forward so he could hear better.

"We could," I said. "It wouldn't be much different than a few days ago." I coughed a laugh. It felt like months since we'd been in the Middle Ages. "It's November, and we'd risk getting soaked again."

"What's the worst outcome we could expect?" Goronwy said.

"We fall in the river," I said. "With all this rain, as at home, the Wye must be running high. We'd float downstream, and someone would come along and fish us out."

"What about these government men?" Llywelyn said. "Will they pursue us?"

"I don't know," I said. "Surely they won't expect us to drive to Chepstow. They don't even know we have a vehicle."

"If we did jump from the balcony, and failed to return to our time, we'd be vulnerable. How likely would it be then that these men from the government would catch us?" Goronwy said.

"It would depend on where we beached, and what shape we were in when we did." I shrugged. "Possibly we could buy life vests and wear them."

"Buy what?" Llywelyn said.

"Life vests," I said. "Flotation devices. Items we stick around our necks so that we don't drown."

"I like that idea," Llywelyn said. "I feel no need to swallow any more water that I don't intend to drink."

"Do you think it will work?" Goronwy said.

"I have no idea about that either," I said. "We've never traveled *to* the Middle Ages except by car."

"So, let's go," Llywelyn said. "If it doesn't work, we still have the car. Maybe we can use it instead."

I didn't want to think about purposefully creating a car accident to get home, like David had done, but I started the car and we drove off again. Nobody pursued us, still, though the closer we got to Devil's Bridge and the road leading from Aberystwyth, the more traffic we encountered. I couldn't see much besides the road in the dark and the rain, but both men looked with interest out the window as we crossed the Devil's Bridge, which spanned a canyon that would have been impassable without it. They'd journeyed in this area at one time and had taken the long way around.

Then we headed east, across the mountains that ran through the middle of Wales, down a road that hardly qualified as a road to my mind. It narrowed to a single lane as we rattled across a cattle guard. The drive was harrowing, between the rain and the sheep, which would appear beside the road unexpectedly and cause me to jerk the wheel every time. Still, we saw only two cars, both going the other way. We reached Builth Wells by midnight.

I'd intended to drive through the town without stopping. Llywelyn didn't need to know that what had once been the great keep of Buellt Castle was nothing more than grassy mounds in the back of a housing development.

But he had a different plan.

"Cilmeri is to the west," he said.

I glanced at him. "What? No—"

"You can't keep it from me, Marged," he said. "I have to see it."

181

I breathed in deeply through my nose and then out through my mouth. "It's dark and it's raining ..."

"You said yourself that we'd reach Chepstow by the time it got light. Surely we have a moment to see where I died."

I would have closed my eyes and said a prayer for patience if I hadn't been driving. Instead, I gave in to my husband. At the next round-about, I followed it around to head west again as Llywelyn wanted. We soon came to the Irfon River, the site where the bulk of Llywelyn's army perished (supposedly) after the Mortimer brothers had ambushed and killed him at Cilmeri.

"This is the bridge?" he said.

"Nobody knows what happened to your army, Llywelyn." At his raised eyebrows, I said, "I'm serious—nobody! All the stories about your death and the battle that followed were written much later. That your men defended and died at the Irfon River makes no sense. Why would they do that when they had the high ground to the west? Besides, the description of the battle bears a disturbing resemblance to the Battle of Stirling Bridge in Scotland."

"If you say so." Llywelyn gazed out the window at the darkness beyond. Trees flashed by, caught in the glow of an occasional streetlight and just visible through the rain, which continued to fall, unrelenting.

I pulled to the side of the road, outside Cilmeri's village center. The windshield wipers flicked back and forth. Llywelyn sat in the car, thinking hard through a long count of ten. "This isn't it,

182

surely? The hill where Anna and Dafydd rescued me is over there."
He pointed to his right. "I think."

I sighed and reached for his hand. "I know that. But history
doesn't. Llywelyn—you have to understand what happened after
you died. King Edward eliminated all mention of your seat at Aber
from the royal records, took the sacred piece of the true cross, your
crown and your scepter, and began a program of cultural genocide.
We don't even know where your body is buried."

"What you're telling me is that somebody guessed as to the
location, and put up a rock in his field," Llywelyn said.

"In a word, *yes.*" I gestured towards the stone pillar in the
meadow to my left. "At first, there wasn't even a sign to tell visitors
what this was. Still ... someone has left a fresh bouquet of flowers."
I pushed open the car door and stood up.

When I'd come here before, twenty years ago when David
was a baby, I'd cried—and despaired. Now, I just felt defeated. I
hadn't wanted to show Llywelyn this, but he was a grown man and
the King of Wales. There was no stopping him.

Llywelyn got out of the car, followed by Goronwy, who'd
been asleep until we stopped. "What is this place?" Goronwy said,
straightening.

"My tombstone, apparently." Llywelyn pulled up his hood
to protect himself from the rain. Not for the first time, I longed for
an umbrella. Now that we had the duffel, I should have gotten out
my cloak. But I didn't move. Instead, I watched the men.

"Interesting," Goronwy said.

Llywelyn smirked and headed for the gate. He pulled on the latch and passed through the opening to stop in front of the stone. Two streetlamps shone down on the field. I didn't think they'd been there when I'd come here last time. Llywelyn walked all around the monument and then came back to me. "And the well? Where is it?"

"Llywelyn—"

He came forward, put a finger under my chin, and bent his head to kiss me. I leaned into him, my arms around his waist.

"I'm not fussed." He eased back after a moment. "This isn't my world, but I want to see it." He gestured towards the monument. "This stone is a reminder of why Dafydd and I do what we do, why you and Goronwy brought me to your world, and why we have to go back."

"Okay," I said, without adding *it's your funeral*. That would have been too morbid, but the thought created a bubble in my stomach—of laughter—and eased the tightening in my chest. "It's over here."

I led them to a path and a short flight of stairs down to a wooden box under a low hanging tree. I lifted the lid, revealing the access to the well, or stream, as it had probably been in Llywelyn's time.

"This is where the Englishman washed your severed head?" Amusement sounded in Goronwy's voice.

Llywelyn peered past Goronwy, studied the well, and then looked to me. "Really?"

Goronwy laughed. Llywelyn, who had been grinning, joined him. Their laughter crescendoed until they both staggered, bending over and holding their stomachs. Llywelyn wiped his streaming eyes. "Don't you see, Meg?"

I was smiling too, though more because of their laughter than my own amusement. "See what?"

"My dear." Llywelyn threw his arm around my shoulders. "We Welsh are a gruesome bunch, aren't we?"

"You two." I shook my head. This was yet another example of their pessimistic optimism that I'd noticed when I'd first come to Wales and had never been able to successfully wrap my head around.

Llywelyn pulled me closer. "What did Dafydd say? There's something freeing about facing that which you most fear?"

"But you don't fear this, Llywelyn," Goronwy said.

Llywelyn had finally gotten control of himself. He straightened. "No. No, I don't. I fear for my people and my country, but this ...?" He nudged the toe of his boot against the wooden frame of the box. "Edward did everything he could to crush us, including cutting off my head. But Wales lives, even in this time." He turned to me. "Doesn't it?"

"It does."

We headed back to the car, Llywelyn with his arm across my shoulders, both of us with our heads down against the driving rain. Llywelyn's laughter had faded, but Goronwy still chortled ahead of us. He pulled open the rear door of the car and got in, but

Llywelyn stopped with one hand on the roof and the other around my waist.

"I'm sorry," he said.

I looked up at him. The light from the lamp post was behind him so his face was shadowed. "For what?"

"For being so hard on Dafydd," he said. "You've stood by and watched, and bit your tongue more times than I can count."

"I never wanted to argue with you," I said.

"You told me about your time and what happened in it." Llywelyn gestured to the stone, but seemed to indicate the world at large too. "I believed you, but never understood. I see now that for all that Dafydd is my son, he still lives here inside his head much of the time."

"Do you think so?" I said. "I wouldn't say that, so much as that his attitudes and responses were forged here. He's never going to compete for the crown of England. You know that, right?"

Llywelyn sighed. "I do. I always did, even when I was arguing with him about it. Maybe it's not possible for me to ever understand him, not having grown up in your world, or lived here long. If I have my way, we won't stay another day. But I'm not sorry you brought me here. It's given me the opportunity to see what's inside you—and him—more clearly."

He kissed me again and then pulled open the car door while I walked around to the other side. Before we sat in the car, he and I exchanged a long look, and then he canted his head. "All will be well, *cariad*, regardless of how this turns out."

I nodded. No matter what happened, no matter how long we were stuck in the twenty-first century, he and I were each other's constant. We were in this together, and neither death—nor time—was going to part us.

15

19 November 2016

Meg

I pulled into the parking lot outside of Chepstow Castle at four in the morning. Llywelyn peered through the windscreen. The rain that had fallen unrelentingly since Ystwyth had tapered off in the last few minutes. With two more sweeps of the wipers, the windscreen cleared.

"It doesn't look too bad." Llywelyn meant the castle, not the weather. In fact, in the years I'd been with him, both when I was younger and more recently, I'd never heard him complain even once about the weather. He only cared about it if it impacted his current plans or strategy.

"In this world, we never took it," I said. "Chepstow was fortified until the 1600's, when the government deliberately made it indefensible."

"What could possibly have motivated them to do that?" Llywelyn said.

I ran a hand across my eyes. "The English crown has had its ups and downs in the last seven hundred years. There was a period in the 1600's when parliament deposed the king and a man named Oliver Cromwell ran the country."

"Ahh," Llywelyn said. "Like Simon de Montfort in the Baron's war."

"Cromwell was more righteous about it, I think, and believed he was chosen by God," I said. "Under his oversight, Parliament executed the king and abolished the monarchy."

"Where was Wales in this?" Llywelyn said.

"Mostly supporting the king." I smirked. "Ironic, I know."

"At what hour can we enter the castle?" Goronwy said.

"If Chepstow is like other castles I've been to, nine o'clock in the morning." I started the car again. "We should try to sleep until then if we can. We'll need to buy the life jackets too, before we go in. And maybe get a good breakfast and some provisions. We never know where we're going to end up, and if it turns out to be like what happened to me the last time, our location could be remote." I pulled out of the parking space and back onto the street.

"Where are we going?" Llywelyn said.

"We shouldn't park so close to the castle," I said. "It's too conspicuous if someone is looking for us."

"*Someone*," Goronwy said.

"How could the government possibly know where we'll be?" Llywelyn said.

"You forget, Llywelyn. They have Ted," Goronwy said.

189

Llywelyn nodded. "I do forget. He wouldn't stand up well to any pressure. A few well-placed punches or a broken finger and he'd talk."

"He did leave us his keys," Goronwy said. "Maybe he's stronger than we think."

I coughed a laugh. "We call such questioning *torture*, and it's illegal in this time." At Llywelyn's scowl, I added, "not that it doesn't happen. Even so, you're right that Ted might still not understand the gravity of our situation. I can see that if his friend were present, Ted wouldn't see a problem with mentioning that we arrived here by jumping off the balcony at Chepstow."

I found a parking space on a one-way street a few blocks from the castle, among a line of other cars parked for the night. I showed Llywelyn how to lean back his seat.

"How are you, Llywelyn?" Goronwy rested against the duffel which he'd propped up against the door as an improvised pillow.

"Four days ago, I was sure I was going to die." Llywelyn reached for my hand. "You saved my life, and I am glad to have finally seen your world. But now I can't get home fast enough."

I leaned over and kissed his cheek. Then I handed him a water bottle and one of the antibiotics from the prescription I'd filled shortly before Ted had arrived. "Take this and go to sleep. We have a few hours until the castle opens."

I intended to stay awake myself, to keep watch, but the next thing I knew, Llywelyn was pushing at my shoulder. He held my car door open and crouched on the curb. My tongue had stuck to the roof of my mouth so I grabbed the water bottle from the cup holder and took a quick swig. "What's wrong?" I twisted in my seat to see Goronwy getting out of the car with the duffel on his shoulder.

"The men in the black vehicles are here," Llywelyn said.

"What?" I straightened and grabbed Llywelyn's hand so he could help me out of the car. I was too pregnant to easily haul myself out of a low-slung vehicle in a hurry. "You saw them?"

Llywelyn nodded. "I walked over to the castle."

"You did what?" The panicky feeling Llywelyn's words had given me wasn't lessening. "Llywelyn—"

Llywelyn pulled me into his arms. "I'm fine. They didn't see me."

I breathed in and out, my forehead on his chest. I calmed and made room for thinking. "How many vehicles?"

"Three, with three men apiece sitting inside."

We are in deep trouble. I thought the words but didn't say them. Why bother? My men were prepped as if for battle, and they'd lived through far more real battles than I. Even so, I wiped the car for prints the best I could. If the men who were hunting us found it, they would know without further inspection who had driven it here, but I wouldn't make it easy for them. As it was, they'd be looking for us earnestly enough. I wasn't even sure that leaving the vehicle at all was the right course of action, but if we stayed inside it, we were sitting ducks.

"We could go somewhere else," I said. "It doesn't have to be here."

"It does," Llywelyn said. "I feel it."

I stared at him. It wasn't unusual for him to admit to a feeling that influenced his actions. He'd won battles by listening to that inner surety that he couldn't rationally explain, rather than to his advisors. In fact, that first night I was with him, twenty years ago, could be ascribed to him going with his gut rather than what made sense.

So I didn't argue with him.

I checked the car a last time. I'd left the keys on the seat and the windows rolled down in the hope that someone would steal it and put our pursuers off our trail. That we had pursuers at all continued to boggle my mind. Regardless of whether or not we jumped from the balcony today, we couldn't come back to this car. According to the car's clock, it was only 7:30—light, but the heavy cloud cover kept it from being bright.

"We should find some food," I said.

Llywelyn rubbed my arms, then took my hand and we started walking. I looked up at him as we strolled down the street, heading for the river. "What are you doing?" I said.

"Walking with you," he said.

"I know that, but you never hold my hand. Ever."

Llywelyn lifted his chin to point to a couple ahead of us. "I'm fitting in."

Which was the truth. He wore his cloak and sword, but the couple ahead of us was dressed more like him than me, and when we turned at the intersection, we encountered five more people in period costume. It dawned on me what was going on. "They're re-enactors," I said.

"They're what?" Llywelyn said.

"They work at the castle," I said, suddenly excited. "We should stick with them."

"It appears that you and I should put back on the clothes in the duffel," Goronwy said.

The people ahead of us headed towards a restaurant that had a sign out front advertising hot breakfasts all day long. With a shrug, I turned into the porch and ducked through the door.

The place was packed with a mix of people—all ages, sizes, colors—most of whom were dressed in medieval garb.

"Nice cloak!" A man bumped into Llywelyn, who turned.

Llywelyn didn't understand the English, but nodded and smiled. I leaned in. "What time do we have to be at the castle?"

"Half eight," the man said. Then he pointed a finger at me and cocked his head. "You're American?"

"Yes," I said. "We've come a long way for this."

"Me too!" He stuck out his hand and suddenly his accent was Midwestern. "Don Jones. We make a special trip every year so we can participate."

"It's an odd time of year for it," I said, still trying to gauge if this was something specific to Chepstow Castle, or part of the Society for Creative Anachronism.

The man shrugged. "You can get cold and rainy any time of year in Wales."

Which was, of course, the truth. Don looked from me to Goronwy, who seemed to understand what the man was thinking without him speaking, because he hoisted the duffel higher on his shoulder.

"If you've got your gear with you, you should get dressed," Don said. "The organizers won't admit anyone without a costume. They have a back room for that over there." At my look of surprise, he added, "we've been coming here for many years."

"Great." I gestured to Goronwy and Llywelyn and went with them to where Don pointed. I opened the door to find a dozen people in various stages of undress. A few glanced at us as we entered, but our presence didn't spark any particular interest.

Goronwy bent his head and I could tell he was trying not to look at the women. "We get dressed all together?"

"Sorry." I tipped my head towards the far wall. "You can go behind one of the screens."

Llywelyn clapped a hand on Goronwy's shoulder. "Let's go."

Amusingly less worried about modesty than the men, I stripped off my pants and shirt in front of God and everyone, and stepped into my shift. After a minute of watching me struggle into my dress and surcoat, one of the other women smiled and came over. "Let me help."

"Thank you." I didn't tell her that I never dressed myself anymore and these dresses weren't designed for me to do so. Oddly, I found myself happy to be back in my medieval clothing. When I first put on the pants I'd bought at the boutique at the spa,

194

they had felt comfortable, and certainly familiar. But I liked how the clothing swished around my ankles and enjoyed the warmth of wearing so many layers. As I belted my knife around my nonexistent waist, I wasn't sure how the other enactors might feel about us wearing actual weapons, but if we didn't unsheathe them, they wouldn't know if they were rubber or real.

"What should we do with the bag?" Goronwy said when he and Llywelyn came around from behind the screen. Goronwy looked much more fit and comfortable in his old clothes.

"Leave it here," I said. "Is there anything in it we're going to need?"

"Not if we make it home," Llywelyn said. "What about the present you bought for Bronwen?"

I smiled and patted the purse at my waist. "I have her lip balm here, along with your pills."

"So, can we eat?" Goronwy said.

We pushed through the crowd and found a table vacating as we approached it. We sat in the booth, Llywelyn beside me, and Goronwy alone on the opposite bench. Goronwy fingered the condiment tray with its display of ketchup, salad cream, and vinegar. This was a more upscale tea shop than some. If we wanted condiments, we wouldn't have to pay 25 pence for them.

"There are too many *things* I don't understand and don't know about to even begin to ask questions about them." Goronwy fingered the vinegar jar. "I do have to ask, however ... this is glass? Like the windows and the cups?"

"Yes," I said. "And that's a change from a few years ago when everything was made of ... well ... plastic." I said the word in English. It didn't matter what I called it, since they wouldn't know what it meant anyway. "At home, we could make more from glass, too. I'm sure that David has instructions in that pile of documents he brought back three years ago."

Llywelyn leaned back in his seat. "He does. It takes time to train men and for them to master the skills, and other items were more pressing."

"Like weapons," I said. "Glass is precious and we needed to focus on spectacles."

Goronwy gazed out the window. It had started to rain again. Then he looked to Llywelyn. "I'm sure he is doing fine. Better than we are."

"I know," Llywelyn said. "I feel it. At times over the last few days, I've felt both him and the presence of our Wales, a finger's-breadth away, as if I could stretch out my hand and pierce the veil between our worlds. And then it disappears again."

It sounded to me like Llywelyn could have been hallucinating. Then again, like the Native Americans in the United States, the medieval Welsh were far more in tune with their spiritual side than most modern Americans. Maybe he *could* feel home.

The waitress stopped by our table and took our order: a full Welsh breakfast for everyone, including fried tomatoes, a food item that neither man had ever tasted before the hospital visit. Tomatoes, along with potatoes, chocolate, and corn on the cob,

196

came from the New World. While we'd talked about the Land of Madoc as a way to explain our strangeness to the medieval Welsh, other than this notion that Madoc had been there and back, it hadn't truly been 'discovered' by medieval Europeans.

The last time I'd eaten a full breakfast was Monday morning, back at our Chepstow Castle. My biorhythms were so off, I didn't know what day it was, much less the hour. But the men would finish my food if I couldn't. I took a sip of coffee, savoring the taste for possibly the last time, and found both men staring at me. I set down the cup. "What?"

"I've been keeping something from you," Llywelyn said.

I moaned. "Oh no! Are you sick? What hurts?"

"It's not that. I'm fine." He covered my hand with his. "It's nothing to do with me."

I heaved a sigh. "Then ... David?"

The men exchanged a glance and Llywelyn nodded at Goronwy. My heart sank a little, because if Llywelyn was getting Goronwy to tell the story, it had to be something I wouldn't like.

"Bevyn came to me six years ago. He asked if he might—" Goronwy seemed to struggle to find the right words "—might organize a separate—even somewhat independent—group of men to protect Dafydd."

"I'm not understanding you," I said. "You mean, besides his *teulu*?"

"Well, yes." Goronwy shot Llywelyn another look. "More secret."

"Like a spy ring?" I said.

197

"Somewhat," Llywelyn said.

"Hmmm," I said. "There has to be more to it than that or you wouldn't have kept it from me."

"Something you said about Ted and his friend, whose wife works for the government, reminded me of it. She's a spy, correct?" Goronwy said.

"So I understand," I said. "MI5 is the internal spy organization of the British government. MI-6 takes care of foreign activities."

"But there are other organizations, secret organizations, that exist in your world as well," Llywelyn said.

"As in yours," I said. "It isn't as if Math or Tudur speak of their network of informants."

Again with the glance. "What are you not saying?" I said. "Did you encourage Bevyn to create a secret order to protect David?"

Both men nodded.

"Ha!" My laugh came out like a bark. "And you didn't tell him?"

"No," Llywelyn said.

"That's because he wouldn't have liked it," I said. "What's it called?"

"The Order of the Pendragon," Goronwy said.

I laughed again. I couldn't help it. David really wouldn't have liked it, but he would have appreciated the symmetry: He gets a secret society and the Land of Madoc becomes Avalon. "Why are you telling me now?"

"Because we may have to rely on them when we return, depending upon where we return, and I didn't want to have to explain where the help came from when we were in a hurry or in danger," Llywelyn said.

"Okay," I said, and it really was okay. We'd been through so much in the last four days that learning about a secret society whose purpose was to protect David seemed like a small matter. "You're telling me that this Order functions in England as well as in Wales?"

"The men are mostly in England," Goronwy said. "That's where connections and information are most needed."

At that point, our food came. I forced myself to eat it, even though I had lost my appetite. My problem wasn't the Order of the Pendragon. I actually thought the idea kind of amusing, even if David might not, particularly if he were in one of his more serious moods.

Thinking about returning had focused my attention on the *where* as well as the *when*. In previous trips, whoever was doing the time traveling had left the modern United States and gone to medieval Great Britain or vice versa. This trip had broken the pattern. We'd gone from medieval Wales to modern Wales. What would happen when we tried to go from modern Wales to medieval Wales? At worst (well, other than finding ourselves on Mars), we'd find ourselves in medieval North America. Medieval Wales would then be completely inaccessible to us—forever. At that point, we really *would* be in the Land of Madoc.

16

19 November 2016

Meg

As we were finishing our breakfast, the restaurant began to clear out. I took one last sip of coffee, paid the bill, and we attached ourselves to a group of a dozen re-enactors, all in period costume.

"Would anyone know what we look like, other than Ted?" Llywelyn said.

"Um ... yes." This was the part where Llywelyn and Goronwy just couldn't grasp the reality of the twenty-first century. While I had been trying to think as a covert operative might (and certainly failing), he was the medieval King of Wales. Modern Wales wasn't as wired as many places in England or in the United States, but the spa had cameras, stop lights had cameras, and for all I knew, the restaurant we'd just been in had cameras. Our faces could be plastered across every television and web page on the planet by now.

Yet here we were, in Chepstow, and we could do nothing about how desperate our situation had become except get through it. I'd relaxed for a while in the restaurant, comfortable among the crowd, but Llywelyn's question renewed my anxiety that our pursuers would descend upon us at any moment. We crossed the street amongst ten or so of our new friends and entered the parking lot in front of the castle.

Here, too, cameras glared down at us. They perched on every light post. One sat above the entryway into Chepstow Castle. My only consolation was that the rain meant that we had an excuse to keep our faces hidden in our hoods, allowing us to blend in with the other re-enactors, and the spots of rain on the camera lenses might blur what watchers could see of us. Although Llywelyn claimed to have seen them earlier, no black SUV lurked in the shadows. Had they given up and gone home? Their absence worried me almost more than the presence of the cameras.

"Are you sure you saw the vehicles, Llywelyn?" I said.

He had a tight grip on my hand. "Yes." He lifted his chin and pointed ahead. "If I had any doubt, there's Ted."

Llywelyn was right. I tugged him and Goronwy to a standstill, allowing the rest of our group to get ahead of us. Ted stood with another man, who was wearing a suit and trench coat. Both men were watching the crowd from the main gate. Each person had to file past him to enter the castle. We had no way of getting by them undetected. As I hesitated, a new herd of people, who had entered the grounds from the grassy area to the west of the castle, overtook us and temporarily blocked Ted from my view.

I pulled my hood closer around my face, unsure of how to proceed, but knowing that Ted would recognize us in a heartbeat if we got close. "I should never have brought you here. I didn't know what else to do."

"This is not your fault," Goronwy said.

"We'll have to use the other gate," Llywelyn said.

"It won't be open," I said.

"How do you know?" Llywelyn said.

"I guess, I don't," I said, "but the last time I was here, admittedly years ago, it wasn't what you might call *accessible*."

"Be that as it may, it's the only way inside," Llywelyn said. "We'll have to wait until someone opens it or find a way to open it ourselves."

More cars drove into the parking lot, the rain fell harder, and, as one, we turned away. We walked around the edge of the parking lot, heading west, so we lost sight of the entrance to the castle as we followed the wall towards the rear entrance. Chepstow Castle stretched along the Wye River, which ran from west to east at this location (in general, the river ran north/south, but it wandered as it did so). We left the main gatehouse behind, heading for the second gate at the far, western end of the complex.

"Why would they post Ted at the front entrance, knowing we'd see him?" Goronwy said. "Maybe they want us to come to this gate so they can capture us quietly."

Llywelyn stopped. We had come fifty yards along the side of the castle and it loomed above us on our right. The rain continued to fall. "What will happen if we are captured, Meg?"

"I don't really know, but I imagine that we'd find ourselves in separate rooms, being questioned by people we'd prefer didn't question us," I said.

"Questioned about what?" Llywelyn said.

"Who we are, what we're doing here, time travel," I said. "That is, if this isn't all a hallucination on my part and I haven't concocted a threat where there is none. I simply don't want to stick around to find out."

"We want to go home, regardless," Llywelyn said. "Let's find a way to do that."

"So, we must enter through the far gate, regardless of what faces us," Goronwy said.

Llywelyn nodded. "The far gate."

The version of Chepstow Castle which Llywelyn had taken from Roger Bigod in 1285 wasn't as fancy as this one. Bigod had continually expanded and upgraded his fortress throughout his tenure, such that instead of the more modest rear gate we'd inherited at home, this Chepstow sported a far more expansive protective structure. A cart path led up to it, along with a ramp that allowed access to the castle through what had become essentially a service entrance. The double doors were closed.

We studied the doors from a nearby stand of trees. Due to the rain, anyone who passed by took no notice of us. "Let's give it some time," I said.

"What time?" Llywelyn gestured to the parking lot below where we stood. A near constant stream of cars turned off the street into it, filling parking space after parking space. "What do you call these people—tourists, right? The more people who fill the castle, the more difficult it will become for us to get to the balcony and jump off it."

"But the more easily we'll be able to blend in with the crowd," I said.

The three of us drifted further into the trees and closer to the rear gate. Despite the rain, it looked to be a big day at Chepstow Castle. "If we wait a while, maybe the soldiers will give up," Goronwy said. "Perhaps they'll decide that we aren't coming and leave."

"We can hope for it," I said, "but we can't depend upon it."

"I can't see anything from here." In his frustration, Llywelyn's brow had furrowed and his mouth turned down.

"I will scout the exterior of the castle." Without waiting for assent, Goronwy strode out of the trees and onto the pathway, headed back the way we'd come.

"Goronwy, wait—" I said, but Llywelyn put a hand on my arm.

"He knows what he's doing. And besides, of the three of us, who do you think these government men noticed the least?"

"Goronwy's noticeable to me," I said, "but of course you're right." I subsided, even as my hands twisted together under my cloak.

We waited what felt like a long time—at least half an hour—for Goronwy to come back. I'd lived with medieval people long enough to know that time didn't mean to them anything close to what it meant to me. Goronwy was scouting. He was making himself knowledgeable about every angle of approach. I would have been surprised if he hadn't surveyed every street in old Chepstow before he came back to us.

When he finally did, he appeared from behind, his finger to his lips. "See them?" He pointed down the slope to two men in black, striding towards the rear parking lot. "They patrol in twos and Ted no longer watches the front entrance."

"Is this crazy?" I said. "Should we even be doing this? Maybe we should find another wall to jump off."

"No." Llywelyn was still insistent. "This is the one we want." As soon as the men had passed out of sight, Llywelyn left the trees and walked up the path to the rear gate, which had remained locked this whole time. He pounded on the door with his fist. I waited, my heart in my mouth, fearing that the soldiers would return and see him, since he was out in the open. But after a minute, someone from behind the door said, "A moment!"

Llywelyn waved at us with his whole arm, and by the time the door swung wide, we stood together on the doorstep.

"You're supposed to enter at the front," said the man who greeted us. He wore brown coveralls and had grease on his hands, which he rubbed at with a dirty cloth.

Since the man spoke in English, I stepped in. Taking a chance, I said, "Don Jones told us to enter this way."

The man didn't balk at my blatant and fraudulent name-dropping. He looked us up and down, seemed to like what he saw, and shrugged. "Come on, then."

"Thank you!" I said. *And thank you Don Jones.* He had said he'd been coming here for many years. Though I hadn't thought much about it at the time, Don had struck me as one of those people who couldn't go anywhere or do anything without getting to know everyone involved.

We passed into Chepstow Castle while the man pulled the gate closed behind us. Once inside, I tried not to gawk, though Llywelyn and Goronwy were swiveling their heads from left to right.

"It's so strange to see the castle like this," Goronwy said. "It's as if the castle is the ghost from the past instead of us."

"It would have been fun if our world wasn't a different one," I said. "Anna could have left us a message and we could have hunted for it."

"Fun—except for the part where I died at Cilmeri." Llywelyn looked down at me and smiled as we hurried through the barbican. "I'm still thinking about the Englishman washing my severed head."

"I don't think she was suggesting a preference for that outcome, Llywelyn," Goronwy said.

We'd reached the upper bailey, which was all but deserted. "Where is everyone?" Llywelyn said.

A handful of tourists had braved the rain to explore the far end of the castle. I didn't see any men in black, for which, of course, I was intensely grateful.

"Not here, anyway," I said. "Maybe it's the rain." Then we entered the middle bailey and stopped short. At least two hundred people filled the space, a number which it easily accommodated. A man near the far gateway stood on a box and lifted his hands. "Welcome!"

He then launched into a speech about the historic occasion this date commemorated.

"What is he talking about?" Llywelyn said.

"I have no idea," I said. "We might have to pretend we care, however."

"Let's lose ourselves in the crowd," Llywelyn said.

I gripped Llywelyn's hand while Goronwy kept close to his other shoulder. We slipped along the margins of the onlookers, but had to stop every few feet to pretend we were listening. The speaker went on to enumerate the day's events, which included archery, periodic firing of the trebuchet, and a medieval feast under the pavilion which had been set up in the lower bailey. The stone building which had once held the great hall was a ruin, but the kitchens hadn't entirely disappeared. That was where we needed to go if we were to get into the wine cellar and out onto the balcony.

That was a big *if*. So far, we'd managed to blend in with the crowd, now composed of equal parts re-enactors and tourists, who continued to swarm into the castle. But once the talk was over and the crowd dispersed, it might be harder to avoid being spotted. "Up there." I jerked my head towards the top of the wall above the bailey. Two men in black rain slickers spoke to each other before looking to a third man on an accompanying tower.

"They should have guarded the rear door," Goronwy said.

"It was locked," I said. "Besides, maybe they felt they couldn't commit their full resources to Chepstow and the nine men Llywelyn saw is all they have. Ted might have told them that the only way we've succeeded in returning to the Middle Ages so far is in a vehicle."

"At which point they would think of his abandoned vehicle and go back for it," Goronwy said.

"And then realize that it's gone and beat Ted until he confessed to leaving us the keys," Llywelyn said, though not without a twitch of his lips and a glance at me.

I spared a second for a grateful thought that the spa had been built in a remote location, and that the road I'd taken from Devil's Bridge had been hardly more than a paved cart track. No cameras. We'd been off the grid until we entered Buellt.

"I liked it better when we decided Chepstow would be considered a long shot and a potential waste of manpower," Goronwy said.

"I liked it better too," Llywelyn said. "But they've committed enough to this endeavor to post men and to keep them watching."

"We should have driven the car into the river," I said. "They'll be on the lookout for it, and if they find it without us in it, they'll know we've come to the castle."

"But not that we've entered it," Goronwy said. "They posted most of their men outside, in the hopes of stopping us before we got inside. From here, I see only three."

"Five," Llywelyn said.

208

"Where?" I said.

Llywelyn tipped his head to point at the two men standing on either side of the doorway into the lower bailey.

My stomach clenched. "We have to get past them if we're going to reach the cellar. We have only fifty feet to go!"

"It could be five thousand feet for all the difference it might make," Llywelyn said.

The speaker ended his speech and at once, the crowd began to break up. "We'll separate," Llywelyn said. "Find someone to talk to."

I let go of his hand and fell into step beside a girl of about twelve who was heading towards the lower door. "Hi." I kept my head bent towards her and my hood up. "Where are you from?"

"Crickhowell." The girl smiled at me. She and I were of similar height and coloring, which is why I chose her. I was hoping that anyone watching would assume she was my daughter. I stayed close enough to her so that our shoulders brushed as we approached the door. I couldn't see Goronwy or Llywelyn but had to hope they were okay.

"That's a pretty dress." I fingered the fabric and she looked down at her skirt. Thus, with two bent heads and in close conversation, we passed through the doorway, straight past the men in black, who'd had to move aside to allow the crush of people through it in a timely fashion. They still watched, but I wasn't going to check their faces and they didn't ask to see mine. I was more and more thankful for the rain with each minute we weren't caught.

209

Now that I was in the lower bailey, I said goodbye to the girl, who was headed towards the pavilion, and ducked through the doorway that led to the kitchens. The passage was crowded with people, and despite the tension whizzing up and down my spine, I noted how closely the crush resembled midday at Chepstow in the Middle Ages. By keeping close to the wall, I slipped down the steps and into the hallway that led to the cellar stairs. Relief rushed through me at the sight of Goronwy, leaning against the wall, waiting for me. He shook his head at my raised eyebrows. *No Llywelyn.*

Goronwy rubbed his chin. "He was right behind me." He peered through the doorway into the kitchen, and then fell back as two women passed him carrying trays of food.

Llywelyn popped out of the doorway that came from what had once been the great hall—in time to almost run one of them over. *"Esgusodwch fi!"* he said, *I'm sorry!* He spied me, grabbed my arm, and turned me towards the wine cellar. "Come on!"

Goronwy's feet clattered on the steps behind me. "How is your heart, Llywelyn?"

"I'm fine."

I glanced at him, hoping he was telling the truth and not hiding his distress under all this activity. He'd been in a hospital *yesterday* and it wasn't like he'd gotten discharged. We swung around the corner at the bottom of the steps that led to the balcony. It was deserted and I stopped abruptly, surprised to have actually made it this far. Goronwy almost collided with my back.

I started moving again. "Don't wait. Don't think. Let's just go!"

Before I'd even finished speaking, with a bit of creaking of the knees, Goronwy had climbed onto the low wall that overlooked the Wye River. I held out my hand to him so he could help me up—

"Stop!"

I froze and looked over my shoulder. A man in a tan trench coat stood in the doorway, his hand reaching toward us. Llywelyn already had one boot on the wall and, ignoring the man, hitched himself all the way up before turning to face him. I clutched my skirt in one hand and gripped Goronwy's hand tightly with my other. "Please. Let us go."

"Don't make another move," he said, "except to step down slowly. You must come with me."

"We can't," I said. "We have to go home." Very slowly, my heart pounding at my nerve, I dropped my skirt and reached for Llywelyn's hand. The two men lifted me onto the wall with the strength of their arms so that I now stood between them.

The man took a step closer, one hand palm out, telling us to stop. His other hand strayed to his pocket and came out with a phone. The three of us sidled closer to one another and Goronwy and Llywelyn clutched me around the waist. I slipped my arms under their cloaks and looped my fingers through their belts.

"Don't do it." The man was only five feet away.

But we did.

Without needing to talk or count to *one-two-three*, we pushed backwards off the wall. At that same moment, the man launched himself towards Llywelyn in a flying tackle. He was too late—Llywelyn's feet had already left the wall—but we'd jumped up as well as out and at the last second, the man's arms came around Llywelyn's knees and he fell with us.

We hit the river with a mighty splash and went under.

17

19 November 1288

Lili

W e wended our way through the London streets, looking this way and that, trying to see at everything at once. Most of Dafydd's entourage had stayed behind at Castle Baynard, where Clare would house them. Dafydd, a handful of retainers, and I were to stay at Westminster Palace. Dafydd had suggested that I rest for a while before facing the intensity of the attention we'd receive, but I had insisted that I was fine, and would come with him despite my stomach.

I would rather face what must be faced than wait another hour.

Baynard's Castle lay below St. Paul's Cathedral on the north bank of the Thames River. Westminster Palace was on the same side of the river, directly opposite Lambeth Palace, which was the seat of the Archbishop of Canterbury. Dafydd leaned into me as we approached the gates of Westminster and said, "This should be fun."

I glanced at him, startled by his cynicism, and almost laughed. The sound caught in my throat, however, when I spied my father standing under the gatehouse. So far he hadn't looked at me, though my skin crawled as if he had. Surely he knew that I was married to Dafydd?

Fortunately, Edmund Mortimer, Gilbert de Clare, and Nicholas de Carew were with us, acting as Dafydd's heralds. Cynan greeted them first.

"I'm sorry he's here," Dafydd said, as we waited to pass under the gatehouse. He glanced at me.

"I can't think ... I can't move," I said.

"Hang on. It'll be okay." He put his head close to mine. "You do realize that I'm meeting your father for the first time since I threw him out of Buellt?"

He smiled at me and touched my cheek, and I found that I could match the laughter in his eyes.

"What has come over you?" I said. "You've been in a good mood ever since we left Chepstow. Maybe you should drink too much mead more often."

"It wasn't the mead," Dafydd said, "but the absurdity."

Dafydd had distracted me sufficiently to allow us to reach the bailey, having ridden past my father without looking at him. Men milled around us to take our horses. Dafydd helped me from my horse and then all of sudden my father was in front of us, bowing. "If I may escort you into the castle, my lord," he said.

Dafydd nodded and I even managed a gracious tip of my head. My father didn't acknowledge that he knew me. Still, we followed him across the bailey and into one of the many large buildings that made up Westminster Palace. It had been built on a grander scale than any Welsh castle—bigger by ten fold. Wales still had far to go if it was to compete with England, or at the very least make an attempt to do so. Maybe all this luxury was a waste of money—Dafydd would argue that it was—but money was power. So far, everything I'd seen in England had indicated that the Normans still had far too much of both.

Bohun waited for us in a resplendent room and was dressed in a robe of equal splendor: deep blue velvet embroidered in gold. He'd come far from the field at Evesham where he'd lost his father and Montfort had lost his head. Bohun was a regent of England, as high a station as he could ever have hoped to reach. And his son might well do better.

"Bohun." Dafydd nodded to him.

Bohun had been standing behind a table, leaning on his hands as he studied the papers in front of him. He looked up at our approach. "Leave us," he said to Cynan who hadn't entered the room and instead had waited in the doorway. My father put his heels together, bowed, and departed. I let out a sigh of relief. That hadn't gone badly at all.

But then I looked into Bohun's face and clenched Dafydd's arm at the hostility I saw there. Dafydd patted my hand, though he had to be feeling the same sinking feeling in his stomach that I was, and that threatened to upend the lunch I'd just eaten.

"What is it?" I said, blurting out the question in a rude and untimely fashion, but we'd been through too much with William and the Bohuns to equivocate.

"You have betrayed me." That was about as blunt as one might expect from Humphrey do Bohun, but not the greeting we were hoping for.

"I most certainly have not," Dafydd said. "And that's a fine welcome for an ally."

Bohun put a fist to his mouth, coughed, and then said, "Welcome to Westminster. I wish you hadn't come."

"You were the one who invited us," I said.

Bohun's chin jutted out and his jaw was clenched tight. "You should not have accepted."

"So my advisors have told me a dozen times," Dafydd said. "We would just as soon have stayed in Wales, but both you and William asked for us specifically. What has changed since then?"

"Everything. It was a mistake."

I eyed him. His throne-like chair sat in front of the fire, but he ignored it and didn't invite Dafydd or me to sit either. Dafydd nudged my side, directing my attention to a spindle chair with a cushioned seat. He led me to it. "Bohun might be heedless of propriety, which is my usual *modus operandi*," he said, "but you don't need to be made uncomfortable. Sit here while I find out what has Bohun in such a state."

I nodded and squeezed his hand. "It will be okay."

Bohun paced in front of the mantle. "Did you really think I wouldn't find out?"

Carew, who had remained to the left of the door, stirred. I glanced at him. He raised his eyebrows and lifted his shoulder half an inch. He was as much at a loss as I.

Dafydd planted himself in front of Bohun. "I have no idea what has discontented you. William marries Joan on Friday. I support that. It's what you wanted."

"I wouldn't have invited you if I'd known that you were planning to claim the throne for yourself!" Between one second and the next, Humphrey's face had flushed so dark it was almost maroon.

I managed not to laugh. No wonder my father stayed with him. Both were irrational and temperamental.

"I have done no such thing," Dafydd said.

Humphrey continued to glare at Dafydd, but as my husband gazed calmly back, some of the fire left him. Bohun moved closer and studied Dafydd's face more carefully. "You're telling the truth."

"Of course I am," Dafydd said. "To whom have you been speaking?"

"How can you—?" And then he stopped, looking to Carew, and then to Edmund, and then Clare, all of whom gazed back without expression. I was impressed that none of these men had leapt to Dafydd's defense. Maybe they finally trusted him enough to know that he could handle himself, no matter the threat.

"You don't know. You really don't know!" Humphrey turned away, paced to the fire, and then came back to stand in front of Dafydd again. "You haven't heard the rumors?"

217

I assumed he was speaking of the way that the legend of King Arthur had dogged Dafydd's steps, but then Carew coughed once, his fist to his mouth. It was the same gesture Humphrey had used earlier, and I thought maybe that many Normans employed it when they were about to impart unwanted truths. "Prince David doesn't know, but I've heard them," Carew said.

Dafydd didn't object or criticize, but merely said, "Tell me all, Carew. I might as well hear it before this gets any worse."

"I didn't tell you because I dismissed the news at first, and then as more people spoke to me of it, I needed confirmation before I troubled you with it," Carew said. "None has been forthcoming." He tipped his head towards Bohun. "His lordship is the first person who seems to know more than rumor."

Dafydd tsked through his teeth. "Will someone *please* tell me what we're talking about?"

"Your claim to the throne, of course," Bohun said.

"Yes, I got that part," Dafydd said, "but I haven't put forth a claim because I don't have one. I have no royal blood."

Again, Bohun put his fist to his mouth and coughed. "Apparently you do, my lord," he said. "The Archbishop of Canterbury reports that you have a claim through your mother. He has proof."

Dafydd scoffed. Of all the answers Bohun could have given, that was the least expected and the most unlikely.

"Did you say that the claim is through Prince David's mother?" Clare said. "What proof could he possibly have when we have none?"

Bohun smirked, enjoying everyone's confusion. "According to the Archbishop, Prince David's mother is the secret daughter of King Edward's father, Henry. I understand that the Archbishop has been provided with documents that contain King Henry's seal and signature testifying to that fact."

Bohun was *serious*.

"I feel like laughing and chucking a chair across the room at the same time," Dafydd said. "Provided by whom?" He turned to me. "Are you hearing this, Lili?"

I rose from my chair and slipped my arm around his waist. "I hear it."

"Could it be true?" Clare had stepped closer to Dafydd, too.

"Of course not—" Dafydd stopped. I could tell that he was bursting to tell them that his mother had been born in the Land of Madoc. I held on tighter, trying to tell him not to, to speak to him without speaking. My husband was honest almost to a fault. He had a conscience and a strong sense of duty. It kept him up at night.

To my relief, Dafydd didn't continue. Instead, he let out a long breath and looked at Bohun. "Who was my grandmother supposed to be? A pig keeper's daughter?"

"Caitir, one of the many illegitimate daughters of King Alexander II of Scotland." Bohun said this with an absolutely straight face. "It is said that she was a great beauty in her time, just like your mother."

Dafydd rubbed his chin and turned to Carew. "I can see why you didn't tell me."

"I apologize, my lord," Carew said. "Please forgive me. It just seemed—"

"Preposterous," Dafydd said. "I know."

Bohun's face was grave. "The Archbishop *believes* it," he said. "You're telling me there's no chance that it's true?"

A knock came at the door to the room before Dafydd could deny the claim again. Bohun pressed his lips into a thin line, but he strode to the door to open it himself. "What is it?"

"My lord—"

My father stood on the doorstep, shifting from one foot to the other, obviously uncomfortable. Bohun softened his expression. "Tell me."

"We have received word that Lord Hywel, Prince of Wales, has died."

Bohun stared at Cynan, speechless. Dafydd stepped forward, bringing me with him and I was able to look into my father's face for the first time without balking.

"Lord Hywel is really dead?" Dafydd said.

Cynan bowed. "Yes, my lord."

Bohun turned to us. "You knew Hywel was here for the wedding, yes?"

"We knew," I said, and then spoke to my father. "How did he die?"

"I was told it was a sudden sickness," Cynan said. "Prince Hywel did not wake this morning."

"Where was he staying?" Dafydd said, without debating the man's use of the title *Prince*. Hywel's paternity had never been proved to King Llywelyn's satisfaction.

"At Lambeth, as a guest of the Archbishop of Canterbury," Bohun said. "He was to attend the dinner here tonight."

I knew there would have to be a dinner and that I would be required to attend. All those smells—meat, vegetables, spices—caused my stomach to roil just thinking about them. But some things couldn't be helped when one was a princess. Although a joust or a tournament was a common way to celebrate too, because this was November and the clouds to the west told me that rain was imminent, I was glad Bohun had forgone that level of display.

I still held my husband's arm. "Do you think you ought to pay your respects? It's not far, right? Just across the river."

Bohun bowed slightly to me. "I'm sure the gesture would be well received." He looked at Dafydd. "Have you ever met Valence? He is also staying at Lambeth as a guest of the Archbishop."

"No," Dafydd said.

"Or spoken to the Archbishop since your father signed the Treaty of 1285?" Bohun said.

Dafydd shook his head.

"Then I should come with you," Bohun said.

"To protect me?" Dafydd said.

Bohun snorted laughter. "Not you. The realm."

I squeezed Dafydd's arm. "I could rest while you go."

"Of course, my dear." Bohun's expression gentled. "Please allow my man to show you to your quarters." He gestured towards my father, who still stood on the threshold. Bohun really didn't know who he was—or who I was, for that matter.

"Lili, are you sure?" Dafydd said.

I didn't hesitate, just stood on tiptoe as Dafydd bent so I could whisper in his ear. "I'll have information for you by the time you return." I even managed a smile.

My father held his arm out to me. I took it, without even an overt shiver or a last glance back at Dafydd, and walked with him towards our rooms.

Cynan cleared his throat. "His lordship does not know that we are kin."

"You mean that I am your daughter?" I said, and then took in a breath to gain control of the sudden rush of temper. Ieaun had described the anger that had boiled through him at the sight of Cynan three years ago. I had felt it just then—years of suppressed rage at what he had done to us and not done for us. "You would prefer he doesn't know?"

"At this late date, if I told him, he would wonder that I had not mentioned it before. I have a new wife, now, and two sons. A new life." He stopped at the door to my room and gestured that I should pass through it. "She does not know either."

I felt cold to the core of my being. I had so dreaded this meeting, fearing his spitefulness and wrath. At the same time, I had almost been looking forward to it—to his disappointment and anger—so I could reveal my anger too, and throw it back at him. Instead, he had spoken cordially.

And denied all connection.

Branwen appeared in the doorway to the room and, because she could sense my distress, moved close and took my hand.

I clutched it. "Goodbye, Cynan," I said.

"Madam." My father bowed and turned away.

I went with Branwen into the room, closed the door, and leaned back against it.

"Are you all right, my lady?" Branwen said.

"Yes," I said. "I think I truly am."

18

19 November 1288

David

"Valence hates you with a passion I've rarely seen, though he hides it behind a cold veneer that has deceived the Archbishop," Bohun said.

"Bohun is right, my lord," Clare said as we headed back through the labyrinth that was Westminster Palace towards the main bailey. "I would also add that you've been in rare humor this week and your wit has become more ..." Clare paused as he thought "... acid of late. We want a wedding tomorrow, not a blood bath."

Now it was Bohun's turn to laugh. "Our boy is growing up."

Given that I censored ninety percent of what actually went on in my head, I thought I was doing pretty well. But I didn't say that either, and was, in fact, somewhat offended since I endeavored not to give offense pretty much all the time. I'd diffused Bohun's anger, hadn't I? And found amusement in this turn of events, not anger.

I said none of this, of course, and in truth, my thoughts were back in the hallway with Lili. That she would willingly walk away with her father stunned me, but at the same time, it was just like her. She was braver than most anyone I knew, and it had nothing to do with her ability to shoot straight.

So it was that despite Bohun's and my own myriad obligations, not the least of which was that Bohun's son was marrying a princess of England tomorrow, he and I rode from his castle after a brief meal in his solar, with a host of retainers and hangers-on.

Lackey. In the modern world, it meant servile hanger-on. Here, it simply meant servant, and they were everywhere. I'd learned over the years to accept assistance, because to do otherwise would be to put whoever was serving me out of a job. Jeeves had been born the fourth son of a fisherman forty years ago. Fishing was an honest day's work, and even though I'd accepted the help of servants since I was fourteen (when my father had claimed me as his son), it was Jeeves who'd taught me that laying out my cloak was no less honest work, even if it sometimes made me feel foolish and I could have done it myself.

But this ... this was servantry on a scale I never could have imagined.

Carew rode with me as before, now joined by Bevyn, Evan and a handful of my men. Both Gilbert de Clare and Edmund Mortimer had left me at the gatehouse, declining to join us, saying that their presence could provide more of a spark than a dampener to Valence's ire. I knew the real reason for their absence: both men despised Valence and didn't want to have to feign respect. The feast that evening would be enough of a trial.

As it turned out, it was just as well that Edmund hadn't joined us, as it was his brother, Roger Mortimer, who greeted us in the foyer to the Archbishop's reception room. I'd often wondered why it was so common for noble brothers to be at each other's throats. I would have assumed it had to do with primogeniture—the practice of leaving the entirety of an inheritance to the older son—*if* Wales had practiced it too, which it didn't. And still Uncle Dafydd, my father's brother, had *hated* him, to the point of betraying him with the Normans multiple times and even attempting to murder him. How could any man hate his brother that much?

Mom had pointed out that while the quest for money and power was ongoing among the Marcher lords, it was made worse in noble families by the practice of fostering out sons to different households. If a child lived away from his family from the age of seven, could anyone be surprised that he had little fraternal loyalty or feeling? Not to mention the fact that growing up male in the Middle Ages was all about competition and one-upmanship. Edmund Mortimer had suffered because his peers—his siblings— viewed him as an inferior man because he was an intellectual. It was his bad luck that his elder brother had died, making him the heir. Roger, the younger brother, had never forgiven him for being born first.

226

Today Roger wore a deep red cloak over highly polished mail. The rings on his fingers reflected the lights of the torches on the wall and it made me glad that once again, Jeeves had cleaned me up before we left Baynard Castle for Westminster. I wore my breeches over my boots, instead of tucked into them like Roger, but my tunic was spotless. And my cloak was lined with fur.

I hadn't seen Roger since we were both in King Edward's pavilion back when I was sixteen. I had never brought up the events of that night with my newfound allies, except perhaps in vague reference to the dangers of overeating. Edmund Mortimer and Gilbert de Clare had been there, too. The only Norman who had stood up for me had been King Edward's brother, who was dead now. None of my current allies, except for Carew, who already had been riding at my side by that point, had tried to stop the king from murdering me in cold blood.

And Bohun wondered that my wit was acid sometimes?

Still, with my newfound resolve to live more lightly, I strode up to Roger who'd been conversing with someone else dressed in equal finery but with a large paunch. Bohun hurried to keep abreast and made the introductions. "Lord Mortimer, Lord Valence," he said, "may I introduce to you Prince David of Wales."

"My lord." Valence accompanied his words with a bow. Roger followed suit.

Their brief reverence left me speechless, actually. It wasn't that I expected them to snub me, but it was certainly within the realm of possibility, given the war Valence had started and into which both men had invested so much energy and money. Bohun filled the gap in the conversation which I was inadvertently leaving. "We heard about Lord Hywel and have come to pay our respects."

"Of course," Valence said and indicated an adjacent corridor. "He lies this way."

I was beginning to see the pattern in how these Norman lords spoke and gestured. I hadn't ever seen so many of them in one place so I hadn't noticed before.

"How did he die?" I said.

"A sudden illness," Valence said, parroting the messenger who'd brought us the news. "The maid found him dead this morning." Valence led us from the foyer, down a corridor to a side wing of the palace. He knocked once and then entered.

My cousin lay in state thirty feet from me, on a table before the altar of a small chapel. A thin white blanket, embroidered around the edges and folded back on itself, covered him to the waist. The other men held their position by the door, and a nudge from Carew at the small of my back had me realizing that everyone was deferring to me. They expected me to go forward to look at him.

I'd seen dead people before, of course, and I felt nothing for this long-lost cousin of mine other than regret that he'd fallen into Valence's clutches. Still, it was disturbing to meet him for the first time as a dead man. When I reached him, I made the sign of the cross, again as everyone expected, and gazed into his face. He wore a neatly trimmed beard, like most of these Normans. His hair and skin were fair, a trait he'd inherited from his father, or so I understood. I had never met Prince Owain, who had died a few months before I came to Wales. At the same time, Hywel hadn't achieved the height of most of the men in our family, and certainly not the six feet of me or my father.

Someone had folded his arms across his chest. His fingers were discolored on the ends, bluish, as was the tip of his nose. If Anna were here, she might have told me what disease could have caused it. As it was, after another minute, I turned away. "Thank you," I said. "I'm sorry that he died so young."

"So sad." Valence said the words through a tightened jaw.

"I would meet with the Archbishop now, if he is willing to speak with me?" I said.

Valence blinked. He should have been expecting that, but he looked as if the very idea was upsetting his stomach.

"He knows you are here and has already asked to see you," Roger said, more smooth than his co-conspirator.

Sometimes I felt as if all I'd done since I'd come to England was follow other men around strange castles, but the Archbishop's solar was next door to the chapel. As Roger had indicated, he was waiting for me, with a carafe of heated wine and two goblets on the table beside him. Like Roger, he wore a red cloak, but underneath, instead of mail, he wore a gray robe, a reminder that he was of the Franciscan order. I wondered what robes, if any, the Order of the Pendragon might wear when they met, and decided that I didn't want to know.

"Archbishop." I took Peckham's hand and bent my head over it, though it irked me to do so. Mom had commented once that it was a good thing everyone usually bowed to me, since I had such trouble bending a knee to anyone, good American that I was. I didn't kiss his ring.

"Son," Peckham said. "Please join me for some wine."

I moved towards a chair next to the fire, but when Peckham didn't follow, I turned. He was looking at the cluster of men in the entrance to his solar.

"I would like some time alone with our young prince, my friends. Please excuse us," he said.

The Archbishop used the word *please*, but it was more than a request. The others filed out, but Carew didn't move until I nodded at him. He tipped his head to me and followed the other men out the door. He would remain on the other side of the door until I finished my meeting, filling in for Bevyn and Evan, who hadn't been invited past the bailey.

"Now." Peckham turned to me—and then to my surprise, grasped both my forearms and held me. He couldn't have been more than five and a half feet tall, about Mom's height, so he had to look up at me as he spoke. "You have grown much in these three years, in both stature and wisdom."

Wow. Really?

I didn't say it, though. Instead, I smiled, and accepted the glass of wine the Archbishop poured me. I waited to take a sip until he drank from his own goblet, however, not trusting this man, for all that he had greeted me as a friend. As I sat in an armchair beside the fire and listened to the Archbishop make small talk, a deep suspicion grew in my belly. I had met

Archbishop Peckham only once, but it was memorable—in 1285 at the signing of the Treaty between Wales and England—and that man would never have welcomed me into his chamber this way. He was bowing and scraping, as if he really believed all that claptrap about my mother.

He *couldn't* believe it. At the time I'd found it staggering that Bohun had given the idea any credence at all. Why was Peckham behaving as if it were God's own truth?

Finally, I broke in. "What's really going on here?"

Peckham wasn't used to being interrupted. "Excuse me?"

"I appreciate your hospitality. Believe me, it's a delightful change of heart compared to the last time we met, but I'm wondering why you are being so solicitous to me?"

Peckham tapped a finger on his lips. "I see before me the future King of England."

So that *was* it. "You see me on the throne of England? On what grounds? I neither want the crown nor have a right to it."

"I beg to differ, my lord. These papers say you do have a claim." Peckham rested his hand on the parchment on his desk. "In fact, yours is more credible than that of any other man in England."

"May I see the papers?" I held out my hand.

Peckham flattened one of the rolls and handed it to me as if it were the crown jewels. I gazed at what was written there. The words were in Latin, which I could read, and said exactly what Bohun had insisted they said. The document read as a testimonial, as if my mother might some day need proof that she was the king's daughter.

I shrugged, unable to explain why the document appeared authentic. It wasn't like a man could digitally alter documents in the Middle Ages. I would have seen the hand of Bevyn's Order of the Pendragon behind it, but given the fewness of them and their limited reach, it would have been stretching credulity that they could have accomplished something so monumental as fooling the Archbishop of Canterbury. What the existence of these documents said to me was that whoever wanted me on the throne had friends in very high places.

"Even if this were the king's signature and seal—"

"I assure you, they are genuine."

"—my mother remains illegitimate. That means nothing to the Welsh, but to you? Haven't you campaigned for years against the Welsh practice of acknowledging illegitimate children? Under the circumstances, why isn't the Church opposed to my succession?"

Peckham put his fist to his mouth and coughed. "It is something we are willing to overlook in this instance. And of course, you yourself are not illegitimate. Before your birth, your parents married in secret, did they not?"

I stared at him. *Very high places.*

"Surely dozens of other men might have an equal claim to the throne, or at least a comparable one," I said. "We could trace the right of kingship back to King Harold and find an English counterpart to my cousin Hywel, if it was necessary to find a worthy successor to Edward. Why am I the horse you're betting on?"

For the first time, Peckham gave me a ghost of a smile. "Who says you're my only bet?"

I let out a breath that was almost a laugh. *Who indeed.* "Touché," I said. "I'm Welsh, the son of the King of Wales. You acknowledged my father only three years ago and reluctantly at that. Again, I ask you, *why me?*"

The Archbishop leaned forward to peer into my face. He gave me a long look, and then sat back in his chair. "For a moment, I was tempted to hurl those words back at you, because I find it difficult to believe that you don't know the reason why— don't know what you've done. Then again—" he gazed at me from under bushy eyebrows, "—Clare warned me about you."

"Clare—"

"So I'll tell you why you have my support," Peckham said, "and my heart."

I swallowed hard. Like Bohun—and Clare, and Carew, and Edmund Mortimer—he was serious.

"When your father claimed you as his heir six years ago, soon after you turned fourteen and by Welsh law became a man, I thought nothing of it," Peckham said. "Well, not *nothing*, but it seemed of little concern. King Edward was in the ascendancy, your father barely escaped Cilmeri with his life, and it appeared to be only a matter of time before all Wales fell to us."

"But we didn't," I said.

Peckham stabbed a finger in my direction. "*You* didn't. Since then, everywhere you have gone, upon whatever you have turned your gaze, you have triumphed. When the name *Arthur* began to be ascribed to you, whether spoken in the countryside or in taverns and street corners from Bristol to York, do you know what my first instinct was?"

"To deny it, of course," I said.

"You think that, do you?" Peckham said. "Six years ago, England was the strongest, most united, and most powerful kingdom in Europe. Then you save your father, and two months later defeat Edward's forces in an epic battle, to the point that his creditors start clamoring for their money out of fear that he has nothing left with which to pay them. Then Edward dies, along with many powerful men, including his brother.

"In three short years, we have fallen into disunity and despair, so far from what we were that most of us can still barely comprehend what we are seeing, even though it is happening before our eyes. At the same time, Wales—a tiny, insignificant country full of sheep herders and pig keepers—has conquered all, simply because you raised your sword and said *God wills it?* The truth is laid bare before us. Rarely in my life have I seen such obvious signs of the hand of God in man's pursuits. How can you ask *me* why I support your claim? Are you that blind to your own power?"

"I am that clear-eyed," I said. "Every Norman in London seeks either to use me for his own purposes, or to murder me. I wanted to know what was in your heart."

So adamant was Peckham as he'd been speaking, that he'd risen to his feet, but now he lowered himself back into his chair. "You can trust no one. I understand that. But it would be a mistake to think that you are alone and without friends."

"It may be that you are telling the truth. You may think that England would be best served by my rule," I said, "but when has what is best for England meant more to those who seek the throne than their own power?"

"It means more to you."

"What's best for Wales means more to me," I said.

"You care nothing for the people of England?" he said. "You care nothing for the Will of God?"

I tapped my lips with one finger, studying Peckham. He sort of had me there, since the English were a conquered people too. I wouldn't wish poor rule or a bad king on them either, in theory anyway. Weak English kings tended to be a good thing for Wales and King Edward certainly hadn't been that.

"Edward tried to thwart God's purpose." Peckham's face was lit from within. "And He smote him down."

"Edward did keep the barons in line."

Peckham allowed himself a laugh. "That he did. And me too." He rubbed his chin as he eyed me. "I would be doing you a disservice if I didn't tell you before you assumed the throne that all has not been well in England since King Edward died."

How had we gotten from my outright denial of interest in the throne to Peckham assuming that I would take it? I thought back over our conversation. Nowhere had I said—or even implied—such a thing. This was so much worse than any conversation I'd had on the subject with my father. Still, I had to answer. "So I have heard. You're talking about money, aren't you? You're in debt. How bad is it?"

"Not in debt, per se, but when Edward died, the regents defaulted on his personal loans," Peckham said.

"I know already that these loans came from the same Italian creditors to whom you owe money," I said.

The Archbishop didn't respond to my barb. "It means that the crown can institute no more wars or building programs until we either find a new source of revenue or increase taxes."

"That would be because your pogroms against the Jews have effectively cut them off as a source of ready cash," I said.

"They are not *my* pogroms," Peckham said. "The Church does not support these laws." The smile that curled on his lips had my heart clenching. "If you were king, you could do something about these heinous crimes against the Jews."

"Archbishop—"

"Think about it."

19

19 November ...

Meg

As I fell, I blacked out for a second, but then I hit the water, went under, and came up, sputtering and gasping for air—and more glad than I could possibly say when three other heads popped up with me. I was sorry that it hadn't worked and we were still stuck in the twenty-first century, but I was happy to be alive. As the current swept me downstream, one of the babies kicked me hard as if to say—*Mom, what on earth are you doing?*

And then it hit me: *three heads?*

I didn't have time to think about our stowaway for more than a second, because I spun around and nearly banged into a floating log. Then a hand grabbed my arm. I blinked away water to see Llywelyn's face in front of me. "I've got you."

"I know," I said. "We never bought those life preservers."

He swung a piece of debris in my direction, a thick branch from a tree, and then grinned at me. "This is what we call a *life preserver* in my time."

I clutched at it, grinning back at him, though it was ridiculous to be happy when we were about to get arrested for attempted time travel and jumping into the Wye River. I'd loved Llywelyn for twenty years. Even cold, wet, and on the run, every day with him was a good day.

"We need to get out of the water before we drown." Goronwy shouted at us from ten yards away.

Llywelyn scoffed. "How is it that we always end up in the water, Meg?"

"I have no idea," I said, and then added. "I'm sorry it didn't work."

Llywelyn didn't answer, just urged me towards a sandbar jutting from the eastern shore of the river. Gasping, I was reminded of our fall from the window at Brecon Castle twenty years ago when we escaped one of Roger Mortimer's assassins (the Roger who was father to the current Roger Mortimer and his brother, Edmund). I'd told Llywelyn I was pregnant with David that morning.

Now, I crawled on my hands and knees out of the water and turned onto my back with one arm thrown across my eyes. The three men followed suit and we lay in a row on the beach. The rain had abated, which was a blessing, and it was warmer on land than in the river. I was happy to be alive.

"We should go," I said, "before anyone comes."

"Who's going to come?" Llywelyn said. "We've left everyone behind."

"What?" I opened my eyes and sat up to look down at Llywelyn. "What did you say?"

At my exclamation, the man who'd tried to stop us, jerked upright too. "Oh, my God."

He pointed at the towers that poked above the trees on the other side of the river. I didn't know to what estate they belonged, but they weren't part of Chepstow Castle. The river in front of me wasn't the Wye, either, and the mountains in the distance weren't in Wales.

I reached out to Llywelyn, who lay on my left, still with his eyes closed, but with a smile hovering around his lips. "Why didn't you say something earlier?" I said.

He sat up and his smile broadened. *Someone* was happy to be home. "I was a little busy getting you out of the water."

"My God, you did it." The man said. His legs sprawled in front of him and somewhere along the way he'd lost his trench coat. His suit and tie, modern and incongruous, contrasted sharply with our medieval clothing.

"What did he say?" Llywelyn said. The stranger had been speaking English.

The man turned his head to stare at Llywelyn and me as if he had to force himself to do it. Upon closer inspection, I placed him in his middle thirties, with just a few lines around his eyes. "We're really—we're really in the Middle Ages?" he said.

"It's what was supposed to happen when we jumped off the balcony," I said, "though honestly, I almost can't believe it myself and it's the third time I've done this."

"My God."

It didn't look like I was getting much more out of him for a while, so I turned back to Llywelyn and Goronwy. "Where are we? Do you recognize those towers, or the river?"

Both men shook their heads. Goronwy pulled off a boot, poured water from it, and then put it on again, to repeat the process with his other boot.

"Isn't that Windsor Castle on the Thames?" the man said. "It's not as elaborate as it is in our time, and the river is flowing closer to it than it should, but the tower is almost right ..."

I was having trouble processing his words and that he, of all people, might know where we were. "You think we're in *Windsor*?"

"Whoooee!" The man laughed, though he sounded closer to hysteria than amusement. "My God. Welcome to the Middle Ages." Then he stuck out his hand to me. "I'm Callum."

"Meg." I shook his hand. "You're not Welsh?"

"My dad's American, mom's Scottish."

Great. "You do realize that the man you were trying to stop is the King of Wales, right?" I said.

Some of Callum's ebullience faded from his face. He looked past me to Llywelyn who was eyeing both of us with what had to be amusement, given the twitch in the corner of his mouth. Callum scrambled to his feet. "Uh, Sire," he said, in English, "It's ... uh ... nice to meet you."

"He said—" I began.

"I know what he said." Llywelyn reached up to Callum, who grasped his forearm and helped him to his feet. Callum was taller than Llywelyn and more broad-shouldered. Even were he to put on medieval clothes, he would stand out in a crowd.

Now that we all were upright, I didn't see how I could have mistaken the little beach or the river for any place near Chepstow. "We should find shelter," Goronwy said. "Meg has started to shiver and we're all getting colder by the second."

Goronwy was right and I clutched my arms around myself, trying to find some warmth. Both babies kicked at the same time, a miraculous rat-a-tat. I put a hand to my belly. "At least we're here and unharmed."

Llywelyn put his head close to mine. "You're sure that you are well?"

I put his hand to my belly, where the drumming duet was ongoing. He smiled. "What were the chances we'd arrive in Windsor, the exact place we need to be to help Dafydd?"

"Honestly, I think the odds were excellent," I said, "if it was going to work at all."

"How so?" Llywelyn said. "When you returned to me four years ago, you arrived at the Wall."

"I did, but this confirms a theory I've been developing," I said.

241

Llywelyn raised his eyebrows. If he were David, he would have said, "Care to share?" but since I could read him, he didn't have to be so flippant.

"I've decided that we don't return to the place we want to be, but to the place we *need* to be."

"But—?" Llywelyn stopped as he thought about what I'd said. "I don't know that I like the idea of you ending up so far from me, but I can see why you might think it was necessary, given what came after."

"David went from Lancaster to the Wall, and then to the modern world where he found Bronwen, who saved your life," I said.

Llywelyn pursed his lips. "Perhaps you're right at that."

Goronwy had already started walking. "It wouldn't be good for you to catch a chill so soon after you've started feeling well."

"Of course," Llywelyn said. "It's time we discovered if Callum is correct in his assessment of our location." Llywelyn led us to a path that followed the river downstream, walking confidently in a way I hadn't seen in months. We came around some bushes to see the wooden bridge that would take us across the Thames River to Windsor Castle.

Before the first William conquered England in 1066, the old Saxon palace for the English kings had been built a mile and a half downstream from the current castle. It no longer existed and I didn't remember why the Normans moved it. You would have thought they would have built right over the old one, as a sign of their power, but they hadn't.

I was a little concerned that Llywelyn was going to march us right into an ambush, but he strode along, head high, unconcerned about his lack of protection or that we were in England. He climbed the bank up to the road with little effort while the rest of us straggled along behind him. He reached for my hand to haul me to level ground. My skirt caught around my ankles and I stumbled. I was really shivering now. My cloak did me no good when it, like everything else I had on, was soaking wet.

"I gather you have a plan, my lord," Goronwy said.

I glanced back at him. That was the first time he'd called Llywelyn *my lord* since I told him not to. We really were back in the Middle Ages.

"I thought I'd knock at the gates of Windsor Castle and introduce myself," Llywelyn said.

Nobody had a response to that, other than open-mouthed surprise. Callum stared at the ground as we walked, and as we approached the bridge, pulled up. "I can't go any further."

"Callum—" I stopped and tugged Llywelyn to a halt as well.

Two soldiers guarded our end of the bridge, while two more watched from the other side. They held pikes which barred the passage across. As I watched, a horse pulling a farmer's cart clip-clopped across the bridge, which was wider than most of the roads I'd spent the last day driving in Wales. Four sheep baaaa-ed at us from the back as it passed by. Once it had gone, the four soldiers went back to watching us.

"Look at me!" Callum gestured with both hands to indicate his clothing and then pointed to the guards on the bridge. "Look at them!"

I turned to Goronwy. "He's fearful for his appearance."

Goronwy unhooked the brooch that kept his cloak closed at the throat and swung it around Callum's shoulders. "I am of the opinion that they will think us odd no matter how we look, but this should help."

Llywelyn surveyed Callum, who clutched the cloak closer around himself, even as it continued to stream river water into the mud at his feet. "Can we continue?" Llywelyn said.

"No time like the present." I walked forward alone and planted myself in front of one of the bridge's guards. "Is the Prince of Wales still in residence?" I said, in their version of English, which Callum probably wouldn't understand any more than he understood our Welsh.

The guard lifted his eyebrows. "They left for London early this morning. What business is it of yours?"

"Prince David is my son."

The man snorted laughter while the other guard glowered at me. "Madam—"

"I am Marged, the Queen of Wales." I gestured to the men behind me. "As you can see, the King and I have run into difficulties in joining our son and require assistance."

Both soldiers had their pikes at the ready, but before they threatened me with them, they looked over my shoulder at Llywelyn, who was by now only a pace behind. For all that he was sopping wet, the fabric of his cloth was still recognizably fine, he wore the crest of Gwynedd on his tunic, and water glistened off the ornate decoration on the hilt of his sword and on his scabbard. An expression of consternation passed across the first soldier's face as he decided that I could be telling the truth.

He stiffened. "My lord." He bowed at the waist. "My lady. Please come with me."

"Geoffrey, wait—!"

The second soldier wasn't yet convinced, but Geoffrey pressed a hand to his chest and hissed, "What if she's telling the truth? We'll let the captain deal with it."

Geoffrey turned and marched across the bridge in double time. "Make way! Make way!"

We followed.

By the time we arrived on the other side of the river, we had an escort of eight, plus a handful of curious onlookers who'd come out of their homes and workshops to see what all the fuss was about. One of the townspeople bowed as we passed, and several more followed suit. The soldiers led us to the entrance to the castle.

I tucked my hand in Llywelyn's elbow. "They seem friendly," I said. "Why are they friendly?"

"I don't know," Llywelyn said. "Given that this is their response to us, it warms my heart to think that Dafydd was greeted properly, too." We had hoped that Bohun would see to that, but David was a Welsh prince—not always the most favorite category of nobleman among the populace of England. One might even venture to say that at times it had been the *least*.

"Even if I would have liked to see him, I'm glad to learn that David left this morning as planned," I said.

"My lord!" A man hustled down the steps of the keep. "You are most welcome here! I am Sir George. If we'd known you were coming ..."

He spoke in French, which was helpful, and Llywelyn was able to answer. "Thank you, Sir George. We didn't know ourselves until recently. There was no time to send word."

"Of course, my lord." Sir George eyed us, with a look just short of askance. We were soaked to the skin, unhorsed, and clearly in great need. "Where are your men?"

"We were ambushed not far from here. We are the only survivors," Llywelyn said, lying through his teeth with an aplomb that had me hiding a grin.

"Lady Mary in heaven!" Sir George had been concerned before, but his solicitousness doubled. "Please come inside!"

"If there was a good place to end up in England, Windsor Castle is clearly it," Goronwy said, speaking low and in Welsh, so only Llywelyn and I would understand. I didn't translate for Callum, who appeared almost comatose. I appreciated his shock at finding himself in the Middle Ages. I'd had some hope for him earlier, given his initial joy at the news, but reality appeared to have set in. He had to be thinking that he was stuck here for the rest of his life, and he might be right. *I* certainly wasn't planning to take him back to his world any time soon.

It seemed that Goronwy was correct about our reception at Windsor Castle. Sir George saw to baths and warm clothes for everyone, including Callum. He also found a maid to help me dress and arrange my hair. Llywelyn returned, looking far too bright-eyed for a man just out of the hospital whose only sleep had been for a few hours in the front seat of a car.

"We should go to David now," I said. "We still have a few hours of daylight left."

Llywelyn tipped his head. "Not yet, I think. The wedding is tomorrow. I see no need to throw Bohun and his plans into disarray. And our sudden arrival would, between the political implications and the security involved. As it is, with only one man—well, two, if we count Callum—to attend us, Sir George will have to provide a hurried escort. Tomorrow should be soon enough."

"You want to appear after the wedding, you mean?" I said.

"Yes. By then, Dafydd might be wishing for my support in dealing with the barons when they meet the next day," Llywelyn said.

Given the disagreement they'd had at Chepstow, Llywelyn might be right to be wary of interfering with David's activities, but I didn't think that things had gotten so bad between them that David wouldn't want his father with him. Besides, although David didn't yet know it, Llywelyn had lived a whole lifetime since they'd parted. Llywelyn had already admitted that he'd pressed David too hard, and his joy at having returned to this time was tangible.

The castellan, for his part, hadn't calmed down. He didn't seem to know what to do with us. Llywelyn was the King of Wales and thus worthy of reverence, but he was an uninvited guest. Windsor Castle had just played host to David's entourage, and the servants were still cleaning up after them. Still, he sat with the four of us at the high table and tried to make small talk.

Callum, our wayward addition, stayed close and silent throughout the meal. In fact, I hadn't heard him do anything more than grunt since we arrived at the castle. He hadn't asked what had happened to his clothing (Llywelyn had hidden it in a rucksack), and he seemed much diminished, for all that the castellan had rustled him up a complete change of clothing, including a mail tunic. He shifted in his seat beside me, sipping gingerly at the beer a servant had placed in front of him.

I scooted my chair closer and had his instant attention. He regarded me through hazel green eyes, fringed by ridiculously long lashes.

"Talk," I said. "In some ways, it doesn't matter now, but I want to know what's going on back in the twenty-first century—why the pursuit?"

"You have to ask?" Callum leaned forward. "I'm sitting at the high table at Windsor Castle and I don't even know *when* it is. How could we not have pursued you?"

"But you had no proof that we could travel in time," I said. "You built your investigation on Ted's word alone?" I held my breath. It wasn't like I could help him from here, but I needed to know what they knew about my brother-in-law.

248

Callum shrugged. "He told his friend, Peter, who told his wife, who happens to be my boss. That was years ago."

"You're in MI5?" I said. At his nod, I added, "But surely you dismissed what he said when you learned of it. You had to have."

"At first," Callum said. "Not me, of course. I wasn't involved, but others looked into Peter's information, which led to new discoveries."

"What discoveries?"

"Ones that added to—and in truth, lit a fire under—a long-existing project." He studied my face. "You know about the images, right?"

"Ted said something about satellites."

Callum sat back in his chair. "That's right. When Ted first reported your story, Peter pursued it on his own. Given that he worked at Cambridge in astrophysics, he had access to imagery from the nineties, when you came to Wales the first time, as well as to more recent data."

"I don't get how our world shifting could be viewed from space," I said.

Callum hemmed and hawed. "I can't explain without going into absurd detail, but suffice to say that what you saw on the camera image at the spa—" he nodded at the widening of my eyes, "—yes, we know about that—is only a fraction of what is happening on the subatomic level."

Great.

At my sour expression, Callum grinned. "This was only one of twenty-five projects on my desk. When MI5 handed me the

249

portfolio, I thought it was a joke. They sent me to Cardiff—a demotion, mind you—and I've been cooling my heels investigating the odd Welsh nationalist group for the last six months."

"Until Ted called his friend from the airport," I said.

"Ted deserves knighthood. When Peter let us know where you were—well, it got real exciting, real fast."

"If what you say is true about the imagery, your people will know we've returned to this time." I bit my lip. "Can they tell how many people came with me so they'll know where you went?"

"No," Callum said.

"Do you have a family?"

"A girlfriend," Callum said. "Cancer got both of my parents too young."

"I'm sorry," I said, and meant it. "I can't send you back. You know that, right? I can't."

"I know." Callum looked away and cleared his throat. "We still haven't figured out the *why* of any of it."

"You and me both," I said. We sat in silence for a bit and picked at our food. "So, you're telling me that you don't speak Welsh, medieval or modern?"

"I guess I'll have to learn." He looked at me sideways. "I do have some Gaelic."

I let out a relieved breath. "That's something. Maybe more than something."

Goronwy leaned across Llywelyn to speak to me. "We should get the king to bed. He was near death a few days ago."

"I am well," Llywelyn said. "It's Meg I'm concerned about. You must be exhausted."

"I am," I said. "But Goronwy is right about you, too." I had continued to make sure he took his antibiotics, but proper sleep was as much medicine as the pills. "We have a big day tomorrow."

With Sir George's hurried (and relieved) acceptance, we returned to the suite he'd allotted us. Llywelyn sat heavily on the bed, revealing for the first time that Goronwy was right and he was very tired. As was I. The desire to be horizontal overwhelmed me and I gave in to it, curling up on top of the covers with my head on a pillow and my hands tucked under my chin. Llywelyn rested a hand on my feet in a sign of companionship. I sighed.

Goronwy surveyed us both, nodded, and then disappeared into the adjacent room. Callum excused himself to use the latrine. Then someone knocked at the door. Llywelyn didn't move. I didn't want to either. I glanced at him, but when he showed no signs of motion, forced myself into a sitting position.

"Come in!" I said.

The castellan opened the door but remained standing in the corridor, with a young man behind him. It was all I could do not to leap up and throw my arms around our visitor. "Huw! Goodness!"

Llywelyn nodded at Sir George. "If you would excuse us?"

"Of course, my lord." Sir George bowed and departed.

At that point, I did rise. "Look at you! A grown man. But ... what are you doing here?" I went to Huw and took his hands in mine.

"He is in The Order of the Pendragon," Llywelyn said.

Ah yes. "But how did you find us?"

"We've been following Prince Dafydd's progression through England closely, of course, but when we heard that you'd arrived at Windsor ..."

I dropped Huw's hands, I was that startled. "How did you hear of it?"

"We guard your son, my lady," Huw said. "Everything that concerns him is of concern to us."

When Llywelyn had told me of this secret order, I had accepted it at face value, but for Huw to know that we had arrived here within hours of our arrival indicated a conspiracy more far-reaching than I'd supposed.

"I had stayed in Wales, because that was my post," Huw said. "However, Bronwen came to me after the Prince left and I had to follow."

"Bronwen! Why?" I said.

"Word came to her of a plot against Prince Dafydd, with a churchman at the center of it."

"Is it Peckham?" Llywelyn said.

"We don't know," Huw said. "The informant didn't know."

"From what I've seen and heard, he has been treated well, and is even beloved. But—" I chewed on my lip. "I've heard 'Arthur' mentioned more than once and we've been here for only a few hours."

"That is why he is in danger," Llywelyn said. "Some of the other barons are jealous. They see Dafydd as too influential, too powerful."

I wanted to scoff, to say that Llywelyn was being ridiculous, but his grave expression stopped me. "I don't understand. He's a Welsh prince. Why would the English care about our myths?"

"Because he is Arthur returned," Llywelyn said, and his voice was gentle. "His people know it."

"*All* of his people," Huw said.

"Huw—" I began, but stopped because I had nothing to say. I couldn't counter Huw's earnestness—which was as genuine as that of the woman who'd dumped the warm water into my tub in the bathing room earlier, or the man who'd stoked the fire in this room half an hour ago. Their French had been halting (and they'd both been happy to switch to English when I'd replied to them in that language), but sincere nonetheless. They had referred to David as *Arthur*, with a light in their eyes that matched Huw's. They were English but spoke of him with reverence, as if they too awaited his return.

"Why are the English happy to see him?" I said. "Didn't we defeat them in a war three months ago?"

Llywelyn smirked. "We defeated a few lords who committed far too many good Englishmen to the endeavor. The average Englishman cares nothing at all for Wales, if its existence has ever entered his mind. But Arthur, now—the legend of Arthur is one that all people know—and to which they can all relate."

"But the men who died—"

"Who do you think the English blame? Our Dafydd for defending his country or Roger Bigod for leading them into a storm?" Llywelyn said.

"People speak of that storm as a sign from God; that God wasn't happy with the challenge to his chosen king," Huw said.

I didn't like the smile of satisfaction on Huw's face. "So what do we do next?" I said.

"Prince Dafydd's party left at dawn," Huw said. "He should have arrived at Westminster Palace hours ago. We have men there to watch over him."

"Does David know ... any of this?" I said.

"No—" Llywelyn began but Huw interrupted with a raised hand, followed by slight bow in Llywelyn's direction.

"My lord, yes, he does. Bevyn brought Dafydd to speak to my father and me in the village of Chepstow before the Prince left Wales for England. We told him about the Order of the Pendragon. I understand that this was your wish."

I heaved a sigh. That was the first good news I'd heard. "And the threats against his life?"

"We're not sure," Huw said. "He has good men around him, loyal men. But we have knowledge of several churchmen who have close access to him, and are powerful in their own right."

"Peckham," Llywelyn said again, and this time the name came out as a growl.

"There are others too," I said. "That other regent, Kirby, for one."

254

"Churchmen abound in England," Huw said. "There are too many to count."

"I'm surprised that it isn't Valence who's of most concern. Plotting against us is what he does best," I said.

Llywelyn slapped his thigh. "It is pleasing to me that his best has not been good enough."

"It hasn't been good enough *so far*," I said.

"I will ride to him tonight, my lord," Huw said. "I stopped here to rest my horse and because the Order knew that my face was one you'd recognize."

"Go," I said, knowing Llywelyn and I couldn't—just couldn't—go with him. "Tell him everything you know."

20

19 November 1288

David

We left Lambeth Palace and crossed the Thames. Before I entered under the gatehouse at Westminster, however, I dismounted. "I need to think." I tugged my cloak around my shoulders. It had grown dark while I'd been speaking with the Archbishop, though the pre-wedding feast was still several hours off.

"There are many places to walk *inside* the palace, my lord," Bevyn said. "No need for you to expose yourself in this way."

"I've never been to London," I said. "I want to see it." I was being stubborn, but the day had presented me with one surprise after another. If I went back to my room, I'd be with Lili (which was all to the good), but the palace was like a fishbowl and I was the fish. Even if I walked in the gardens, I'd have the eyes of every nobleman and servant in the place on me. In Wales, I knew the exact length and width of my cage. Here, I was struggling with it being so much smaller.

The men around me exchanged the kind of glances that I didn't have to read to know what they said. They didn't want me to go, and ninety percent of the time—maybe ninety-nine percent of the time—I would have done as they asked because I didn't want to inconvenience the people who looked after me. I wasn't feeling reckless, not like when I'd followed William into England. I just wanted to walk.

I grinned, deciding to do what I wanted, for once, whether they liked it or not. "Come or don't. It's of no matter to me." I set off walking north, heading away from the palace along the road that fronted the Thames River.

I imagined the mad scramble that ensued behind my back, and wasn't surprised that it was Carew who surfed up beside me: he spoke English and French, he was a nobleman, so dressed similarly to me, and he belonged to the Order of the Pendragon. To Bevyn, he would be the perfect choice.

"Are you feeling guilty yet?" Carew said.

"Ha!" I said. "You have me down pretty well, don't you? And yes, I was justifying my walk to myself, on the way to avoiding guilt."

"Think nothing of it, my lord," Carew said. "It's good for the men to have something to think about. Protecting you will keep them busy and hone their skills. There's nothing to do at Westminster but stand around and listen to gossip."

"I noticed," I said, "and I was inside the palace for all of an hour."

Carew was silent a moment as we walked. I side-stepped a pile of refuse in the road, managed not to get run over by three ruffians chasing a fourth down the street, and avoided a prostitute on the corner. We were passing through a seedy section of London (which was what I wanted to see, I admit). Still, I carried a sword and had Carew at my side. I was safe, especially with Bevyn's minions surrounding me on all sides, even if I couldn't see them. Knowing him, he'd have sent them running at double-time to catch up.

What I wasn't safe from was my thoughts. "Who has been speaking to the Archbishop, Carew?" I said. "It's this business with my mother's lineage which bothers me most. Whoever has falsified her origins has to know that her real parentage is obscure. The information had to come from someone very close to me, but who also has the Archbishop's ear. I can't think of anyone who fits that description."

"I don't know the answer, my lord," he said. "It is a strange turn of events. I support your claim to the throne of England because you are Arthur reborn, whether or not you admit it. But this? It's reaching."

"Peckham showed me the documents," I said. "They look real. The signature and seal of King Henry looks real."

"Could ... could it actually be the truth?"

I tsked at him. "No."

"Did you say as much to the Archbishop?"

"Of course," I said. "He didn't believe me, and gave me a long explanation as to why, which sounded credible even to me. I fear another few days of this and I'll start believing it myself."

"You should, my lord, you of all people."

"Don't say that, Carew." I pointed to a building on the left. "Let's turn in here."

We'd passed half a dozen taverns in the few minutes we'd been walking, but we now approached a more well-to-do area of the city and this tavern looked more upscale than the others. I might have wanted to walk, but I wasn't stupid. Even so, Carew looked askance at me as I pushed through the door.

Fortunately, men weren't waiting three deep at the bar. We asked for beer and got it. I paid, much to Carew's surprise since he didn't expect me to carry coins. I didn't tell him that in the modern world, celebrities and presidents rarely carried cash. Even if the Arthur myth was going to swallow me whole, I didn't have to fall into that trap. A table in the corner opened up and we sat. I chose the stool that put my back to the wall. The open stool would have had Carew's back to the door, so he edged it around the table until he could see the room too.

I surveyed the room with him. "What do you think?" I spoke in English. I didn't want to flaunt our Welshness more than our clothing already did.

"I miss Wales already," Carew said.

A man at the next table swung around to look at us and pointed a finger at Carew. "Did you say Wales? Are you from

Wales?" The two men sitting beyond him at the same table looked daggers at us.

I decided to brazen it out. "Yes."

"Did you come with that prince?" The man snapped his fingers. "David, right?"

"Right," Carew said, without answering the man's question.

The man held up the finger he'd used to point at Carew and shouted to the bar. "They're from Wales!"

"Oh, Christ—"

But the man cut off Carew's lament by snapping his fingers at one of the barmaids. "Two more for those Welshmen in the corner!"

A minute later, Carew and I found ourselves surrounded by a half dozen men. The original talker pulled his stool closer so he could rest his elbows on our table. When our new drinks came, the barmaid placed them in front of us and said, "On the house."

The man who'd called for the beer gave her a thumbs up. For a second, I feared it meant *cut off his head!* but it appeared to have the same meaning in medieval England as it did in modern America. The Welsh didn't use that sign, so I hadn't seen it in years.

"Tell us about him," the man ordered. He tapped his chest. "I'm John." He pointed at each of his friends in turn. "That's Tom, Rob, another John, Henry, and Will."

Carew and I lifted our hands in a tentative 'hi'. "What do you want to know?" Carew said.

"What's he like? Is he as brave as they say? As tall as they say?" John said.

Carew glanced at me and I decided to play along. I got to my feet. "He's as tall as I am. I don't know about brave—"

"When he was fourteen he stood his ground against a charging boar and killed it by ramming a spear down its throat," Carew said.

I sat down again.

The man nodded. "I heard that story. It's true?" At Carew's assent, John added, "What about when he defeated old King Edward in single combat, without wielding a sword?"

"I was there," Carew said. "I saw it."

"You saw it?" The six Englishmen leaned forward.

I elbowed Carew in the ribs, trying to get him to stop. He winced but otherwise ignored me. "He had Edward at his mercy, but refused to kill him, since he was a kinsman. Edward then ordered his men to chain Prince David. King Edward knew who David was, you see, and rightfully feared him."

"Arthur." One of the men to John's left, Rob, breathed the name first.

Carew nodded.

I rolled my eyes. "He's just a man—"

John glared at me. "You doubt that Prince David is the return of Arthur? Your own liege lord?"

"Well ... I ..." I swallowed. The eyes of the Englishmen had turned hostile.

261

"Of course not." Carew clapped me on the shoulder. "My friend here witnessed the storm last summer, and what it did to the men in the boats who meant to invade Wales from the sea."

I had to play along. I had no choice. "I did."

John and his companions grunted and nodded to themselves. "I hear it was a grandfather of a storm."

"The winds and water were so strong, the Severn flowed the wrong way, upstream," Carew said.

I barely managed not to snort into my beer. The Severn Estuary was tidal. It flowed 'upstream' twice a day, every day, as did the Wye River.

The men didn't know that, however. "It's one of the signs," Will said.

"What signs?" I said.

"That Arthur has returned, of course," Will said.

"I thought it was when the Tham—"

Carew stamped a foot on the toe of my boot. "Thanks for the beer, gentlemen. We'll be off. Big day tomorrow."

"The wedding." John's tone was sour. "Bohun's thinking we'll have a King William soon, don't he?"

"That is, I believe, his plan," I said, not worrying about giving Humphrey de Bohun away. Everyone knew by now that this was his plan.

"We'll see about that," Tom said, to more nods all around.

Carew had gotten to his feet, but now leaned over the table. "How will you see about that?" he said.

262

Tom shrugged, but his eyes slid sideways to look at his friends. "The people of London have always had a say in who's to be king, and we don't want William."

"He's a nice boy—" I began.

Tom stabbed a finger at me. "Exactly! A boy."

"Who would you have as king instead?" Carew said.

"I think we ought to stick that crown on this David," John said. "He's got mettle—more than most. And we've heard he's the grandson of old King Henry, which ought to satisfy those lords we've got sitting up there at Westminster."

And with that comment, I finally understood—really understood—what was in these men's minds. They were English. The Normans had conquered them and taken all of England for their own, just as they'd done to the Welsh in my old world, and Edward would have done to our Wales here if my father and I hadn't defeated him. If the Welsh in the twenty-first century could remember their losses after more than seven hundred years, it wasn't surprising these Englishmen held onto their grief after only two hundred. If they couldn't have a king of their own choosing, maybe a Welsh prince who carried the mantle of Arthur was better than any Norman they already knew.

Trouble was, they wouldn't be getting Arthur. They'd be getting me.

So I asked them: "You'd prefer to crown an upstart Welsh Prince with a half Scot, half Norman mother, who happens to be the illegitimate child of King Henry?" I said. "You think he'd be better than William de Bohun or any other baron?"

"He wasn't ever as young as this William, even when he was that age," Rob said. "Didn't you say he killed a boar at fourteen?"

"He knows how to fight," John said.

"And he isn't Spanish neither," Henry said, speaking for the first time. "That Alfonso fellow that's betrothed to Eleanor is up to no good. Before you know it, we'll have Spanish folk taking over."

I tugged on Carew's sleeve. "We need to go."

Carew nodded. "Thank you, gentlemen, for a most instructive evening." The men in the room rose to honor our departure. As we left the pub, I could hear them discussing the future of their country among themselves. Once outside, Carew turned to me, his face split by a grin. "This was your idea, my lord."

"Don't remind me."

21

19 November 1288

David

"There he is." Humphrey de Bohun leaned in from the left to whisper close in my ear. I had returned from the tavern with an hour to spare to wash and dress—and make sure Lili was okay—before the feast.

"Who?" I looked up from my meal, eyed Lili and William, who were talking together on my right side, and then glanced down the hall to where Humphrey indicated.

"Alfonso of Aragon."

"And that must be Eleanor," I said, "the would-be bride. And look who arrives with them."

Humphrey's face darkened. "Valence." He practically spat the word. It was odd that he was allowing his emotions to show so easily tonight, given his title and station. I'd tried (probably unsuccessfully) to cultivate a look of impassivity, especially when presented with bad news. Maybe Humphrey was presented with bad news so often that nobody noticed any longer the constant reddening of his face.

"You knew Valence was going to be here," I said. "We can't avoid him."

"When I learned that he had Alfonso in his pocket, too," Humphrey said, "it became clear to me that he would barely notice the loss of your cousin, Hywel."

As far as I could tell, nobody was mourning Hywel's loss at all. When I'd returned from Westminster, Lili (having survived the encounter with her father) had been full of court news, including the gossip about my dead cousin. She reported that he had been accepted at court well enough, but neither liked nor disliked—it was more that he had very little personality. Given the huge egos and personalities of so many of the barons, that could have been construed as a good thing. Though it wouldn't have made Hywel a very good King of Wales.

Alfonso, on the other hand, had nothing but personality. He swept towards the dais with long strides, Eleanor on his arm. He wore a hat—felted perhaps, since knitting hadn't been invented yet—with a huge floppy brim and a three foot peacock feather. Wales was certainly on the edge of the fashionable world, even with our current relative wealth, but I had never seen anything like that hat before. Lili and William both snorted into their soup. Lili glanced at me, her eyes streaming with unreleased mirth. "Quite a confection," she said.

Evan and Bevyn had found places against the wall near the entrance to the hallway that led to our suite. Carew, who was sitting at the near end of one of the long tables stretching down the cavernous hall, stood as Alfonso passed him. In the last few days, Carew had taken upon himself a position of close advisor to me, much as he had when we'd gone to England to meet King Edward three years ago. Now, he'd gone on alert. It seemed I had many people watching out for me.

Alfonso approached the high table where Lili and I sat with the Bohuns, Princess Joan, the Archbishop Peckham, both Roger and Edmund Mortimer (sitting at opposite ends of the table), and several other high-ranking Norman barons. Clare hadn't yet put in an appearance, nor had Kirby, the other regent. Alfonso, Eleanor, and Valence had been given seats on the far side of Bohun and the Archbishop, who sat in the central position on the dais. Bohun had ceded it to him tonight because, with all these people who hated each other in the same room, Peckham might be a steadying influence.

Alfonso looked directly at William, who stood with Joan to greet him and Eleanor. "Congratulations," Alfonso said. "I am delighted that we are about to be brothers."

"It is an honor, sir." William gave Alfonso a stiff bow. At thirteen, he was ten years younger than Alfonso and had to be feeling that difference acutely. Alfonso was everything you might want in a Spanish nobleman, with jet black hair, a strong jaw, and a wild light in his eyes. In my old world, he had died at the age of twenty-seven, having never even met Eleanor, and certainly not gotten this close to marrying her. The death of King Edward had changed many fortunes, not only that of Wales.

Alfonso's eyes tracked to mine. He tipped his head stiffly, and I nodded back. "Welcome to London," I said. It was hardly my place to welcome him to a city to which I'd just arrived, but I had to say something.

Carew had warned me about the protocol here. So many of us were equals or near equals in station, it was a matter of constantly negotiating who should be bowing to whom. I hadn't risen to my feet alongside William, which implied that I thought I was better than Alfonso and William. But then, neither had Bohun or anyone else at the table. Alfonso was the King of Aragon, with lands far more expansive than Wales, but in this case, I was happy to go along with the general sentiment. These Normans had French ancestry. To them, the Spanish didn't count.

With a pinched smile in my direction, Alfonso walked to his seat beside Valence and Eleanor, and gradually the general conversation at the table re-ensued. Bohun sat staring at Alfonso for another minute, however. It was no wonder Bohun's face had darkened. If Alfonso succeeded in marrying Eleanor, he would not only outrank William for the English throne, but put Valence back in power.

Towards the end of the meal, as some of the diners began to depart, Clare nudged me as he slipped into the chair recently vacated by Lili, who'd had enough of the official meal and needed to lie down. Bevyn had escorted her to our chamber and returned. Bohun, still seated on my left, was in close conversation with the Archbishop. Carew had found himself a seat at the high table next

268

to Edmund. People had drunk enough of the very good beer not to care anymore who outranked whom.

"How goes it with you?" Clare said.

"Well enough," I said.

"And your bride?"

"She is well, too."

"No problems at this stage, then?" Clare's face was earnest and intent. "The pregnancy goes well?"

"Yes," I said. "What is it, Clare?"

"I'm concerned about Hywel's death—"

He broke off at a sudden uproar coming from the other end of the table. We both stood. Alfonso had his hands to his throat and appeared to be choking.

"I think it's a bone! I warned him—" Eleanor was on her feet too, clutching at Alfonso's sleeve.

I reached Alfonso in two strides. Kicking away his chair, I grabbed him from behind, clasped my hands underneath his diaphragm, and jerked upward. An olive pit popped out of his mouth and skittered under the table. Alfonso gasped real air. I set him down gently, onto his hands and knees. His breath came in ragged gasps, but it was breath.

"My God," he said.

I crouched beside him. "You should be okay now." I held out my hand. He clasped it and levered himself to his feet. I eased him back into his chair beside Eleanor, whose hands fluttered and shook.

"Thank you, my lord! Thank you." Eleanor leapt to her feet and threw herself into my arms. Then she embraced Alfonso, who patted her shoulder and leaned back in his chair. Eleanor reached for the wine goblet they were sharing and offered it to him.

Alfonso shook his head. "Give me a moment for my breath to return before I eat or drink anything, my dear." He looked up at me. "Thank you, Prince David."

Meanwhile, Eleanor took a long drink from the goblet, which seemed to steady her. A servant reached between them to refill the cup. At that exact moment, Alfonso looked away from me and jostled his arm. Wine spilled to the floor and Alfonso cursed.

"No problem." I turned back to my seat, not wanting to witness another display of poor behavior on the part of a nobleman towards someone he viewed as beneath him. Clare sat sideways in his chair, one arm draped across the back and an elbow on the table.

"That was noble of you," he said.

"That's me, noble to a fault." I pulled out my chair while Clare smirked.

And then Alfonso cursed again, louder this time.

I spun around. Eleanor held her hands to her throat, but not because she was choking on an olive pit. She'd flushed red and staggered, her eyes hugely dilated. Alfonso sat useless, staring, so I bounded forward. This time I could do nothing to help. Still, I grabbed her as she toppled from her seat and felt in her mouth with my fingers, just to make sure I couldn't clear a blockage in her throat. Nothing. She stopped breathing. It all happened so fast

I found myself staring down at her in horror. I whipped around to look at Alfonso.

"What happened?"

"I-I-I don't know!" Alfonso gazed at me blankly. "One moment she was well, caring for me, and the next ..."

"Perhaps the wine." Clare had come to help.

Nobody seemed to know what to do. The Bohuns stared at Eleanor wide-eyed, Alfonso was cursing steadily, and even Valence had both hands in his hair, running his fingers through it. I stepped back and away to allow others to crowd closer. I eyed the row of abandoned food and drink. Every chair on the dais had an empty trencher and accompanying goblet in front of it. I waved at Bevyn and Evan. They skirted the dais and approached.

"I need you to work fast. Gather all the goblets on this table. Handle them carefully, with the tips of your fingers. Do not let anyone else touch them and I want you to remember which goblet went to which man or woman." They had no idea what I really wanted, but after a quick glance, they obeyed. The nobles would be surprised when they returned to their seats and found their drinks missing. Clare eyed me, but he didn't argue either. If I could have used modern techniques, I would have dusted the goblets for fingerprints. As it was, I simply wanted no more poisoned nobles tonight.

The dozen shocked men and women continued to huddle around Eleanor's fallen body, gazing at her in stunned silence. It was Valence who was the first to recover, and instead of expressing sympathy to Joan, or Alfonso, he shouldered through the crowd to

271

stand between me and the corpse. He put his face right into mine. "What did you do to her?"

My hands came up. "Hey—"

Edmund Mortimer stepped in front of me and put his hand on Valence's chest. "Back off, Valence. The Prince saved Alfonso's life. You saw it. He had nothing to do with Eleanor's death."

Others of Valence's allies, including Roger Mortimer, Edmund's brother, pulled on Valence's arm, trying to get him to retreat. Valence glared at me over Edmund's shoulder, his mouth working and his face flushed so red I feared his heart might fail him. He was a stout man, used to fine dinners and rich foods. "Don't think I can't see what you're doing! All of your rivals fall like dead flies!"

I blinked. Eleanor had hardly been a rival. In fact, I'd given her as little thought as possible, thinking her a fluttery, spoiled noblewoman, like most of her kind.

The Archbishop himself interceded. "Valence. This is unseemly."

But it was honest. At long last, the real Valence was revealed, and he was angry and ambitious. "Get out of my way!" Valence brushed at his handlers' hands. He pointed at me and shook his finger. "You—" If he could have seen himself, with his usually coifed hair standing on end and his color high, he would have subsided immediately. His carefully managed image had been undone in thirty seconds of uncontrolled anger.

I stood steady, watching him, and maybe he saw something in my expression that gave him pause, because between one instant and the next, he calmed himself. He straightened his tunic with a jerk, swung around, and strode off the dais, heading down the hall without a backwards glance at Alfonso, his distraught ally. Alfonso, unlike everyone else who'd forgotten about Eleanor in favor of gawking at Valence, knelt at her feet. Joan sobbed quietly beside him, clasping her sister's dead hand.

I looked toward Bohun, who also gazed down at the body. He lifted his head and met my eyes. That same mistrust from earlier was in his face, coupled with something else, something I couldn't put my finger on—surprise?

"Not you, too," I said. "I had nothing to do with this."

Bohun's shoulders sagged. "I know it. Once Valence calms down, it is I he will accuse. You understand that, don't you? You would do well to distance yourself from me from this moment."

"Did you cause Eleanor's death?" I said.

Pause. "No. But you can understand why people will think I did. Why I could have."

Clare came up behind Bohun and clapped a hand on his shoulder. "Get your son and his bride out of here. This wedding tomorrow can't come soon enough."

Bohun jerked his head at William, who went to Joan and gently pulled her away from the body. She was sixteen, not thirteen like William. Nobody had asked her what she thought about marrying a boy who was not yet a man, but she responded to him well enough. If history had gone the way it had in my old world, William would have married not Joan but Elizabeth, Edward's youngest daughter, born in 1282. She was only six,

273

however, and Humphrey de Bohun was angling for the throne of England.

Humphrey's wife, Maud, wrapped an arm around Joan's shoulders and the girl left the dais with the Bohuns without protest. I hadn't heard Joan open her mouth once so far. She seemed a little mouse and looked it, with her pointed face and lifeless brown hair that she'd styled as plainly as possible. Her looks had presented a sharp contrast to the blond Eleanor, who stood out in any company of women, no matter how beautiful.

A servant covered Eleanor's body with a tablecloth, and then two guardsmen carried her from the hall, with Archbishop Peckham in attendance at her side. The hall remained full of diners, all gossiping among themselves about what they had just witnessed. Alfonso staggered off, still in a stupor, leaving Clare, Carew, Edmund Mortimer, and me on the dais. Valence and his allies were by now long gone.

Edmund's wife had not come to the wedding—like Roger's wife, she was pregnant again. Clare lifted a hand to him, and he came over. "We have much to discuss," I said as Edmund planted himself in front of us.

"How is that?" Edmund said.

Clare gave a tsk of disgust. "Edmund—"

Edmund lifted his hand to me. "I apologize, my lord Prince. I am still in shock that Eleanor is dead."

I glanced down at the place the body had lain. Traces of white foam remained on the floorboards. I looked up at my three companions. "Do we all agree that she died of poison?"

Clare pursed his lips. "How can we doubt it, given what we witnessed? Do you think it was in her wine? Is that why you sent Bevyn and Evan away with the goblets?"

"That is for the castle herbalist to determine," I said. "I know nothing of poisons."

I was turning away when a man appeared from a side door in the hall. I hesitated, feeling that I knew him, and then at his raised hand, recognized Huw and waved him to me. As he approached the dais, he took in the chaos in one glance and then bowed to me. "I have good news, my lord."

"It would be a relief to hear some," I said.

"Your parents are at Windsor," Huw said.

My breath whuffed out of me. *Thank God!* And then I laughed, even though it was completely inappropriate under the circumstances.

"I have bad news, too," Huw said. "Bronwen sent me."

"Talk to me as we walk," I said. "We have much to do."

22

19 November 1288

Lili

"It could have been Alfonso as easily as Eleanor who died tonight," I said. Dafydd had stormed into the room with Huw and Carew and poured the story out in a long, uninterrupted stream, almost before Huw had a chance to close the door. Fortunately, I'd been dozing by the fire instead of in bed. "They shared a cup. Maybe the poison was meant for him and not Eleanor."

"In that case, do you think the incident with the olive was a true accident?" Huw said.

"It was an opportunity," Carew said.

"How so?" Dafydd said.

"While you were busy saving Alfonso's life, and all attention was on the two of you, someone poisoned the wine," I said. "How else would it have poisoned only Eleanor? Wine is poured from a communal jug, which the food taster sampled before it was served. Only Eleanor died."

Dafydd rested a forearm on the mantle and leaned into it. "You're right."

I didn't add that I was always right and my husband should know it by now. Instead, I nodded. "This was a cold act of a desperate man—or men."

Dafydd shook his head. "I can understand that someone might murder Alfonso, but Eleanor? A woman?"

I reached out to Dafydd and he gave me his hand. He saw the best in people; he couldn't help it, but that made it hard for him to comprehend evil. "With Eleanor's death, Joan is the next princess in line for the crown. The murder of Alfonso would have merely delayed Eleanor's ascension until another candidate for her hand was found."

"Your lord husband told me about the poisons from Shrewsbury, my lady," Huw said. "With them so freely available, anyone could be responsible."

"I checked with the herbalist earlier today. He knew nothing about the shipment from Shrewsbury and never took them into his possession," I said.

"They are in the wind," Dafydd said.

Before he'd come to see me, Dafydd had disposed of the goblets of wine. It wasn't his task to find Eleanor's killer, but because Dafydd had seen no signs of anyone else taking charge, he'd set the wheels of discovery in motion. He'd left the bulk of his men at Baynard's Castle, as had Clare, but Clare had sent his constable to ask questions of the kitchen and to interview the servers and the wine steward. Bevyn and Evan were interviewing guests.

Dafydd hadn't let me near any of the goblets. Instead, Edmund had woken the castle herbalist who had sniffed the offending liquid and postulated that the juice of belladonna berries had been added to the drink.

"Valence was very angry." Dafydd fell into the chair opposite me and held out his hands to the fire. "I'm sorry I cannot blame him for the night's events."

"You said Bohun denied having anything to do with Eleanor's death. Do you believe him?" I said. "I wish I could have been there to read his face."

"I'm glad you weren't," Dafydd said. "You didn't need to see that."

My husband was protecting me again, but I supposed I was glad, too, that I hadn't seen Eleanor die.

"He's an obvious candidate," Carew said. "As Lili said, the death of Eleanor clears the way for William to ascend the throne, even if he is only thirteen." Carew shrugged. "It also makes Bohun the least likely candidate to commit murder because he's the most obvious one."

"I can attest that he was nowhere near that goblet." Dafydd sighed and scrubbed at his hair again. "You and Huw might as well know, too, that the Archbishop expressed concern to me today about Valence and his motives."

"Did he?" Huw said.

"He felt that Valence didn't have the best interests of England at heart," Dafydd said. "Peckham said that he would be sorry to see a Spaniard on the throne."

"Are you saying that the *Archbishop* might have murdered Eleanor?" I said.

"He was sitting right next to Alfonso," Dafydd said. "He has motive and opportunity. And Bronwen did say that a threat would come to me from a churchman."

Carew's chin firmed. "I hadn't considered that."

"What are Peckham's ambitions?" I said.

"He's the Archbishop of Canterbury," Dafydd said. "He can't rise any higher in the Church and remain in England. He doesn't appear to want the throne for himself."

"Then what does he want?" I said, and then answered my own question because I should have known the answer without having to ask. "Power—and the ability to wield it."

"Humphrey de Bohun isn't on good terms with Peckham," Dafydd said. "We know that."

"Peckham *is* fond of William," Carew said. "The Order reports that in the last week, he has asked for several audiences with William and Joan."

"To counsel them on their marriage?" Dafydd said.

"So we would assume," Carew said.

"Why else would he meet with them?" I said. "William isn't involved in affairs of state."

"It is my guess that he is actively attempting to woo the couple towards his way of thinking and away from Humphrey's," Dafydd said. "That is Peckham's way."

"It's ironic, then, isn't it, that Valence wooed Peckham so successfully before?" I said. "Because of Peckham, Valence wasn't imprisoned in the Tower of London after the debacle in the Estuary."

"Perhaps Peckham regrets that now." Dafydd leaned forward. "Has the Order learned anything about Kirby, the other regent? He's a *churchman* too."

Before Carew could answer, a knock came at the door. After a glance at Dafydd, who nodded, Huw strode to the door and opened it. Bevyn stood in the doorway and Dafydd waved him inside. "You might as well come in. Huw's been a delightful fount of information, but either he or Carew would have immediately turned around and told you everything anyway."

"I have learned something, too, my lord," Bevyn said.

Dafydd nodded. "You first."

"I know who murdered Eleanor, though I can't see how I could prove it, short of a confession." Bevyn came to a halt in front of Dafydd. "It wasn't Bohun."

"It was Peckham?" Huw said.

Bevyn glanced at him, his brow furrowed. "No, no, why would you think that?" He let out a sharp breath. "It was Maud."

"Maud de Bohun?" I covered my mouth with my hand in my surprise. "You're sure?"

"As I said, I have no specific proof," Bevyn said. "Although nobody saw her take possession of the herbs, Maud was the one who asked to be sent word when the cart from Shrewsbury arrived. More importantly, one of the guests noticed her reaching across the table towards Peckham while Alfonso was choking. Her hand passed right over Alfonso's goblet."

"That's awfully specific," Dafydd said. "Why would anyone notice her actions in particular?"

Bevyn cleared his throat. "Apparently the man to whom I spoke finds her beautiful. He watched her every move all evening."

I blinked. Maud was attractive, certainly, but with grown children, I'd not considered her the object of chivalric attention.

Dafydd let out a sharp breath and leaned back in his chair. "I can't go to any of the barons and suggest that Maud de Bohun poisoned Eleanor. It's just not possible."

"Does it make it better if my guess is wrong and she meant to kill Alfonso?" I said.

"I don't think so." Dafydd rubbed at his forehead with his fingers. "This has gotten way out of hand."

"Why did Huw think Peckham was responsible?" Bevyn said.

"Because of some things he said to me today," Dafydd said.

Bevyn tapped a finger on his lips. "Other members of the Order would be very interested to hear of your conversation."

"I'm sure they would," Dafydd said, which is why he hadn't told Bevyn anything about it earlier. To do so would be to convey the information instantly to a hundred others. But now that three members of the Order were present, Dafydd gave way. "He said that he found the documents supporting my mother's birth credible."

"What did you say to him?" Huw said.

"I told him flat out that the whole thing was absurd."

Bevyn eased out a sigh.

"What?" Dafydd said. "It's true."

"And what was his reply?" Carew said.

I could tell that Dafydd didn't want to answer. As the silence stretched out, I put a hand on his arm and said, "Peckham laughed and said that he'd been told that Dafydd would deny any claim to the throne of England, because Dafydd has never sought to place himself above others, even if he deserves the acclaim. Peckham said that a time would come, however, when Dafydd would consider the needs of his people greater than his own."

When I had asked Dafydd how he'd replied to Peckham, he'd shrugged and turned away. The truth was that he had no reply to make. He'd spent the last six years striving to deserve the trust that the people of Wales—and his father—had placed in him. He knew exactly what Peckham was saying but resented that Peckham meant the *English* people were somehow his to care for as well.

Carew had once accused Dafydd of caring so little about his own power that he doubted he was even a prince. It wasn't that nothing had changed since then. Dafydd was used to *being* a prince and it would be hard to go back to not being one, but he'd never asked for it—neither for it nor for the acclaim, as Peckham put it.

"Tell me now if you or your Order had anything to do with these documents," Dafydd said. "I need to know."

"We didn't," Carew and Bevyn said together, without hesitation.

From the look on Dafydd's face, I wasn't sure that Dafydd believed them. Still, he clasped my hand and said to me, "Don't worry. The papers don't matter. I would not take the throne on false premises, no matter who swore to the truth of these documents or supported me because of them."

"Carew says that Peckham called you *Arthur* at your departure," Bevyn said.

Dafydd ground his teeth. "He did. And that is a claim I cannot shake, no matter how I try."

* * * * *

Dafydd, my love. Wake up!" I prodded him, and he rolled over.

"Why?"

"I couldn't sleep and—" I broke off, too much in a hurry to explain what I had seen and overheard. He had to hear it for himself. "Can you please come with me?"

Dafydd opened his eyes and looked at me. I didn't try to hide the fact that I was anxious and he touched my cheek. "Okay." He swung his legs out of bed, pulled on his breeches, and then reached for his boots, but I gestured that he should follow me out the door without them.

"You don't need them and they make noise."

He eyed me, a smile on his lips, but nodded and allowed me to lead him on tiptoe along the corridor from our room. Castle building had evolved in England faster than in Wales, and even though Dafydd and his father had added luxuries as they could afford them and felt them worthwhile, King Edward had done the same on a much grander scale, as a monument to his power.

Westminster Palace, which had been the seat of the Norman kings since William Rufus built the first castle here, had been the object of much of Edward's largesse. In addition to the enormous great hall, corridors within the twelve-foot-thick walls made it possible to travel anywhere within the castle without going outside. Meg had told me that in her old world, after he'd conquered Wales, Edward had built this feature into the castles he built at Caernarfon and on Anglesey. If those castles looked anything like Westminster, they would have dominated the landscape, and I was glad he hadn't had the chance to build them.

Our suite was on the second floor of the palace, and I led Dafydd past half a dozen latrines and smaller rooms until we approached a small chapel. "In here." I drew him into an alcove, protected by a curtain, in which a brazier burned but no man guarded.

"They sent the sentry away." I kept my voice to a whisper.

"Who's they—?" Dafydd stopped because he could hear them himself. I pointed to a slit in the stones that separated the alcove from the chapel. He peered through the crack. The brazier was the only light in the alcove and it flickered behind us but wasn't as bright as the lights in the chapel.

Gilbert de Clare, Nicholas de Carew, and Edmund Mortimer stood in a circle ten feet from us. They appeared to be arguing, their voices low, but not so low that we couldn't hear them.

"The key question remains," Clare said, "does Kirby know that we know that he forged the papers?"

"No." Carew shook his head. "How could he?"

"What about Eleanor?" Mortimer said.

"Her death has nothing to do with us," Clare said. "We stay the course as planned."

Dafydd's throat worked. "Kirby forged the papers?" He drew his eyes away from the slit. "Why would he do that?"

"It seems that like Peckham, he has weighed his options and chosen you," I said.

"I must talk to them—"

"No!" I caught his arm and tugged hard. "No, you mustn't!"

"What? Why?" Dafydd had pulled aside the curtain, but now let it drop and came back to me. "I hate all these secrets."

I crowded him up against the wall of the alcove. He was much larger than I, so he could have continued with his original intention of confronting his Norman allies, but he didn't push me aside.

I peered into the slit. "They're leaving." I pressed a hand on Dafydd's chest, holding him still until the sound of the men's footsteps had faded down the corridor.

"Lili—"

"Let them have their secrets," I said. "You heard what they said, didn't you? They are loyal to you but fear how you might react if you knew the truth."

"I understand that, but now that I know the truth—"

"You can't control everyone, Dafydd, and you must choose your battles. What would have happened if you'd burst in on them?"

"They would have had to admit to their deception," Dafydd said, "and they would have known that they couldn't pull the wool over my eyes."

"No." I shook my head. "You would have embarrassed them—and yourself—and they would have lied through their teeth, pretending they were speaking of something entirely different. And then they would have gone further underground. These men plot as easily as they breathe. This time, they are plotting *for* you. Let them."

"It feels wrong, Lili," Dafydd said.

"I know." I stepped back. "But now you have the advantage. There may come a time when you find the need to whisper into Clare's ear, to mention the conversation he had in the chapel at Westminster Palace. It might not be for a month from now, or a year, but he will remember, and wonder how you knew, and why you kept silent, and what long game *you* are playing."

"I'm not playing any game," Dafydd said.

I laughed and threw my arms around my husband's neck. "*I* know that. But you don't have to let everyone else know it, too."

23

20 November 1288

David

As we arrived at St. Paul's Cathedral, I leaned down to whisper in Lili's ear: "I thought we'd never make it."

Lili humored me by giggling and squeezing my hand. The wedding was due to start at any minute. Once it was out of the way, along with the council meeting tomorrow, we could go home.

Lili and I had defied our handlers once again. Although we'd ridden from Westminster, we'd left the horses at Baynard's Castle because it was so much easier to walk from there than navigate London traffic with two dozen horses. Clare and Edmund Mortimer had looked at me askance when I'd suggested it, but then Edmund's mouth twitched—that ever-present, dry amusement rising to the surface—and they both had agreed. It was my guess that neither man ever mingled with the people of

London. Like the rich in the modern world, they didn't want to contaminate themselves by contact with commoners.

I had to remind myself that ruling England was about power and fortune, and to try to discuss quality of life issues with a Norman was futile. It was bad enough that they still spoke French among themselves, though more were learning English every year. Peckham was the only Norman I'd ever heard talk seriously about the English as a people, as if he were one of them instead of a foreign overlord perched atop a conquered populace. But then again, most of my interactions had been with Marcher lords, who held on to their Norman ancestry more strongly, and looked down on the English (as well as the Welsh) over whom they ruled.

St. Paul's Cathedral was ancient, even by medieval standards, having been built in Saxon times when Christianity had no more than a foothold in Britain. It occupied the highest of London's three 'hills', which were puny by Welsh standards at a whopping 60 feet above sea level. But still, the Cathedral had a view.

Clare walked up the steps to the front doors with us. "The Bishop of London has been busy," he said.

"I can see that," I said, noting the construction materials surrounding the cathedral and the uncompleted spire. Mom had told me that this particular version of St. Paul's would burn down in London's great fire of 1666. I didn't mention it to Clare. It might not even happen in this world and wouldn't be our problem if it did.

289

The nave was already full of people. I could never get used to the way churchgoers were expected to stand for an entire two hour service, when they weren't kneeling on cold stone. Today, William stood in front of the public altar. It was common practice these days to marry at the church door and not inside the church itself, but it was cold outside and too fraught with security issues for the future King of England and Princess Joan to expose themselves in that way. It was unseemly for them to be getting married at all, given Eleanor's death last night, but Bohun would not be gainsaid, not with the throne of England within his grasp. In fact, it wasn't unusual among the Normans to claim a crown before the body of a fallen ruler had gone cold.

The Bishop of London, Richard Gravesend, stood beside William at the head of the nave. Gravesend had to be ambitious to have achieved his position in life, but not so much that he had taken part in the back and forth of politics and succession that had consumed Peckham.

Clare approached so Lili could take his arm. He led her to a spot near the front of the worshipers, while I made my way to William's side. He had several other lords—some younger than I— standing up with him today. Humphrey de Bohun stood close by too, and he sidled over to me. I could see the glee in his face as he rubbed his hands together. "Are you ready for this?"

"I have nothing to fear. I'm already married," I said. "How's William?"

"Nervous," Humphrey said, "not that I can blame him. Tomorrow he could be the King of England."

"Do you think the barons will approve his ascension at the council meeting?" I said.

"How can they not?" Humphrey said. "With Eleanor dead, all other claimants fall to the side." He paused. "Except for you, of course."

"I've told you that I will not challenge William's claim," I said. "I am a loyal friend."

Humphrey acknowledged that pledge with a bow. "As we are loyal to you, my lord."

Which was the first admission I'd ever wrung from Humphrey that our relationship went beyond momentary convenience. Not that I made the mistake of trusting him, and especially not if Maud had poisoned Eleanor, as Bevyn suspected. One thing this trip had made me realize, almost more than anything else, was that *trust* was something precious, and not to be bestowed lightly. I was pretty sure the only person I trusted completely here today was Lili. My father would no doubt have said it was high time I'd come to that realization.

A wedding was easily the most commonplace medieval ceremony still in existence in modern times, and for that reason, the format of William's wedding was familiar to me. I found a spot to William's right, facing inwards, towards the center of the church. William and Joan had actual chairs to sit on (they resembled nothing less than thrones—coincidence? *I think not*) and sat facing the audience.

Gravesend, since it was his church, performed the ceremony. He stood in front of William and Joan, facing the audience too, which made more sense than what we did in the twenty-first century, which was spend the whole service staring at the couple's backs.

I stood at parade rest, trying not to shift from one foot to the other while Gravesend droned on in Latin. At least there was music, a boys' choir, which I could have joined once upon a time. I didn't sing nearly enough these days. It wasn't without precedent for a Prince of Wales to sing. Hywel, the son of Owain Gwynedd, had been known throughout Wales as a warrior-poet. I would have liked that role, as long as I didn't have to sing any songs about King Arthur.

St. Paul's Cathedral was laid out in typical medieval fashion, though bigger than any church I'd ever been in. It was hugely long from east to west and the service was taking place with Gravesend standing in the exact middle, at the intersection of the north/south and east/west transepts. The main altar lay at the eastern end, behind him—behind William and Joan—in the choir, which was off-limits to common folk. Churches like this were built so that the rising sun would shine through an eastern window, but as this was November, there was no sun to speak of.

Giant columns supported the roof and a narrow second floor balcony protected by a solid railing with wooden panels, not spindles, ran all around the interior of the nave. It culminated in a larger space above the porch which allowed people to look down on the churchgoers below. Humphrey had cordoned off that area today for security purposes. Given the events of last night, I couldn't blame him—nor blame him for following through with the wedding today, even if it was shockingly soon after Eleanor's death.

Joan, for her part, was keeping it together better than anyone expected. She sat a foot from William, her hands on the arms of the chair. I couldn't see her face, since she wore a veil, but she wasn't sobbing. Maybe she and Eleanor hadn't been close. English royal families were often as cutthroat as Welsh or Marcher ones.

Gravesend lifted his hands in conclusion to a prayer and then turned around to face William and Joan. Finally, it was time for the actual vows, after which the pair would be officially married in the eyes of the Church. William reached for Joan's hand and helped her to rise. As she did so, I caught a flash of movement from the second floor balcony at the far end of the church, a hundred feet away, which was supposedly off-limits. A man appeared, lifted a bow over the railing, and nocked an arrow into it.

Too much had happened in the twenty-four hours since we'd arrived in England for me to hesitate, and the only thought that passed through my head was that the assassin was in my line of sight and no one else's, now that Gravesend had turned his back on the crowd.

I coiled my body and launched myself at William, like a goalkeeper stretching for a ball that was headed towards the upper corner of the goal. My arms wrapped around his shoulders and I brought him down. As we fell, we cannoned into Joan, who screamed as we came down on top of her.

I rolled off of William and he rolled off of Joan, ending up with all three of us lying flat on the floor. The force of the fall had knocked the air from my lungs and I felt a searing pain in my left hip, which was odd since I'd landed more on my right side than my left. Gravesend's face swam above me. "Son! Son! God be praised you're alive. Help is coming!"

That's good. I tried to say it, but my mouth felt thick and cottony. Lili appeared above me too and pressed her cheek to mine. I pushed onto one elbow and turned my head. Joan and William had sat up as well, though Joan was sobbing into William's chest. He gazed at me with a stunned expression, but all I could see was the yard-long arrow to the left of his head, buried in the headrest of Joan's chair. If I hadn't knocked William into Joan, thinking the arrow was meant for him, she would have been skewered through the chest as she rose to her feet.

The crowd in the nave was in an uproar. Over the commotion, I could hear Bohun shouting, ordering his men to seal the cathedral, find the archer, and secure William and Joan. I gathered my wits and put a hand on Lili's shoulder. "Can you help me up?"

"My lord, you should lie still!" Gravesend was aflutter with concern and reminded me very much of Eleanor when Alfonso had choked last night.

"Why?" I said as Lili pulled me upright, but then I wavered on my feet. Lili pulled my cloak aside and then showed me her hand, which came away bloody from my thigh. "The arrow hit you before it went into the chair."

I looked down. Sure enough, the arrow had scored my flesh just below my hip. Now that I knew what had happened, the pain I'd been feeling became focused. I swallowed hard, tasting bile.

"Thank goodness it was a bodkin arrow and not a barbed one," Lili said.

I tried to nod my agreement, but ended up gazing down at my feet instead, trying to get a handle on the pain. "Get the arrow, would you Lili?" I said, in Welsh.

"What? Why?" she said, but at the look on my face passed me off to Carew, who tugged my arm over his shoulder and put his arm around my waist.

"I've got you, my lord," he said. Within a minute, a circle of friends had surrounded me, including Edmund, Clare, Bevyn, and Evan. The latter two hadn't been invited to the wedding officially, but had formed part of the security detail for the church, joining men from the corteges of the dozens of other noblemen who'd come to see William and Joan married this morning.

Meanwhile, the audience had turned into a raucous mob. Half the crowd seemed to be clambering for the exits, fighting Bohun's men in the process, while the other half had surged forward, encircling Gravesend, William, Joan, and me. I lost sight of Lili, which was all to the good if it meant she was going to dig the arrowhead out of the chair and spirit it away.

Then a hand came down on my shoulder and I turned. All of a sudden, I didn't care about the wedding or my wound. The weight of the world lifted from my shoulders as my father gave me a twisted grin. "Good to see you, Son. Just as we feared, England has turned out to be a treacherous place."

24

20 November 1288

Meg

"This way! This way, my lord!" The Bishop of London himself herded us from the nave into the sacristy, where he and the priests who served the cathedral changed into their robes and kept the items sacred to the Church.

Gravesend gestured David towards a chair with thick arms and back, and David didn't protest when Carew and Llywelyn guided him into it. David's eyes had narrowed over the pain and his breeches were soaked with his own blood. I studied his profile in quick glances as I ripped the fabric from hip to knee. I hadn't even gotten a chance to hug him yet. I glanced around for Lili, surprised that she wasn't hovering over her husband (though she was hardly the hovering type), but didn't see her.

Then David smiled down at me and the lines around his eyes and on his forehead smoothed, revealing a face more akin to the twenty-year-old he was. "I am so glad to see you."

He leaned forward and pulled me into his arms. We held on, and then I released him so I could get back to tending his wound and he could hug Llywelyn. They gripped each other tightly, both men fighting tears.

"You're okay?" David said. "Huw said you looked tired last night."

"I am well, Son," Llywelyn said. "Your mother fixed me right up."

"How about you, Goronwy?" David grasped Goronwy's hand. "I suppose you've had quite an adventure. Did you try the coffee?"

"I surely did, my lord. Ieuan and I will have much to discuss." Goronwy's mouth twitched beneath his mustache.

David rested his head against the back of his chair. "I *am* glad you're all safe," he said, softly.

I glanced into his face and then back to my work. "We're good. We have a lot to tell you." I turned to Gravesend, who still hovered in the doorway and was the only one not of David's entourage to enter the sacristy. "I need clean cloths, hot water, and white alcohol."

Even in his distress, David smirked at the way I gave the order, with no regard for Gravesend's station. He was lucky I hadn't said, *RUN!*

It wasn't like I'd forgotten where I was living after a few days in the twenty-first century, but David was my son, and I had no time or patience for formality as long as he was hurting. To Gravesend's credit, he tipped his head to me and turned away, giving orders to those who waited outside as he left the room. At worst, someone could find what I needed at Clare's Castle Baynard.

David looked past me and his brow furrowed. "Who's that?"

I checked behind me. "Callum. He came back with us. He's MI5."

David raised his eyebrows. "You do have stories to tell, don't you?"

I nodded.

"Can we trust him?" David said.

"He doesn't speak Welsh, French, or English," Llywelyn said. "I don't see how he could harm us."

David lifted his chin. "Callum? Come here."

I didn't know if I'd ever get used to the way David ordered men far older than he around. At the same time, given his wound, he wasn't worrying about other men's feelings any more than I was.

With a wary look, Callum approached. He put his heels together and bowed. "My lord."

"Sorry about that," David said in American English and waved a hand. "It's who I am at present. You've been caught up in a mess which I can't fix for you."

"I know," Callum said.

"Mom says you're a spy," David said, "not a historian."

"That is correct." Callum cleared his throat. "While my mother was Scottish, my father was an American who worked for the U.S. State Department. After my parents' divorce, I moved with my mother back to England. My degree is in politics and international studies from Cambridge." He flushed red, as if he thought he was boasting unnecessarily by giving David his resumé. He didn't add, though he could have, *I'm not completely ignorant!*

"He speaks Gaelic," I said.

Callum gave me a sharp nod. "Only a little."

David pursed his lips as he studied Callum.

"You've glossed over the fact that you were in the military, too," David said.

Callum's eyes narrowed for a second. "You can tell?"

"When and where?" David said.

"Afghanistan, for the two years before we pulled out."

"So, you're smart and can handle yourself. If you can bear with us, you may find that you do fine here. It'll just take a bit of getting used to."

Callum bowed, and this time it even seemed natural. "Thank you ... my lord."

I bent my head and thought about Marty, my pilot friend who'd flown away and left me near Hadrian's Wall four years ago, never to be heard from again. Even with our help, this was going to be hard for Callum and I didn't have a way to make it easier.

Then Lili entered the sacristy on the heels of the servants who brought the bandages and water. I caught her eye as she scanned the room and she trotted over. Callum moved aside.

"Hi." She leaned down and kissed my cheek. "I'm so glad you're here." Then she touched David's shoulder. "Are you okay?"

"He's going to be fine." I swabbed at David's wound with alcohol.

David took in a sharp breath at the pain of it and nodded, even as he reached for Lili's hand. Ever observant, Llywelyn leaned in close. "Did you send Lili on an errand?" he said.

"I asked Lili to get that arrow." David's face had gone pale from my ministrations, but he answered his father steadily.

"Why would you want her to do that—?" I stopped as Lili showed him where she'd hidden it under her cloak, and then I understood.

During battle, an archer would fire any arrow that came to hand. Lords and common folk alike stockpiled arrows as a matter of course. Every castle had men who made arrows: a man who could forge the points, another to heat the wood to make it straight, and a fletcher to affix the feathers so the arrows would fly true. That said, skilled archers often fletched their own arrows when they could. I certainly didn't recognize the fletching on the arrow that had been shot at Joan, but arrows were Welsh weapons. In the old universe, it had been only after he'd learned the importance of archery through his wars with the Welsh that King Edward had instituted a nationwide program of archery among the English populace.

"May I see that?" Edmund edged closer and took the arrow from Lili.

He stared at the fletching, and then at David. "It's the same, my lord."

"You're sure?" David said.

Before I could say, *The same as what?* Edmund snapped the arrow over his knee. "You'd think I'd remember seeing a similar arrow sticking out of three of my men!" He tossed the two halves on the floor and glared at David. "I believe you know who did this."

"I do, Edmund," David said, "but if I tell you, you must not confront him. Not yet."

"Who is it, my lord?" Edmund said. "You must tell me."

"Valence," David said, "with the full knowledge of your brother."

Edmund's chin jutted out. "I will kill him." He spun on his heel, without indicating whether it was Roger or Valence he meant to kill.

Perhaps it didn't matter.

Before Edmund reached the door, David said, "Edmund!"

I'd never heard that kind of authority before in David's voice. He expected Edmund to obey him. Accordingly, Edmund stopped, his hand on the frame of the door and bowed his head, holding the position for a count of five. And then he nodded. "As you wish, my lord."

He marched from the room.

Llywelyn bent to pick up the two halves of the arrow. "You have true knowledge that Valence is behind the attempt on Joan's life?"

"Valence planned an ambush for me on the road to Gloucester." David looked up at his father. "Edmund says this arrow was fletched by the same hand as those who killed his men."

302

Llywelyn shook his head. "But to kill a princess—"

"I must ask you something now, Dad, even though it might make all of us uncomfortable."

"Anything, Son," Llywelyn said.

"Bevyn may have conceived of it first, but you called it into being. Did the Order of the Pendragon have a hand in anything that has happened this week, to clear the way for my rule of England?"

I kept my expression steady, focusing on the bandages, and didn't look at either David or Llywelyn. I wasn't sure exactly what David was asking, what he meant by *anything*. Llywelyn gazed at David for a long moment. "No, Son. Whatever troubles you have found in England, they are none of my doing."

"Thank you, Dad." David bowed his head. "I believe you."

"What concerns me," Lili broke in, "is how many different people have developed plots and plans that affect Dafydd. Bohun, the Order of the Pendragon, Peckham, all of you." She gestured with one hand to the room at large.

"I'm sure we don't know what you mean," Carew said.

David eyed Carew, and then bit his lip as I cinched a cloth more tightly around his leg. "Duct tape."

"What was that?" I said.

"Since you and Dad left, I've thought a lot about Valence," David said, "about the fact that I could picture him running around behind the scenes, patching his elaborate plot together with duct tape whenever a hole appeared in it. What if it's happening again?"

"Surely it's not Valence who wants to put you on the throne," I said.

"Not Valence," David said, and he shot a second glance at Carew that went by so quickly I wasn't sure I'd even seen it. Had David and Carew fallen out in some way during our absence? "But others do, while still others want to prevent it from happening, and each man ends up being far too clever for his own good. Valence, at least, seems to be able to conjure a way out whenever fate throws up a brick wall."

Llywelyn looked from David to me. "Do you understand what Dafydd just said?"

I shook my head, and it was Lili who tsked through her teeth. "Regrettably, I do. And I think he's right. We have multiple conspiracies, all working at the same time."

"And at cross-purposes," David said.

"I'll tell you what I'm most worried about," Lili said, speaking louder, not just to Llywelyn, David, and me. "What if Dafydd were to accept the Archbishop's challenge and take the throne of England—and then it is discovered that the papers that put him there were forged?"

I looked around at the other men in the room, fingering their chins. *Was I crazy to think that no one wanted to meet my eyes?* I glanced at Llywelyn. He lifted one shoulder. Neither of us knew what Lili was talking about. "What do you mean by *papers*?" I said.

David directed a rueful look at me. "I forgot that you wouldn't have heard about Peckham's papers yet."

"What papers?" Llywelyn said.

"The Archbishop has in his possession evidence that Mom is the result of a secret liaison between King Henry and a granddaughter of Alexander of Scotland." At the look on my face, David added, with a lopsided smile, "It defies all logic, doesn't it?"

"I can't believe it! Who would do such a thing?" And then as I studied my son, I said, "Do you know that answer, too?"

"I won't say here."

"Why would someone go to such effort to put you on the throne?" I said.

"That I can answer," Llywelyn said. "What the noblemen of England fear most is losing power. For a baron to choose Dafydd over a fellow Norman means that particular baron has no other play to make. He has reached the breaking point and is asking himself *who am I going to back? How am I to come out of this endless strife on top?"*

David gave his father a brief nod.

Llywelyn put a hand on David's shoulder and straightened. "As you said, we shouldn't discuss the specifics here."

I wound a final bandage around David's leg and tied it.

"I can walk. Help me up." David held out a hand to his father, who pulled him out of the chair. David balanced on his right leg before testing his left with his weight.

"You shouldn't be walking, my lord," Carew said.

"It's not that bad and I have no choice," David said. "I can't stay here all day."

Llywelyn inspected David's bandage. "Hurts like hell, I imagine."

"It's a stupid surface wound," David said. "I imagine that arrow you took to the gut was far worse."

"True," Llywelyn said, "but I wasn't trying to walk afterwards either."

"The hip I landed on actually feels worse," David said.

Llywelyn and I helped him hobble back towards the nave. As we left the sacristy, Peckham and Gravesend stood with their heads together near the chairs where William and Joan had sat earlier. William, absent Joan, leaned against one the pillars with his father beside him, ten feet from us. I had assumed that the cathedral would have emptied in the time we were gone, but if anything, more people filled it now than before.

As the three of us stepped again into the nave, the crowd went from boisterous to hushed in a single second. We hovered in a cleared space between two pillars, and I was conscious of David's blood on my dress, his torn breeches, and the white bandage around his thigh that was impossible to miss. The rest of our family and friends backed up behind us.

Then Peckham and Gravesend bowed. "My lord." And they meant David, and only David.

Llywelyn patted David's back and let go of him. However, David left an arm loosely around my shoulders, more for emotional support than physical. We limped together towards the two churchmen. "I'm sorry the ceremony was interrupted," David said. "Were you waiting for me to return before you continued it?"

Peckham glanced at Gravesend and then cleared his throat. "Uh ... no, my lord. We were simply anxious for your welfare. I am glad to see that your wound was not more severe."

I looked past the churchmen to the press of people. The noble men and women who'd come for the wedding mingled with their attendants, the elite of London's merchant class, and even a collection of commoners. More than one local entrepreneur had set up shop selling pies, sweetmeats, and beer to the guests.

"I don't understand." David glanced towards his father, who was talking urgently with Clare. Llywelyn lifted his hand but didn't come over. David turned back to Peckham, who seemed to be warring with himself as to what to say.

Peckham opened his mouth, closed it, hesitated again, but before he could speak, a man in the crowd called out—"Arthur!"

The surprised scoff caught in my throat as other voices took up the call. "Arthur! King Arthur!"

"My lord David," Peckham said. "They mean you."

"They have no idea what they're saying," David said.

"So you have said, but are you going to mock their faith by telling them so?" Peckham said.

I'd heard him mock plenty in private. David swallowed hard, looked down at his feet, and then up again at the Archbishop. I saw the moment he realized that he couldn't mock them—no more than he could disappoint the people of Wales. My stomach tightened for him. I'd lived in the Middle Ages—and been misunderstood by medieval people—for too long not to know what he was feeling.

David straightened his shoulders and lifted a hand to the crowd. "Peace, my friends. You honor me with your trust, but we must not speak of this here." He spoke first in English, and then in French.

These few words didn't satisfy anyone (least of all David, I was sure), but the shouts tapered off when everyone realized he wasn't going to say anything more. The people began to talk again among themselves.

Gravesend cleared his throat. "I apologize, my lord, that you were injured in my home."

"Did your men capture the archer?" I said.

"Not exactly," Peckham said.

"What does that mean?" I said.

"The archer is dead," Peckham said. "He attacked the soldier who cornered him. Our man had no choice but to put a sword into his belly, lest he lose his own life."

"Did he get anything from the archer before he died? Anything at all?" David said.

"No," Peckham said, "other than that he was an Englishman."

Huh. "Are you sure?" I said.

"The man who caught him was one of mine." Humphrey had been hovering on the edge of our conversation and now stepped forward. He met neither my eyes nor David's as he spoke, undoubtedly irritated by all the Arthur talk and the news of my fraudulent bloodline. I couldn't blame him for that, any more than I could prevent people from speaking of it.

"I would like a look at him," David said.

"Of course, my lord," Humphrey said. Then he lowered his voice, "Given that he shot an arrow, you rightfully fear that the man was Welsh. Believe me, I share your concern, but it seems he wasn't."

Lili slipped her hand into David's free one. "Shouldn't we continue the wedding?" And then she added, with that sweet smile that disarmed everyone who encountered it, "The least we can do is put William out of his misery."

Peckham coughed into his fist. "Joan has taken the attempt on her life ... rather hard."

"I can only imagine," Lili said. "Where is she?"

Humphrey jerked his head towards the southern transept. "Here she comes now."

A pathway cleared for Joan as she walked towards us. The girl who approached us at this hour, however, was a very different person from the quiet child she'd appeared to be up until now. She'd removed her veil and her fur-lined cloak, and either she or someone else had torn off the lace that adorned the sleeves and bodice of her wedding dress.

Joan halted in front of William and put a hand to his cheek. Then she removed a ring from her finger. "This, I believe, is yours." She grasped William's right hand, turned it palm upwards, and closed his fingers over the ring.

"Joan—" William tried to speak but Joan put a finger to his lips.

"Shh."

Joan left him and turned towards us. Stopping a few feet away, she said, "I have foresworn this marriage and all marriage, forevermore. I have spoken with the Abbess of Barking Abbey and will enter her convent as a novice, effective immediately."

If Joan had said that she was really St. George and planned to head into the wilderness to slay a dragon, she couldn't have stunned her listeners more.

Humphrey sputtered something that sounded like, "You can't—you won't," but he couldn't get the words out properly.

Peckham reached out a hand to her, but Joan took a step back so he couldn't touch her. "My decision is final. I will no longer be a pawn in your game of chess."

I wanted to tell her that she was magnificent in her indignation and certainty. Very few people could render a roomful of Norman barons speechless. I would have laughed, too, if not for the grave expressions on the faces of everyone within hearing distance. Joan tipped her head to David. "My lord."

He bowed his head, and for the thousandth time, I was proud of my son for the way he handled himself in an unpredictable situation. "Princess."

She turned on her heel and marched back across the nave to where a woman in a nun's habit waited for her.

Even from a distance, I could make out the concern on the woman's face. When Joan reached her, the woman wrapped a brown blanket around the girl's shoulders and turned her away, but not before she saw me watching her. The nun nodded her head to me, and then led her charge down the length of the southern transept and out the door into the November rain.

Bohun had recovered from his initial shock and now his face flushed red. He snapped his fingers at William. "Go after her! She's your bride."

But William didn't move. "No, Father. Didn't you see her? There's no changing her mind, not by me, anyway."

Bohun spun towards the crowd and fisted his hand above his head. "We'll see about that." He strode after Joan. By the time he entered the southern transept, a dozen of his men had fallen into position around and behind him. He disappeared through the doors too. Joan hadn't bothered to keep her voice low, so many of those closest to us heard her declaration. The noise level rose again as the news disseminated throughout the nave within a minute.

Peckham turned to David. "What say you now about your claim to the throne, my lord? Or should I say, *King Arthur*?"

25

21 November 1288

David

The barons' long-existing, underlying dislike of one another had exploded into full blown disagreement and anger. The debacle of William's wedding had laid bare every slight that any of them had ever inflicted on each other, and every grudge they'd held.

"You!" The gloves had come off for Bohun and he pointed at Valence. "That Joan has joined a convent is *your* doing. You have spent the last three years plotting against me and everything we regents have tried to accomplish for England."

"Now, now." Kirby stepped in. "That's going too far, surely."

"Shut up, Kirby," Bohun said. "We may be the only regents in the room, but you deserve the station far less than I. I know what you've done!"

"What I've done—?"

Roger Mortimer pointed a finger at Bohun. "Bohun, it is *you* who murdered Eleanor. Don't try to deny that you have plotted and connived—"

"As if you haven't!" Bohun said.

"—to elevate yourself and your offspring far beyond what might please God—"

"I name Bohun as a murderer!" Valence said. "Let all men of understanding—"

"God's own truth, Valence," Edmund Mortimer said, "for you to stand there and accuse someone else of murder when you yourself—"

"Stop!"

To my surprise, I found myself stepping into the center of the circle of men. Far more nobles than just Valence, the Mortimers, and the Bohuns stood at the far end of Westminster Hall, but most had stood by and watched their leaders implode without interfering. Perhaps they didn't feel they could. But quite frankly, it had reached the level of ridiculousness, especially when I knew the truth.

I hadn't revealed to everyone Bronwen's information about the origins of the poison at Shrewsbury, nor Valence's perfidy, just as I hadn't accused Kirby of forging the documents, or Maud of poisoning Eleanor. I had accumulated secrets, not even sure within myself when—and if—I might speak of them.

The hall wasn't packed—I didn't think it was possible to pack Westminster Hall, ever—but plenty of people mingled close by, only a few of whom I knew well. Peckham had called the meeting, and even Kirby had come out of hiding for the council. Like Peckham, he was a man of the Church. Two years ago he'd been ordained the Bishop of Ely (in addition to serving as regent to the crown and Lord High Treasurer) despite his pluralist views. A pluralist was someone who believed that a religion other than Christianity might share some of its universal truths. If this was his true feeling, such beliefs would be astounding in a medieval man. I wished Aaron were here to tell me what he thought of him, because I liked him already.

My most vocal supporters spread themselves evenly among the crowd: Carew, Clare, Edmund Mortimer. Dad settled himself close by and I was very glad to have him with me. He and I were two of the tallest men in the room, which I wasn't sorry about either. For better or for worse, the bigger a man was, the more intimidating he could be. I might need that advantage later.

"How dare you!" Valence pointed at me. "You who murdered Lord Hywel and started this madness—"

"I did not murder Hywel," I said, keeping my voice mild in contrast to Valence's high dudgeon. "You know that very well."

"You ordered it—"

I stepped in close—far closer than was comfortable for either of us—and lowered my voice so only he could hear me. "As you ordered my death? And Joan's? Is that it?"

"I did no such thing—"

"The arrow, my lord, the arrow," I said.

Valence snapped his mouth shut. "The arrow disappeared after the wedding," he said.

314

"It disappeared into my possession." I turned to face Peckham. While he had called this meeting, I was disappointed that he hadn't been able to control it. Bohun and Valence sputtered in the margins while Roger Mortimer's foot tapped out a staccato on the stone floor. I shot him an annoyed look, and he subsided.

"I would speak," I said.

Peckham bowed. "Of course, my lord."

Kirby canted his head. "You honor us with your presence today, my lord. Your bravery in saving William and Joan—"

"I haven't come here to talk about that." I seemed to be interrupting everyone, but Peckham had summoned the barons to discuss what to do with the throne of England. Since chucking it in the Thames, which had my vote, seemed to be off the table, we had to do *something*. If we didn't, whether these barons wanted to admit it or not, civil war loomed.

Bohun and Kirby held the regency now for King Edward's three remaining daughters: Margaret, Mary, and Elizabeth, ages thirteen, eleven, and six. If Valence had his way, Alfonso would soon be betrothed to one of them, as would William, if Bohun could twist his arm tightly enough behind his back. None of the barons wanted such an event to come to pass. Many would oppose Bohun; they all would oppose Valence. And these were the schemes I could guess at. Did Thomas de Berkeley have a favorite? What about some of the northern barons? Other players danced around the margins and at any moment, one might change the game.

I realized now that William's betrothal to Joan had been nothing more than a sop, a gesture of appeasement, to Bohun for losing his lands in Wales as a result of our treaty of 1285. Edward's death, and then Eleanor's, had pushed the other barons to a state bordering on insanity in their horror that William de Bohun would become the King of England and Humphrey would have a say over them for the rest of their lives.

"I came to London to support my friend, William, at his wedding," I said. "Instead, I find myself in a council so unruly that every man is at another man's throat, and no one is left to claim the throne of England."

"My lord—" Peckham started to speak, but I cut him off, no longer willing to listen.

"Four events have occurred in the last week to which I would draw your attention." I pointed my index finger in the air. "One, an attempted ambush of my company; two, the discovery of forged papers detailing my antecedents; three, the death of Princess Eleanor; and four, the attempted murder of Princess Joan." I had ticked them off on my fingers and now waved a hand to encompass them all.

"While I know the name of the one responsible for each of these acts, it does me no good to accuse the guilty, nor us to accuse one another. Everyone here has plotted and planned, schemed and devised. Each seeks to raise himself higher than his peers. Some of you have even sought to raise *me* higher."

"My lord, surely you sell yourself shor—"

Again I cut Peckham off. "So you say," I said. "I'm getting to that."

As I gazed around the room, looking from face to face, I saw that these barons believed me when I said I knew the truth. They feared what I knew, the power I might wield, and the men who had pledged their loyalty to me. It was an odd feeling, and not one I enjoyed. But I would use it if I had to. "What England truly needs to affect justice is a king."

Kirby raised a hand. "Justice, mercy, and faithfulness. We have been entrusted by God to rule with these virtues, and we have forgotten them."

I was surprised at him, though perhaps I shouldn't have been. "Matthew 23:23," I said. "Thank you, Kirby."

Valence wasn't having any of it. "What is this? Mercy towards murderers. Bohun—"

"No, Valence," I said. "How can there be justice when the men meting out punishment are also the guilty? It is an impossibility. When we choose him, justice will be the jurisdiction of the King."

Valence snapped his mouth shut. "I don't have to listen to this." He glared at me and then turned on his heel to pace down the hall towards the doors.

I let out a sharp breath. I hadn't expected him to abdicate so quickly—if I'd allowed myself to hope for it at all.

The other barons watched Valence's progress towards the doors and murmured among themselves, equally surprised. "Of what did you accuse him?" Bohun said in my ear.

"I will not say," I said, "though I meant what I said. He is as guilty as any of us. As guilty as you."

Bohun swallowed hard. "My lord—"

"I know who killed Eleanor," I said. "Do I need to say her name here? Is that what you wish?"

"No, my lord." Bohun stepped two quick paces away from me. I had the sense that he couldn't leave my side quickly enough. Clare took his place.

"You're letting Bohun go, too?" Clare said. "If you know the truth, you should speak—"

"I know lots of truths." I turned my head. "Would you like me to speak of the other night when you met with Carew and Edmund Mortimer in the chapel?"

Clare froze beside me. "My lord, we never—"

"You've let Kirby get away with his forged papers because it served what you saw as my interests," I said. "I say the same to you as I said to Bohun and Valence. It is only the king who can dispense justice."

Clare bowed his head.

"My lords," Peckham raised his voice to call everyone's attention to himself again. "As Prince David has asked, it is finally time to discuss our future ... and the man we will crown King of England." He gestured with his right hand towards me. "He stands before us."

Clare prodded me in the small of my back.

"No, Clare," I said.

Peckham didn't hear me, and wouldn't have taken no for an answer if he had. "If you would come forward, my lord David."

Roger Mortimer coughed into his fist while Kirby smiled beneficently. "Given that your mother is the daughter of our beloved King Henry—" Kirby said.

That got me moving when nothing else could have. "No." I wondered how many times I could cut off one of these barons before he overrode me. It hadn't happened yet.

"My lord—" Peckham said.

"This has gone on long enough," I said. "We must dispense with the mythology of my mother's birth now."

"But your mother was—" Kirby tried again.

"You can believe that her father was King Henry all you want, but it isn't true."

"The people believe it," Peckham said, managing to finish a sentence.

I shook my head and gestured towards the door, miles away down the hall. "The people of England believe something else of me entirely."

It had been impossible to miss the gathering that had begun outside Westminster with the dawn. Many of the men around me had passed through their ranks to enter the palace. The Londoners had been quieter before the meeting, but now I could hear them, calling to one another and clamoring for news.

And for me.

I didn't want what they wanted, but I couldn't just walk away either. I could hear my father's words, said to me on the balcony at Chepstow a lifetime ago, echoing in my ears: *You could be that strong king.*

Archbishop Peckham's eyes crinkled in the corners, as if he could read my thoughts. It irked me that he saw me as some kind of protégé, someone he had brought along until I could stand before a council of men and display my power over them. That's not why I had come.

And yet, it was Kirby's expression that interested me more. In him I saw curiosity, as if I was someone entirely different from the man he'd imagined me to be, and he was interested in finding out what exotic thing I might do next.

I decided to oblige him. Peckham had been slapping the roll of parchment signed by King Henry in the palm of his hand. I grabbed it from him and waved it in the air, not specifically at Kirby, but so everyone could see it. "Someone was paid to create these so-called proofs. When was he to come forward and reveal me for a fraud? At the crowning? At the opening of Parliament? Or was the plan to blackmail me to ensure that I did what he wanted, under threat of exposure as a charlatan?"

Two dozen barons, holding the highest stations in England, gazed back at me with various degrees of surprise and consternation. "Prince David—" Clare had come up behind me. His voice held a gentle warning. I'd done well so far keeping my temper contained. It wouldn't be wise to pull a Valence.

"You need to decide what it is that you want. What you see here—" I held up the papers again, "—is ephemeral—a fictive right of birth. You hold that dear, I know. All your power and titles and strength are based on the family into which you were born."

In two strides, I reached one of the tall candles that lit the room and thrust the parchment into the flame.

"My lord!" William de Bohun leapt towards me and batted the parchment from my hand. It hit the stones and continued to burn until another man, one of the Bigod cousins, stomped on it.

I'd shocked the barons. I could see it, but short of running me through, there was no stopping me now. I'd been wanting to speak my mind for years, and I was going to take my chance, whatever the consequences. I didn't need this crown. I didn't need the power that they thought to hand me so blithely. They had to know now that if they crowned me King of England, I wasn't going to be controllable.

I met my father's eyes. He nodded his encouragement.

"William the Bastard took this land by force," I said. "It took him four years to subdue the people who were here first. I speak to you today in French because many of you barely speak their language, and yet you claim lordship over the English by right of birth? It's by strength of arms that you sit atop your pyramid of power. And those people out there?" I lifted my chin. "They accept it not because of your birth, but because they fought your ancestors and lost.

"The Bastard's line has wavered at times, threatened to be rent asunder by civil war, but never failed. Not until now. These past three years, I imagine many of you have envisioned yourselves on his throne."

A half dozen men shifted from one foot to another. Others stood solidly, impassive. And a few shared Peckham's expression—a crinkling in the corners of their eyes and lips.

That amusement which Edmund Mortimer never seemed to quite suppress rose to the surface. "Young pup!"

He elbowed his way through the crowd and came to a halt in front of me, inspecting me up and down. He bowed his head, and then turned to look at his fellow barons. "We must bring order to the chaos that has engulfed England. Without a strong king, we fight among ourselves, jostling for power, rending the countryside asunder in our quest for ascendancy. Do I want to fight Bohun or Bigod or my own brother every time we have a dispute about our borders? What would that gain me and how much would I lose? As Prince David has said, without a king, we have no justice."

Clare moved to stand shoulder-to-shoulder with Edmund. He threw out a hand. "Who among you would take the throne?"

Silence.

"Who among you believes that Arthur has arisen in this man before us? Your people believe it. Do you believe despite yourself? Or does your pride intervene?"

Too late, I realized I'd lost control of the council meeting.

Clare turned to face me. "By right of birth or not, by the right of Arthur or not, I acknowledge you as my king." He went down on one knee in front of me and bowed his head.

Carew, Edmund Mortimer, William, and my father followed immediately, along with Humphrey de Bohun (never a sure thing) and the Bigod cousin whose name I didn't know. Others followed, though at least half hesitated before capitulating.

I shook my head. I could see the steps that had brought me to this point, to the barons of England bowing down before me, but how could I accept what they were offering?

Peckham caught my arm. "Come with me."

He tugged at my elbow and after a second of silent struggle, I went with him down the long hall. Though I didn't look back, I could feel the other barons processing behind me. Dad appeared on my other side. It was a long walk on a wounded leg. Neither of us spoke. As we reached the doors, Peckham flicked a hand at the two men who guarded them and they flung them open. Beyond, hundreds of people thronged the courtyard and the street, which I could see because the gates to the palace were open too.

At my appearance in the doorway, a roar went up. Mom and Lili had been hovering nearby and Peckham made room for them on either side of me.

"These are your people," Peckham said. "They believe in you. Will you deny them what they need: your leadership and the crown of England upon your head?"

I closed my eyes. This really was too much to ask of any man, but hadn't I known when I entered the hall today that this could happen? And I'd gone anyway, maybe still not believing, but willing to believe. "Live more lightly, isn't that what you said, Mom?"

"I did," Mom said.

"I'm thinking about calling their bluff," I said.

323

"What?" Mom said. "David—no—they don't understand what they're asking of you."

"But I do, finally, I think." I turned to Peckham. "All right. You win. I'll do it."

Peckham's eyes lit but Dad grasped my arm. "Dafydd—"

I turned to my father and spoke in Welsh so I could shut Peckham out. "Isn't this what you wanted? We've discussed it dozens of times."

"Yes ... no!" Dad backtracked. "It's what I thought I wanted, but Dafydd—" he shook his head "—now that it comes to it, I don't want this for you. Not with the way it's come about, not if you have any doubt at all. You are my son, and I love you. If you accept this crown, your life will never again be your own. You fought me so you could marry Lili, and you were right. You fought me on this, and you were right. We'll figure something else out."

I grasped Dad's shoulder, the weight I agreed to take onto my shoulders already lighter. "I can't tell you how much I needed to hear you say that, but it's you who were right this time. Wales does need me to take this step. God knows why any man in England thinks this is a good idea, but this one act on my part will protect Wales for generations to come. I do need to do it. Right, Lili?"

Lili had squeezed between Dad and me and stood with both arms around my waist. I stretched my arm across her shoulders and pulled her closer. "You're crazed if you think I'll make a good Queen of England," she said.

"The fact that you don't want it makes you the best woman for the job." I lifted a hand to the crowd and waved, and God help me, the people roared their approval back at me.

* * * * *

That evening, everyone was in a state of shock, me as much as anyone. Even with the celebration and the adulation of the barons seated at the table with me and throughout the hall, I had one last question I needed to ask—one last person with whom I needed to speak.

Near the end of the dinner, I rose to my feet and pushed in my chair. Lili had already gone up to our rooms, but Dad looked up at me. His cheeks were pink—from the warmth and the wine— and he was smiling. I thought his face was fuller and more healthy-looking than I'd seen it even as far back as last August. "Son?"

"I have to do something," I said.

Dad's eyes narrowed, but he didn't stop me or question me further, just nodded. I walked off the dais and came up behind Bevyn, who sat on the far side of one of the long tables further down the hall. I put a hand on his shoulder. "Come. Walk with me."

I'd kept an eye on him all evening, trying to keep track of the number of times he'd had his goblet refilled. I'd lost count at six. I found it oddly poetic that it was I who was putting a stop to the drinking tonight.

325

Bevyn stood, though he didn't meet my eyes, and followed me through a side door near the dais, down a long corridor and out into one of the numerous courtyards at Westminster Palace, and then to the top of the curtain wall that overlooked the Thames.

I took in a deep breath, allowing the cold air to wash over me. We had no stars or moon to light the sky, but London was a city and a pioneer in light pollution. Lambeth Palace lay across the river, lit to the heavens as the Archbishop prepared for my coronation.

Bevyn came to rest beside me, his forearms on the flat top of the wall and his back hunched over them.

"Did you hear me speak to my father at St. Paul's about his possible role in all this?" I said.

"I did, my lord," Bevyn said. "I assure you, he told the truth."

"I know," I said. "But you have lied by omission, haven't you?"

Bevyn didn't answer at first, and the silence dragged out until he finally said, "If I have displeased you in some fashion—"

"I need you to answer this one question, Bevyn," I said. "I trust you with my life. You would never harm me. But you are smarter than you let on, and devious, and you *believe* in me in a way I can never understand. If you love me, tell me the truth."

Bevyn swallowed. "I did not order the death of Eleanor and Joan." He bowed low. "I apologize, my lord, for I did not think to aim that high."

"Ah," I said. "So the death of Hywel is another matter, isn't it? You poisoned him, then?"

Bevyn picked at the mortar between two stones with one finger. "How did you know?"

"From the discoloration in his fingers, at the very least," I said. "And because it was too much of a coincidence to believe that Hywel could possibly die so conveniently."

"I did what I thought was best," Bevyn said.

"I know you did," I said. "Who else knows?"

"Three of us, no more than that," Bevyn said.

"Both of these others are in the Order of the Pendragon?" I said. "Is one of them Huw or Aeddan?"

"No, my lord."

"Where are the other two?" I said.

"I sent them back to Wales the moment the deed was done," Bevyn said. "They won't talk."

"All men talk, eventually," I said. "I am about to take the throne of England. Tell me why I shouldn't throw you to the wolves?"

Bevyn wiped at the corners of both eyes with his thumb. "I have no answer, my lord."

I sighed and watched a boat slide downstream, heading towards the center of London. The barons were going to crown me king and in so doing cover up murder, deceit, and conspiracy. I could not condone what Bevyn had done, but at the same time, if I let Bohun or Valence go free, how could I punish Bevyn for believing in me too much?

"Go home, Bevyn," I said.

Bevyn straightened and stepped back from the wall. "My lord?"

"You have a wife and child. See to them."

I stared out at the river and the city for a long time after Bevyn's footsteps had faded into the distance.

26

24 November 1288

Meg

"My lady." William de Bohun cleared his throat. "Madam. If I might speak with you?"

I brushed a hand across my eyes. None of us had gotten to bed until after two in the morning any day this week, and this morning we'd slept only until six. David's capitulation had been wholly unexpected. Not even the Archbishop of Canterbury could believe his good fortune. He'd rushed around, making plans and sending out messengers with the good news. The people had spoken, Parliament had been summoned and put their stamp of approval on David's ascendancy, and Westminster Palace swelled with men of importance. Every single one wanted a piece of David, and he'd had no more than a few moments to breathe in three days.

Even Humphrey de Bohun, after an initial cold look, had accepted what we should have known was inevitable. David had stuck out his hand to him and he'd taken it—reluctantly, but he'd taken it. He'd said, "My lord David. I knew this day would come. My attempt to put William on the throne was doomed to fail from the start, wasn't it?"

"I had no role in any of this—"

Humphrey scoffed. "God is on your side, remember? You need do no more than hold up your hand and the world falls at your feet."

To my surprise, Bohun had grinned then, and his eyes had lit. "I'm not going anywhere, Sire."

"I wouldn't have it any other way," David said. "I'm counting on your vocal, even outspoken opinions on all matters, large and small."

"You will hear them," Bohun had said.

I knew what Humphrey did not, that he had been a thorn in King Edward's side up until the day of his death, always demanding more say in the running of the country and the taxation of the barons, to the point of withdrawing his forces from fighting in Scotland in order to force the king's hand. The man had power—he exuded it—and more importantly, he loved to wield it.

In the old universe, he allied with Bigod to write *The Remonstrances*. Of similar tone to the *Magna Carta*, the document was a complaint against Edward for heavy taxation and for forcing his barons to participate in his French wars, about which the Norman lords had come to care nothing.

Now, I gazed at Humphrey's son with no idea what to say to him. Humphrey hadn't actually accused David of usurping his throne, but William had to feel that he had. I couldn't even tell him that David didn't want it. It would be unfair.

"I would ask that you thank your son for saving Joan's life," William said.

"You really should speak to him yourself," I said.

"He has other concerns," William said. "If not for him, she would be dead and I still wouldn't be the King of England."

I shook my head. "I'm sorry, William. You know it wasn't David's intent—"

"Don't you think I know that?" William drew himself up to his full height and took on an air of pomposity that reminded me very much of his father. "I am not a child any longer. I can accept hard truths."

After Humphrey had gone after Joan, William had eventually followed, but she had refused to reconsider her decision to join a convent. Afterwards, she had written William a letter and included the Archbishop of Canterbury in the greeting, indicating that her choice was final. What could Peckham—or anyone else— say to that? She was a princess and could be coerced, but not away from the Church, not in the Middle Ages.

Llywelyn came up behind me and slipped my hand into the crook of his arm. "It's time, *cariad*."

Time to see my son crowned.

William the Bastard (or more politely, William the Conqueror) was crowned King of England on Christmas Day, 1066, at Westminster Abbey. The last Saxon king, Edward the Confessor, was buried here, and because King Henry idolized the old king (he'd named his eldest son for him, after all), he'd begun a rebuilding program in 1245 and was buried here too. And so it was at the Abbey that David was to be crowned King of England—not, however, on Christmas Day. David's advisors, including Peckham, were in too much of a hurry to get him started.

So it's a crowning: blah, blah, blah. Get on with it already...

Those had been David's exact words. My son could be most irreverent sometimes. Thank goodness he said it in private and only to me, in American English, and then shut up about it.

I appreciated his perspective. Like funerals and some weddings, the ceremony was less about *him* than it was about those watching. It was a public statement of his ascendancy, and he had a miniscule amount of patience for any of it, even if he understood why he had to go through it.

Llywelyn and I had front-row seats. Callum settled himself against a side wall next to Evan, whose mustache twitched as he glanced at the newcomer. Evan didn't move away, though, and nodded a greeting. Maybe David had been right to tell Callum that it would get better. He was looking more comfortable with each day that passed. It helped that David had let it be known that Callum had been a soldier. I missed Bevyn, but he'd already returned to Wales, spreading the news of David's coronation.

As David walked down the aisle, I had a terrible feeling that he was walking to the gallows instead of his crowning, but as he passed me, he shot me a grin and his blue eyes sparked with laughter. The Archbishop presided, and while to my eyes the accoutrements of the ceremony bore a striking resemblance to the aborted wedding of William and Joan, the people in the church appeared more joyous than they had on that occasion.

Once he reached the Archbishop, David turned to face the packed church. The Archbishop raised his hands, and the people cheered. David nodded his head, and they cheered some more. David took his seat—on the throne—on the raised dais so everyone could see him. The Archbishop and various lords then went to the four corners of the Church, proclaiming David's sovereignty and asking the people if they willingly acknowledged him as their King.

They did.

As the Archbishop returned to David, ready to hear his oath, I leaned my head against Llywelyn's arm, near to tears. He patted my hand and put his arm around my shoulders.

David repeated the oath from memory—in Latin, then in English, and only then in French:

I will grant and keep, and by my oath confirm, to the people of England, the laws and customs given to them by their previous just and God-fearing kings. I grant and promise that in all my judgments, so far as it in me lies, to preserve to God and the Holy Church, and to the people and clergy, entire peace and concord before God. So far as it in me lies, I will cause justice to be rendered rightly, impartially, and wisely, in compassion and in truth. I will grant and observe the just laws and customs that the people of my realm shall determine, and will, so far as it in me lies, defend and strengthen them to the honour of God. This is my promise.

* * * *

"The scepter and crown weigh a ton, Mom, and my leg hurts like hell."

"We can't leave yet," Llywelyn said. "You have …" Llywelyn stood on tiptoe to peer over the heads of the people in the crowd, "… approximately three hundred more people to greet."

"Excellent," David said, without sincerity.

"The mantle is nice," Lili said. "I'm warm for the first time in days."

Lili wore a golden circlet on her head because, naturally, she had become the Queen of England.

The ceremony had gone off without a hitch. No stray arrows struck my son; no poisoned goblets of wine were presented to him. The Archbishop Peckham, who'd put the crown on David's head, had tasted the ceremonial wine before he'd given it to David to drink. I was tempted from now on to allow David only to eat food that I made with my own hands. It wasn't possible, of course. Truth be told, none of us were really sure what was.

Llywelyn, Goronwy, and I were headed home tomorrow, even if I had to walk the whole way, given my advanced pregnancy. If I didn't go home now, I would have to stay in London until the babies were born, and that I refused to do. I needed Aaron and Anna. I needed these children to be born in Wales.

David, Lili, and their burgeoning entourage would stay in London for a few more days and then begin a month-long circuit of England. Their trip would culminate in the celebration of the Christmas Feast at Caerphilly with us. The purpose of the trip was to show David and Lili off, receive the homage of some of the northern barons who hadn't traveled to London for the crowning (or for William de Bohun's wedding), and proclaim to all and sundry that England had a new king.

His royal name was *David Arthur Llywelyn Pendragon,* King of England.

My son.

The End

Thank you for reading *Children of Time*. All of the books in the *After Cilmeri* Series are available at any bookstore. For more information about dark age and medieval Wales, please see my web page: www.sarahwoodbury.com

Acknowledgments

First and foremost, I'd like to thank my lovely readers for encouraging me to continue the *After Cilmeri* Series. I have always been passionate about these books, and it's wonderful to be able to share my stories with readers who love them too.

Thank you to my husband, Dan, and my children, who have been nothing but encouraging, despite the fact that their mother spends half her life in medieval Wales. Thank you to my mothers, who read versions of the books and approved them. Thank you to N. Gemini Sasson, for her invaluable suggestions, and my writing partner, Anna Elliott. As Piglet says, 'It's so much more friendly with two.'

About the Author

With two historian parents, Sarah couldn't help but develop an interest in the past. She went on to get more than enough education herself (in anthropology) and began writing fiction when the stories in her head overflowed and demanded she let them out. While her ancestry is Welsh, she only visited Wales for the first time while in college. She has been in love with the country, language, and people ever since. She even convinced her husband to give all four of their children Welsh names.

She makes her home in Oregon.

www.sarahwoodbury.com